CONSPIRACY JUSTICE IS BLIND

When Power Decides Who Is Guilty.
A Political Crime Thriller

BY: DR NAEEM MEO

ISBN: 978-1-971178-06-6

Table of Contents

Disclaimer

Conspiracy – Justice Is Blind is a work of fiction. All characters, locations, institutions, families, political figures, law enforcement agencies, judicial officers, and events depicted in this novel are **entirely fictional**. Any resemblance to real people, living or dead, or to actual events, towns, families, or legal cases is **purely coincidental**.

This novel explores themes of **systemic injustice, abuse of power, political influence, and racial inequality** through a fictional narrative. It does not allege or assert wrongdoing by any real individual, family, government body, law enforcement agency, or judicial institution.

The legal proceedings, political dynamics, and law enforcement actions portrayed are **dramatized for storytelling purposes** and should not be interpreted as factual representations of real-world cases or systems.

This book is intended as a work of fiction that raises ethical and social questions—not as legal, political, or historical commentary.

Reader discretion is advised.

Conspiracy – Justice Is Blind is part of the **CONSPIRACY series**, a collection of fictional thrillers examining how power, privilege, and influence can distort institutions meant to protect truth, fairness, and human dignity.

Each novel in the series focuses on a different system—justice, medicine, politics, or media—and reveals how corruption operates not through chaos but through structure.

These stories are fictional.

The questions they ask are real.

More truths will be uncovered.

Chapter 1: The Golden Ticket

Jordan had never felt lighter.

That morning, after practice, his sports teacher pulled him aside and shared the kind of news that changes a life. Jordan had been offered a full athletic scholarship to one of the top basketball colleges in the country.

No student from their high school had ever reached that level before.

By mid-morning, word had already spread. The principal called Jordan into his office, stood up to shake his hand, and said something no one from Haiti, Missouri, ever expected to hear.

"We are proud of you."

Caruthersville High School had never won back-to-back state basketball championships before Jordan arrived. Truth be told, it had rarely been noticed at all. That changed with him. Jordan was not just a standout on the court. He had a natural ability in almost every sport he touched. Basketball came easily, but so did track, swimming, boxing, and even precision shooting at the range. Coaches admired him. Teachers respected him. Students looked up to him.

Almost everyone liked Jordan.

Almost.

The only exception was Mitch Callaghan.

Mitch was everything Jordan was not.

He was the son of Mr. Callaghan, the region's largest farmer and one of its most powerful businessmen. The Callaghan family owned more than one hundred thousand acres of farmland. They controlled rice and cotton processing plants, held major stakes in the local steel mill and power facilities, and even owned the only casino in Caruthersville. They had their own bank.

Their money touched everything.

Schools, churches, hospitals. The Callaghans were always the biggest donors, always present, always influential. But their reach went far beyond money. One brother served in Congress. Another was a state senator. Power moved through the family as naturally as blood.

Mitch had been born into that world, raised with advantages he never had to question. And he was white.

Jordan's story was different.

He was born into a poor Black family. His parents worked the Callaghan land, like many others in the region. They lived in Haiti, a small town with fewer than two thousand residents in Pemiscot County, Missouri, one of the poorest counties in the state. Most of Haiti's population was Black, and poverty there was not something you passed through. It stayed, generation after generation.

After elementary school, Jordan enrolled at Caruthersville High School, the only high school in the county. Caruthersville sat along the Missouri River, a town of around ten thousand people and the center of what little economic activity the region had.

It was also the heart of the Callaghan empire.

The casino.

The rice mills.

The cotton plants.

The corn processing facilities.

All of it tied back to the same family.

Mr. Callaghan had two brothers and two sisters, all living within a fifty-mile radius. Together, they held influence across six counties. Financially. Politically. Socially. One sister was married to a magistrate judge. Another to a county sheriff.

Formal education had never been their strength.

It did not need to be.

Money and power had taught them everything they required.

In Pemiscot County, everyone understood one simple truth.

If the Callaghan family wanted something, they got it.

And now, for the first time, something had slipped beyond their reach.

Jordan.

Chapter 2:
The King of the School

Before Jordan ever set foot in Caruthersville High School, Mitch Callaghan already ruled it.

Mitch dominated nearly every sport the school cared about. Basketball, track, boxing, weightlifting. His name came up everywhere, not just because of his ability, but because of who he was. Teachers, including the coaches, favored him openly. No one bothered to question it. Being Mr. Callaghan's son carried a kind of weight that talent alone could never match.

He moved through the school with an easy arrogance, the kind that comes from never being told no. There was always a group around him, boys trying to stay close, girls drawn in by his confidence. He carried himself less like a student and more like someone in charge. Even teachers handled him carefully, choosing their words, avoiding conflict. Everyone knew he was different, and everyone treated him that way.

Jordan noticed it right away.

As the oldest of four, with one younger brother and two younger sisters, he had learned early how to read people and situations. By the time he reached ninth grade, it did not take long to figure out how things worked. One name kept surfacing in conversations, in locker rooms, in classrooms, in the quiet exchanges between students.

Mitch.

Students talked about him. Teachers protected him. The school, in many ways, bent around him.

But not everyone accepted that.

Tiffney didn't.

She had already had her own experience with Mitch, and it was enough to make up her mind about him. She was not afraid, and more importantly, she was not willing to pretend.

During the first week of school, she walked past Mitch in the hallway. As she passed, he reached out and slapped her buttocks, laughing with his friends as if it were nothing more than a joke.

Tiffney stopped.

Then she turned, stepped back toward him, and slapped him hard across the face.

The sound echoed. The hallway went quiet.

No one had ever done that to Mitch before. Not a girl. Not anyone.

The shock hit him first, then the humiliation. Being struck in front of his friends cut deeper than the slap itself. His face tightened, and anger took over.

"Do you know who I am?" he shouted.

His voice carried down the hall. "I'll teach you a lesson later. That slap will cost you."

Tiffney didn't flinch. She didn't apologize or try to explain herself. She looked at him with clear disgust, then turned and walked away as if he no longer mattered.

Behind him, his friends moved in quickly, trying to steady the situation before it got worse.

"Just ignore her," one of them said. "She's new. She probably doesn't know who you are yet. Once she finds out, she'll come back and apologize."

Mitch's jaw tightened. His eyes stayed fixed in the direction she had gone.

"She'd better," he said quietly. "If she wants to stay in this school."

But Tiffney had no intention of apologizing.

Instead, she went straight to the principal's office. When she spoke, her voice was calm and controlled. She told him she had been sexually harassed. When he asked who the student was, she shook her head.

"I don't know his name," she said. "But he's arrogant and acts like he owns the school."

The principal already had a strong idea.

He stood and walked with her into the hallway. "Can you show me who it was?" he asked.

Tiffney pointed without hesitation.

Mitch.

Mitch and his friends noticed the principal approaching almost immediately. The laughter faded. The energy shifted. The principal slowed his steps, then stopped.

"Why don't you head back to class," he said to Tiffney, choosing his words carefully. "I'll speak with him. We'll make sure this doesn't happen again."

Tiffney didn't move right away.

"This is sexual harassment," she said, steady and direct. "And my father is an attorney."

The principal stiffened slightly. He knew exactly who she was talking about.

"Yes… I know your dad," he replied quickly. "There's no need to involve him. I'll handle this."

Tiffney studied him for a moment, then gave a small nod and turned back toward her class.

Behind her, Mitch stood exactly where he was, untouched once again.

But something had shifted.

For the first time, someone had stood up to Mitch Callaghan and walked away without backing down.

And Jordan had seen it.

The following week, Jordan sat alone at a corner table in the cafeteria, eating his lunch the way he usually did. Quietly. He preferred it that way. Watching people was easier than trying to fit in too quickly.

That day, someone stopped at his table.

It was Tiffney.

"Mind if I sit here?" she asked.

Jordan looked up, a little surprised, then nodded. "Sure."

They sat in silence at first, the noise of the cafeteria filling the space between them. After a minute, she smiled.

"I've been noticing you this past week," she said.

Jordan glanced at her. "Noticing me?"

"Yeah. You're always quiet. You sit alone most of the time. I was just wondering if you're okay."

He gave a small shrug. "I'm fine. I just don't know many people yet."

He hesitated, then added, "Most kids here don't really like Haiti."

Tiffney tilted her head slightly. "So you're from Haiti?"

"Yeah. Born and raised."

"That explains it," she said, not unkindly. "People here can be… ignorant sometimes."

She paused, then leaned forward a little. "What do you like to do?"

Jordan's expression shifted, just a little. "Sports," he said. "Basketball, mostly. But I also box, swim, run track."

He hesitated again, then added, almost under his breath, "Rifle shooting… and deer hunting."

Tiffney blinked, then laughed softly. "Okay… I didn't expect that."

He smiled, just slightly.

"You're definitely not boring," she said.

For the first time since starting at Caruthersville High, Jordan felt the edge of something different. The cafeteria didn't feel as heavy. The space around him felt a little less empty.

And for the first time, he didn't feel quite so alone.

Chapter 3:
Lines That Were Crossed

Within six months, Jordan and Tiffney had grown close.

Not in a rushed or careless way, but slowly, with an understanding that neither of them ever had to say out loud. Jordan respected boundaries. He carried himself with a kind of quiet discipline that was rare in a place where confidence often crossed into arrogance. Tiffney noticed that early. It was one of the reasons she stayed.

She was widely considered one of the most beautiful girls in the school.

And Mitch noticed that too.

Mitch Callaghan had never been used to being denied anything. Attention came easily to him. So did admiration. Girls rarely turned him away, and no one had ever embarrassed him in front of others.

Until Tiffney.

What stung him most was not just the rejection, but the way it happened. She had humiliated him, openly, without hesitation, and then walked away as if he didn't matter. Since that day, they hadn't spoken. Not once.

A few of Mitch's friends tried to fix it, thinking it was something that could be smoothed over with time or pressure.

Tiffney made her position clear.

"I'll talk to him," she said, steady and unmoved, "only if he apologizes in front of everyone."

That condition didn't just frustrate Mitch. It insulted him.

A public apology was out of the question.

What he felt hardened into something deeper than anger.

I'll teach her a lesson, he told himself.

While all of this simmered beneath the surface, Jordan kept moving forward.

In those same six months, he made something clear to everyone paying attention. He wasn't just good at basketball. He was different. His ability carried across everything he touched. Track, swimming, boxing. Even the toughest conditioning drills, the ones that left most players bent over and gasping, barely slowed him down.

Jordan had talent.

Mitch had always relied on something else.

And people were starting to see the difference.

Caruthersville High's basketball program had never been strong. It lacked structure, discipline, and fairness. Favoritism had shaped it for years, and Mitch had benefited from that without ever having to question it. His place on the team had always been assumed.

Jordan saw the cracks almost immediately.

During a private conversation with the coach, the truth surfaced.

"Honestly," the coach admitted, lowering his voice as if someone might overhear, "Mitch usually decides who makes the team."

Jordan didn't react with anger. He didn't need to.

"That shouldn't be his decision," he said calmly. "It should be yours. Based on merit. Talent. Nothing else."

The coach hesitated, caught between habit and truth.

Jordan didn't push. He didn't raise his voice or try to force the moment. He simply said what needed to be said.

Something about that stayed with the coach.

Two days later, everything shifted.

"There will be open tryouts in two weeks," the coach announced to the gym. "Four teams will be formed. Anyone interested must sign up."

The reaction was immediate.

When Mitch heard, his anger flared.

He went straight to the principal's office.

"How could the coach do this without asking me?" he demanded.

From there, he confronted the coach himself.

"Why didn't you come to me first?" he snapped.

This time, the coach didn't look away.

"You're welcome to try out," he said, his voice steady. "Like everyone else."

He paused, then added, "Teams will be selected based on performance. Talent. Effort."

Nothing more. Nothing less.

For the first time, Mitch felt something unfamiliar.

A shift.

Jordan had not confronted him directly. There had been no scene, no challenge thrown in public. But the system that had always worked in Mitch's favor was starting to change.

And Mitch had never had to deal with losing control.

Two weeks later, the tryouts began.

From the moment Jordan stepped onto the court, the difference was obvious. His movement, his timing, the way he read the game. It set him apart almost instantly. Even the older players struggled to keep pace with him.

By the final session, there was no debate.

Jordan was the first name called for varsity.

The remaining spots went mostly to seniors, with a few strong players from the tenth and eleventh grades. When the freshman roster was posted, Mitch's name appeared there. Not because of what he had shown on the court, but because of who he was.

Without that name, he wouldn't have made the team at all.

The realization hit hard.

Mitch couldn't accept it. A kid from Haiti, Missouri, someone with none of his advantages, had gone straight to varsity while he remained on the ninth-grade squad.

Around the school, Jordan's name spread quickly.

Students talked about him in the halls. Teachers mentioned him in class. Coaches from other sports began approaching him one after another. Within days, he had qualified for varsity basketball, and also for track, boxing, rifle shooting, and swimming.

No one at Caruthersville High had ever done that before.

Tiffney didn't try to hide how proud she was. She showed up to practices, cheered louder than anyone, and watched him in a way that said more than words ever could.

Jordan didn't let it change him.

If anything, he pushed himself harder.

He spent extra time with the basketball coach, helping rebuild the program. Practices became more structured. Conditioning improved. Discipline tightened. What had once been a loose, inconsistent team began to take shape.

By the end of the season, something unexpected happened.

Caruthersville High reached the state championship.

Their opponent was a powerhouse from St. Louis, the defending champions for two consecutive years. The game itself was everything people expected. Fast, physical, demanding from start to finish.

In the end, Caruthersville fell short.

But it didn't feel like a loss.

For the first time in school history, a team that had once been overlooked had reached the final. The gym filled with pride. Students, parents, teachers, everyone celebrated as if they had won.

At center court, Jordan stood exhausted, catching his breath, but there was no regret in his expression.

He had changed something real.

And Mitch knew it.

That understanding, more than anything else, made Mitch dangerous.

Chapter 4:
The Price of Influence

Mr. Callaghan visited the high school the week after the state championship.

Standing at the podium in the auditorium, he spoke with practiced ease. He congratulated the students, praised the basketball coach, and thanked the principal for guiding the school to its first appearance in the state finals. Parents applauded. Teachers nodded in approval. It was the kind of speech people expected from a man in his position.

But there was one name he never mentioned.

Jordan's.

The silence around it was noticeable.

When Mr. Callaghan stepped away, the principal moved forward, adjusting the microphone before speaking.

"Since Jordan joined our high school," he said, his voice steady and deliberate, "our rankings across multiple sports have improved significantly. He is a gifted athlete, and we are proud to have him at Caruthersville High."

The room filled with applause.

Mitch sat still in his seat, his jaw tight, his hands clenched out of sight. The sound around him felt distant. Jealousy pressed in, heavy and constant. Jordan had surpassed him in every way that mattered. Faster. Stronger. More disciplined. And somehow, without trying, he had taken something Mitch wanted just as much as recognition.

Tiffney.

That thought followed Mitch home.

That night, he found his father and didn't bother easing into the conversation.

"I hate Jordan," he said, his voice sharp with frustration. "Ever since he showed up, everyone talks about him. Especially the girls."

Mr. Callaghan looked up from where he sat, calm as ever.

"Who is Jordan?" he asked.

"That Black kid," Mitch replied. "The one who plays basketball."

Mr. Callaghan paused, thinking for a moment.

"I believe his parents work for us," he said casually. "They live in Haiti."

Mitch's fists tightened.

"Even Tiffney likes him."

Mr. Callaghan's expression shifted slightly, his attention sharpening.

"Who is Tiffney?"

"Her father's an attorney," Mitch said. "They live in Steele."

Mr. Callaghan nodded slowly.

"Yes, I know him. Handles some minor legal matters for us." He leaned back in his chair. "Is she pretty?"

Mitch didn't hesitate. "She's the most beautiful girl in the school. I like her. But she's close to Jordan."

A faint smile touched Mr. Callaghan's face, the kind that rarely meant anything simple.

"Don't worry," he said. "I'll take care of the Tiffney situation."

Relief spread across Mitch's face.

"Thank you, Dad. You're the best."

Mr. Callaghan gave a small nod. "Anything for you. You're my only son. Everything I've built will be yours one day."

The next morning, he called for his secretary.

"Get Mr. Moreland on the line," he said. "Set up a meeting for tomorrow."

She hesitated just enough to ask, "May I ask what it's regarding?"

Mr. Callaghan's tone cooled. "No. Just arrange it."

"Yes, sir."

The following day, Mr. Callaghan met Mr. Moreland in his office overlooking the river, just steps away from the casino. The space itself made a statement. Floor-to-ceiling glass, polished surfaces, quiet luxury. Everything in its place.

They began with casual conversation. Business updates. Legal matters. Nothing unusual.

"I've been thinking," Mr. Callaghan said smoothly. "We'd like to involve your firm more. Expand your role with us."

Mr. Moreland nodded, clearly pleased.

"That would be… very welcome."

Then, without warning, the conversation shifted.

"I understand your daughter and my son attend the same school."

Mr. Moreland smiled politely. "Yes, they do."

"My son is interested in your daughter," Mr. Callaghan said, his tone direct. "I'd like to know how she feels about him."

Mr. Moreland hesitated, choosing his words carefully.

"As you know," Mr. Callaghan continued, "Mitch will inherit everything I own. The farms, the businesses… all of it."

He paused, letting that settle.

"We're traditional people. We don't see anything wrong with early arrangements. After high school, of course."

Mr. Moreland felt the shift in the room.

"Tiffney wouldn't need to worry about work or education," Mr. Callaghan added. "Anything she wants would be between her and Mitch."

He leaned forward slightly.

"We've known each other a long time. I think it's time we made that relationship more permanent."

Mr. Moreland kept his expression steady, though his thoughts were racing.

"Mr. Callaghan," he said carefully, "we're honored. But we're not in the same financial position. I wouldn't want that to create issues later."

He paused, then added, "Just as your son is your only child, Tiffney is mine."

Mr. Callaghan dismissed the concern with a small wave of his hand.

"That doesn't matter to me," he said. "My son wants your daughter. That's what matters."

Mr. Moreland swallowed, buying himself a moment.

"I'll need to speak with my wife. And with Tiffney."

"Of course," Mr. Callaghan replied. "Take your time. A month is fine."

He stood, signaling the end of the meeting.

"Lisa will be sending more work your way," he added casually. "Soon enough, you'll be handling most of our legal matters."

Mr. Moreland forced a polite smile and shook his hand.

As he walked out of the office, the river stretching out beyond the glass and the casino lights reflecting against the walls, the weight of the conversation settled in.

This hadn't been a simple discussion.

It had been a direction.

And somewhere far from that office, Jordan had no idea that something far more dangerous than rivalry had begun to take shape.

The building itself stood as a reflection of the Callaghan family's reach.

The ground floor was reserved for business. Offices, staff, operations. The first floor housed a large conference room used for corporate meetings, political gatherings, and private negotiations. Mr. Callaghan's main office sat there as well, along with another office that had been set aside for Mitch.

He rarely used it.

The second floor was something else entirely.

It was built for entertainment. Private parties, loud music, heavy drinking, and things that never made it into any official record. At the far end were two executive bedrooms, each with its own bathroom, designed so guests never had to leave once the night began.

By Friday evening, the place came alive.

Cars lined the riverfront. Music carried through the building. Influential guests arrived quietly and left just before dawn. What happened there stayed there, protected by money, silence, and influence.

At some point, Mr. Callaghan set a boundary.

"It's better if you use the space during the week," he told Mitch. "I host my own gatherings on weekends."

Mitch didn't take that well.

In his mind, everything in that building already belonged to him.

After a series of tense arguments, they reached a compromise.

Mitch would have the second floor on Friday nights.

Mr. Callaghan would take Saturdays.

Even within the same family, control had to be negotiated.

And in that building, control was never given freely.

Chapter 5: The Lottery Illusion

Mr. Moreland left Mr. Callaghan's office carried by ambition.

For the first time in years, he did not feel like a small man standing in the shadow of someone else's power. As he drove home, his thoughts moved faster than the road in front of him. He imagined his modest law practice growing into something influential, something respected. He saw himself stepping into rooms that had always been closed to him, invited to private dinners, political gatherings, and boardrooms where decisions were made before the public ever heard a word.

This was more than an opportunity.

To him, it felt like fortune had finally found his address.

He was so consumed by the future he was building in his mind that he missed his turn, something he almost never did. By the time he pulled up to the house and stepped into the office he ran from home, the smile was still there.

Inside, Liz looked up from her desk.

For years, she had been more than his wife. She had been the steady force behind the life they had built, handling the books, answering calls, keeping the office running, and holding him together when the pressure of it all wore him thin.

"You seem unusually happy," she said. "Usually when you come back from seeing Mr. Callaghan, you're irritated. What happened?"

Mr. Moreland let out a short laugh.

"Sit down," he said. "This is important."

Liz studied him for a moment, then sat.

"We just won the lottery."

Her eyebrows lifted. "How much?"

He smiled wider, pleased with himself.

"Tiffney," he said. "She's the lottery."

Liz frowned, not following him.

"What is that supposed to mean?"

"Mr. Callaghan wants Mitch and Tiffney to marry after high school," he said, almost proudly. "His only son likes her."

Liz did not answer right away.

"Do you understand what that means?" he continued, leaning into the moment. "Do you know what that family owns? Over a hundred thousand acres of farmland. A bank. A casino. More businesses than most people can count."

Liz's face stayed still.

"I know exactly how wealthy they are," she said. "That doesn't mean this is going to happen."

The edge in his expression sharpened.

"Why wouldn't it?"

Liz drew a breath and kept her voice calm.

"For one thing, Tiffney doesn't like Mitch."

"That can change."

"No," Liz said, more firmly now. "It won't."

She held his gaze before continuing.

"During her first week at school, Mitch touched her inappropriately in the hallway. She slapped him."

Mr. Moreland dismissed it with a wave of his hand.

"Teenage foolishness. Things happen."

Liz shook her head.

"No. Things don't just happen. Choices do."

Then she added, "And there's something else. Tiffney likes Jordan."

Mr. Moreland went still.

"Jordan?"

"You know who he is," Liz said. "You were praising him yourself when the school made it to the state finals."

A frown settled across his face.

"That Black boy?"

He paused, thinking it through. "I didn't know she was seeing him."

Liz corrected him at once.

"She's not dating him. They're close. That's all. And from what I can tell, they behave with more maturity than most adults."

He looked at her for a long moment.

"Have you met his parents?"

"Yes," Liz said. "His mother works in Haiti. They're humble people."

Mr. Moreland let out a slow breath.

"They're not at our level."

Liz's eyes hardened.

"They are exactly at our level," she said. "And they are nothing like the Callaghans."

Silence settled between them.

Finally, Mr. Moreland spoke, but some of the confidence had left his voice.

"I'm not trying to argue. I'm just saying we need to guide Tiffney. Mitch could secure her future."

Liz stood then, as if she could not stay seated for the rest of this conversation.

"Her future is hers to choose."

"She's only fifteen."

"And still more mature than a lot of grown people," Liz replied. "We cannot force her into something like this."

Her tone softened, but her meaning did not.

"This is her life. Not ours."

Mr. Moreland looked away.

"I don't believe marrying Mitch would make her happy," Liz continued. "Money and power do not make up for character. This is not a small mismatch. It is a dangerous one."

Mr. Moreland said nothing after that.

But inside him, the struggle had already begun. Conscience had spoken plainly. Ambition had heard every word.

And once ambition wakes up, it rarely steps aside without a fight.

Chapter 6:
Lines That Cannot Be Crossed

Liz did not bother lowering her voice. There was no point in pretending discretion mattered. Everyone in the county already knew how the Callaghans lived, whether they admitted it publicly or not.

"You know exactly what that family is," she said firmly. "Their drinking, their excess, their scandals. None of it is hidden. People talk because there is always something to talk about."

Mr. Moreland looked annoyed, but Liz kept going.

"That building they own is not just an office," she said. "Everybody knows what goes on there. The parties. The drinking. The people coming and going at all hours. And Mitch…" She paused, then shook her head. "Tiffney could tell you more about him than I ever could."

She fixed her husband with a steady look.

"All you can see right now is Callaghan money."

Mr. Moreland's jaw tightened, but he said nothing.

"And while you're looking at that money," Liz continued, "don't forget who our daughter is. She wants to go to law school. She wants to stand up for people who get pushed aside and denied justice. She cannot stand the kind of entitlement Mitch represents."

Her voice sharpened.

"She is the opposite of everything that boy stands for. She does not believe money excuses bad behavior. She never will."

That was enough for Mr. Moreland.

"Enough," he snapped. "Stop lecturing me."

He drew in a breath, trying to steady himself.

"We'll talk to Tiffney and lay everything out for her. The advantages. The risks. She's only fifteen. She doesn't understand real life yet, not the way we do."

Liz gave a slow shake of her head.

"She understands more than you think."

Mr. Moreland ignored that.

"What time does she get home?"

"Around 3:20," Liz said. "Sometimes later if Jordan has a game, but there's no game today. She should be here by 3:30, maybe 3:45."

He nodded once.

"Fine. We'll talk tonight. After dinner."

That evening, Liz began carefully, trying to ease into the conversation before it turned into something heavier.

"How's school going?"

"Good," Tiffney said. "Final exams are in a month, and then we move up to tenth grade."

A small smile touched her face.

"I've been thinking about getting a part-time job this summer. Maybe working as a secretary in a law office in Kennett."

That immediately brightened Mr. Moreland's mood.

"That's an excellent idea," he said. "I'll talk to Larry Smith tomorrow. You could spend a couple of months shadowing his staff and learning how things work."

He looked at her more closely.

"How's your Spanish?"

"Fluent," Tiffney replied.

"Good," he said. "That could help. They've been having trouble with Spanish-speaking clients."

Liz smiled, then asked, "How are your friends?"

"They're fine."

"And Jordan?" Liz asked, watching her daughter's face.

"He's fine too," Tiffney said. "We decided to focus on exams for now."

Mr. Moreland nodded, clearly approving.

"That's smart."

Then his tone changed.

"Do you know Mitch?"

Tiffney stiffened almost at once.

"Everyone knows Mitch," she said flatly. "He's arrogant, spoiled, and disrespectful."

There was not even a second of hesitation.

"He acts like the whole school belongs to him. Teachers are scared to challenge him. Honestly, I wouldn't be surprised if he already has the exam questions."

Liz studied her expression.

"How does he treat other students? Other girls?"

Tiffney's face hardened.

"I know enough," she said. "That's why I stay away from him and the people around him."

"Is he dating anyone?" Liz asked.

Tiffney frowned.

"Why are you asking me about his personal life? I don't care who he parties with."

Mr. Moreland leaned forward, deciding there was no point circling around it any longer.

"Let's get to the point."

Tiffney crossed her arms.

"What point?"

"Mitch's father met with me yesterday," he said. "They like you. Mitch wants to marry you after high school."

The room went completely still.

Then Tiffney stood up so quickly her chair scraped against the floor. Her face flushed deep with anger, and when she spoke, her voice trembled, not with fear, but with disbelief.

"What?"

"According to Mr. Callaghan," her father continued, forcing the words out as if saying them calmly might make them sound reasonable, "Mitch is in love with you."

Tiffney stared at him. Her hands had started to shake.

"Are you serious right now?" she demanded. "After what he did to me?"

Liz was on her feet immediately.

"That's enough," Tiffney said, her voice rising now. "I do not care how rich they are. I do not care what they own."

She turned and looked directly at her father.

"I will never marry Mitch. Not now. Not ever."

There was no uncertainty in her voice. No room for discussion. The decision had already been made.

And for the first time, Mr. Moreland felt something he had not expected to feel in his own home.

Fear.

Because this was no longer just about money, status, or opportunity. It was about control.

And the Callaghans were not a family that accepted no.

Chapter 7:
The Answer That Changed Everything

A couple of hours later, after the tension in the house had settled just enough to make conversation possible, Mr. Moreland tried again.

"Just calm down," he said, keeping his tone measured. "Mitch likes you. He's young. He's immature. People change. He'll grow out of this."

Tiffney shook her head, not in anger this time, but with certainty.

"This isn't about love," she said. "It never was. This is about his ego."

Her voice was steady, controlled.

"He doesn't know how to handle rejection. He's angry because I embarrassed him. That's all this is."

She held her father's gaze.

"He told his friends that one day I'd come back, fall at his feet, and beg for forgiveness."

Mr. Moreland shifted slightly, the words clearly landing harder than he expected.

"I was shocked when I found out he went to his father," Tiffney continued. "This isn't normal. They're trying to box me in, to make this feel like something I can't say no to."

She paused, letting the weight of that sink in.

"If he can go this far just to get what he wants now, imagine what that would look like later. After marriage."

She folded her arms, her posture firm.

"And there's something else you should know. One of the girls he's been seeing is already pregnant."

The room went quiet.

"Do you really want me to marry someone like that just because he's rich?" she asked.

Mr. Moreland exhaled slowly, choosing his words carefully, but not backing away from his position.

"Yes," he said, more quietly now. "They have money. Influence. You wouldn't have to struggle the way we did."

Tiffney didn't raise her voice, but something in it hardened.

"Money doesn't make a life," she said. "It doesn't make a marriage work."

She shook her head again.

"I already know how this would end. He'd use me, get bored, and move on. And I'd be the one left dealing with it."

She stood then, her decision clear.

"I'm not for sale."

Her eyes moved from her father to her mother.

"Please tell Mr. Callaghan that I'm not interested. Not in dating Mitch. Not in marrying him. Not now, not later."

Liz, who had been listening quietly, finally spoke.

"I agree with her," she said. "You should tell them she isn't interested. Keep it respectful, but make it clear."

She looked at her husband, her expression softening slightly.

"But you also need to be realistic. Once you say no, they may pull back. Professionally."

Mr. Moreland rubbed his temples, the pressure building in a different way now.

"Can you at least think about it?" he asked, his voice lower. "Maybe not now. But later?"

Tiffney didn't hesitate.

"No. Never."

She took a breath, then added something she had not said before.

"I like Jordan. And after law school, I plan to marry him."

That settled it.

Mr. Moreland didn't argue again. He wasn't happy, but he understood something had shifted. This wasn't a discussion he could control, and for the first time, his wife wasn't quietly supporting his position.

Liz spoke again, more calmly now, thinking ahead.

"There's no need to respond right away," she said. "Give it some time. A month, like he suggested. Say you're considering it."

She glanced at the calendar in her mind.

"Exams are coming up. Then summer break. Let things cool down."

Mr. Moreland nodded slowly.

"That makes sense," he said. "I was thinking the same thing."

But even as he agreed, he knew the truth.

Waiting wouldn't change anything.

The answer was still no.

And the Callaghans were not the kind of family that accepted rejection without consequences.

Somewhere beyond that house, Mitch was already thinking ahead, already turning over what came next.

Chapter 8: His Way or No Way

Tiffney buried herself in her studies.

She made a deliberate choice not to think about Mitch, his father, or the quiet pressure that had started to close in around her. Books gave her something steady to hold on to. Focus gave her space to breathe. It was easier to concentrate on pages and exams than on everything waiting just outside her control.

Still, she noticed things.

Mitch had a way of appearing where he wasn't supposed to be. He lingered in hallways longer than necessary, showed up near her locker, watched her across the cafeteria. When she changed her route between classes, he adjusted his without making it obvious.

She didn't confront him.

She found other ways around him.

Nearly two weeks after Mr. Callaghan met with her father, Mitch finally caught her alone near the back stairwell, away from the usual noise and movement.

"You belong to me," he said, as if stating something already decided.

Tiffney stopped.

"No one touches you except me," he went on. "I've been patient."

She turned slowly and looked at him, steady and unafraid.

"Before this turns into something messy," Mitch added, his tone shifting, "it's better if we just stay on good terms."

A faint smirk crept across his face.

"I'll forget the slap. You join my group. We move forward."

For a moment, Tiffney just stared at him, almost unable to believe what she was hearing.

"I need to go," she said quietly.

Mitch stepped closer, lowering his voice.

"It's my way," he said, "or no way."

She didn't argue.

She walked past him.

And she didn't tell Jordan.

Not about her parents. Not about Mr. Callaghan. Not about what Mitch had just said. Jordan already had enough on his plate. Finals were coming up. Scouts were watching him closely. She refused to be the distraction that pulled him off course.

Two weeks later, exams ended.

As expected, Mitch finished with the highest scores in the class. Tiffney came in just behind him. Jordan passed comfortably, balancing school and sports without losing his footing.

Mr. Callaghan celebrated the way he always did.

He spoke about it openly, praising Mitch to anyone who would listen. Friends, relatives, business partners. Everyone around him knew how those results had been achieved, but no one said anything.

That evening, he called Mitch.

No answer.

He tried again.

Still nothing.

On the third call, Mitch finally picked up.

"Dad, I'm busy," he said. "Can we talk later?"

Mr. Callaghan softened his tone.

"We don't spend much time together," he said. "I'd like to talk about your summer."

There was a pause.

"Come to the office tomorrow night," he continued. "We'll sit down. Have a drink."

"Not tomorrow," Mitch replied. "The day after. Nine o'clock."

Mr. Callaghan hesitated, then agreed.

"That's fine. I'll adjust my schedule."

He ended the call without realizing something had already shifted. Mitch was no longer waiting.

And what he wanted next was not something he planned to ask for.

Chapter 9: A Promise Made

By the time tenth grade began, Jordan and Tiffney felt something they had not felt in months.

Relief.

Exams were behind them. Summer had come and gone. The constant pressure that had followed them through the school year had finally eased.

They sat together on the bleachers after practice, the late afternoon sun stretching long shadows across the empty field.

"We're sophomores now," Jordan said with a small smile. "And you did well. Congratulations."

Tiffney smiled back.

"Thank you," she said. "But I still came in second."

Jordan let out a quiet laugh.

"Everyone knows Mitch cheated."

She turned toward him, surprised.

"What do you mean?"

"One of the history teachers handled his exams for him," Jordan said, calm but certain. "The principal funneled all the quizzes to that teacher. Mitch paid him. Ten thousand. Another five for the teacher."

Tiffney stared at him.

"How do you even know that?"

Jordan shook his head.

"He was drunk. Talking too much, like he always does. He brags about it every year."

His expression tightened.

"He said the teachers work for him. The school works for him. The whole place does. He even said the girls belong to him."

Tiffney let out a slow breath.

She hesitated for a moment, then decided.

"There's something I didn't tell you," she said. "I didn't want to distract you during exams."

Jordan turned fully toward her.

"What is it?"

"Mr. Callaghan spoke to my father," she said. "He wants me to become part of their family."

Jordan's expression went still.

"What does that mean?"

"Mitch wants to marry me after high school," she said. "And he expects me to be… friendly with him now."

Jordan's jaw tightened.

"He stopped me a couple of weeks ago," she added quietly. "He said it was his way, or there would be consequences."

Jordan took a breath, choosing his words carefully.

"That family has power," he said. "What did you tell him?"

Tiffney met his eyes.

"You already know."

She didn't hesitate.

"I hate Mitch. I don't care how much money they have. I'm not afraid of him."

Jordan nodded, but his expression stayed serious.

"They're dangerous," he said. "They could pressure your dad. His work. Everything."

"I know," she replied. "But I'm not going to accept something like that just because they're rich."

Her voice softened then.

"I love you, Jordan. After law school, I want to marry you."

He swallowed.

"I don't have anything," he said quietly. "My parents work for his family."

Tiffney smiled, gentle but certain.

"Are you afraid of him?"

"No," Jordan said. "I'm not afraid. I just don't think they'll stop easily."

He looked at her, steady and serious.

"I'd stand for you. No matter what."

Tiffney reached for his hands, holding them tightly.

"Then we face it together," she said. "How long are people like us supposed to live under people like them?"

She held his gaze.

"I'm not for sale."

Jordan smiled, something firm settling in him.

"I'm with you," he said. "Whatever comes."

Tiffney laughed softly.

"You're my best friend," she said. "And I'm lucky that someone like you treats me like an equal."

Jordan shook his head.

"And I'm lucky that someone like you sees me for who I am."

She stood, glancing toward the parking lot.

"I should go. My mom's been waiting."

He watched her walk away. Her mother gave him a small, knowing smile.

For a moment, everything felt normal.

Neither of them understood that the promise they had just made, quietly and without witnesses, had already begun to shape what came next.

***

Liz glanced at her daughter as they pulled away from the school.

"Did you tell him?" she asked.

Tiffney nodded.

"Yes."

Liz tightened her grip slightly on the steering wheel.

"What did he say?"

"He said whatever decision I make, he'll stand by it," Tiffney replied. "We agreed not to provoke anything. No arguments. No confrontation."

She looked out the window.

"With the kind of influence they have, they could hurt Dad's practice. They could even go after Jordan's family."

Liz sighed.

"I know. People like that don't take rejection lightly."

She paused, then added, "Your father is worried. We're already stretched thin. If Mr. Callaghan pulls back his support, things could get harder."

She glanced over.

"But I'm with you. Whatever happens, we'll deal with it together."

Tiffney leaned over and hugged her.

"Thank you, Mom."

After a moment, she spoke again, quieter this time.

"Maybe we leave after high school. Start somewhere else."

Liz nodded.

"I've been thinking the same."

She hesitated.

"Your dad's been drinking more. The pressure is getting to him."

Tiffney's voice firmed.

"We'll talk to him. He needs to stop."

That evening, after dinner, Tiffney sat down with her father.

"It'll be okay," she said gently.

Mr. Moreland rubbed his forehead.

"Mr. Callaghan wants to see me tomorrow," he admitted. "I've tried to push it back, but he's not letting it go."

He looked unsettled.

"I don't know what to tell him anymore."

Tiffney thought for a moment.

"Tell him I'm young," she said. "Sixteen. Not ready for anything serious."

She chose her words carefully.

"Say we need time. A year or two. Let us grow up first."

She met his eyes.

"You're not rejecting him outright. You're not agreeing either."

Mr. Moreland listened.

"Tell him we'll revisit it later," she added. "That's all."

Liz nodded in agreement.

"And remind him they're both minors," she said. "Any pressure could turn into a legal issue."

Mr. Moreland let out a slow breath.

For the first time in days, he felt like he had something to work with.

"That makes sense," he said. "I can do that."

The next day, he met Mr. Callaghan again.

He opened with praise.

"Congratulations on Mitch's results," he said. "Top of his class. Impressive."

Mr. Callaghan smiled.

"He takes after me."

He leaned back.

"So. What have you decided?"

Mr. Moreland chose his words carefully.

"My wife and I have talked it through. Tiffney is still young. Sixteen. Not ready to make decisions like this."

He kept his tone steady.

"Legally, they're both minors. We can't push anything. It could create complications."

Mr. Callaghan's expression shifted slightly, but he said nothing.

"We've started guiding her," Mr. Moreland continued. "Helping her understand your family, your stability, what the future could look like."

He raised a hand gently.

"One request. Please ask Mitch not to approach her directly. She gets overwhelmed easily. I don't want her to feel pressured."

He held his gaze.

"Let us handle it. We can revisit everything in a couple of years."

Mr. Callaghan sat quietly for a moment.

Then he nodded.

"That's reasonable," he said. "We'll wait."

He paused.

"But I can't promise Mitch will feel the same way in two years."

Mr. Moreland inclined his head.

"I understand. Let's keep things respectful and see where it leads."

They shook hands.

As Mr. Moreland walked out, he felt a brief sense of relief.

But it didn't last.

Because deep down, he knew exactly what this was.

Not an ending.

A delay.

And for a family like the Callaghans, delay was rarely the same as letting go.

Chapter 10: Father and Son

Mitch walked into his father's office without knocking.

"Why did you want to see me?" he asked.

Mr. Callaghan pointed to the chair across from his desk. "I met with Tiffney's father," he said. "They're trying to persuade her."

Mitch gave a short, contemptuous laugh. "That's nonsense. She isn't immature, Dad. She's smarter than most people in that school, and she knows exactly what she's doing."

He leaned forward, irritation sharpening his voice. "Her parents are playing games with us. She likes Jordan. She's already told her friends she plans to marry him after law school."

Mr. Callaghan's expression hardened. "She's a minor," he said. "We can't force her into anything. And don't forget, her father is an attorney."

He settled back in his chair, speaking as if the matter were simple. "Law school takes years. Let her dream. In two years, we can revisit it. Until then, leave her alone and let her parents manage her."

Mitch's face darkened. "So that's it?" he snapped. "I asked you for one thing, and you can't even make it happen?"

He pushed back his chair and stood. "I'm leaving."

"Sit down," Mr. Callaghan said.

The sharpness in his father's voice made Mitch pause. After a moment, he dropped back into the chair, though the anger never left his face.

"I didn't call you here to talk about Tiffney," Mr. Callaghan said. "I want you to spend the summer with me. It's time you started learning the business."

Mitch rolled his eyes.

"The farms, the mills, the bank. All of it," Mr. Callaghan continued. "When you finish high school, this will all be yours. But if you're going to inherit it, you need to start now. Three months every summer."

He paused, as though expecting that to carry weight. "I started shadowing my father when I was twelve."

Mitch laughed, but there was no humor in it. "That's because you dropped out in eighth grade," he said. "Grandpa didn't have a choice."

The words hit harder than he intended, or maybe exactly as hard as he intended.

Mr. Callaghan stared at him for a long moment. "What are your plans, Mitch?" he asked quietly. "Do you even have any?"

Mitch stood again. "I'll tell you later."

He turned toward the door, then stopped as if remembering something more important.

"And I want the party floor every Friday and Saturday night this summer."

Without waiting for a response, he walked out.

Mr. Callaghan sat alone after the door shut, staring at nothing for a while before he reached for the phone and called his wife.

"Why did you tell him I dropped out of school?" he demanded the moment she answered.

"I didn't mean it like that," she said evenly. "I was trying to show him how successful you became in spite of it."

"Don't tell him my weaknesses," he snapped.

She ended the call without another word.

It was not a good day.

For the first time in years, Mr. Callaghan could feel his authority slipping, not just with his son, but with his wife as well. Once, she had been afraid of him. That was gone now. After years of his affairs, his drinking, and the women he entertained who were barely older than Mitch, whatever respect had once existed had worn away completely.

Their marriage had never been built on love. She had been seventeen. He had been thirty-two. It had been arranged, like so many other things in his life, with money and expectation standing in for choice.

She had endured him for years. For the land. For the family name. For their son.

But when she realized he had started drinking and partying alongside that same son, something in her finally broke. The arguments became more frequent. His arrogance became even harder to live with. And Mitch, in so many ways, had become a younger version of him.

As Mr. Callaghan stared out at the river below his office window, one truth settled over him with unusual clarity.

He had built an empire.

But he had not built a family.

And the consequences were already beginning to show.

Chapter 11:
Discipline and Dreams

Jordan, meanwhile, threw himself deeper into basketball than ever before. From the first day of preseason training, his goal was clear, both to himself and to everyone around him. This year, they were going to win the state championship.

The coach shared that determination. Practices grew longer, harder, and more demanding. The team trained five and sometimes six hours a day, pushing themselves well past what the school had ever required before. Jordan still wanted more. After practice ended, he stayed behind to swim laps, lift weights, and run track drills until his body was drained. Over time, exhaustion stopped feeling like weakness. It became part of his discipline.

Winning was no longer just something he hoped for.

It was the standard he had set for himself.

Tiffney saw it, even from a distance. Once or twice a week, she sat quietly in the stands and watched him work. What drew her was not just his talent, but the way he carried it. He was focused without being arrogant. Driven without needing attention.

Her own life was moving forward too.

She had started an externship at a small law firm in Kennett, going there four or five days a week. Her mother dropped her off in the mornings before work and picked her up in the afternoons. Tiffney loved the routine almost immediately. She helped the secretary answer calls, especially when Spanish-speaking clients needed help. She organized files, searched case information, and listened as real legal problems unfolded in front of her.

Mr. Smith, the attorney there, noticed how seriously she took everything. Before long, he trusted her with more responsibility and began giving her a small stipend. It was not much, but to Tiffney it meant something far larger than money.

It meant independence.

It meant a future beginning to take shape.

While Jordan trained for championships and Tiffney leaned further into the life she hoped to build, Mitch went in the opposite direction.

His summer belonged to parties.

He surrounded himself with boys and girls, mostly upperclassmen, many from wealthy families like his own. Social lines existed in every school, and Mitch sat squarely at the top of his. Some of the people around him did not truly belong there, but they stayed close anyway. They were not drawn by friendship or ambition. They came for the food, the alcohol, the rides, and the freedom that money could buy.

Everyone knew Mitch would pay.

There was just one rule.

No one challenged him.

He was not only their host. He was their center of gravity. The money made that clear.

One night, a senior named Jay introduced him to cocaine. Mitch hesitated at first, but the others laughed off his caution and told him he could handle it.

"Just try a little," they said. "You'll be fine."

So he did.

The rush hit him harder than he expected. His head spun. His face flushed. For a moment, he nearly collapsed. The room shifted from laughter to worry as they rushed him to a chair, fanning him and waiting for it to pass.

About half an hour later, the dizziness faded.

Mitch started laughing.

"What the hell was that?" he said. "I feel incredible."

The party surged back to life around him. Music got louder. People loosened up even more. Mitch liked the feeling, and almost immediately he wanted more of it.

He pulled Jay aside and wrapped an arm around him in a quick, excited embrace.

"We need this at every party," he said.

Jay hesitated. "I can get it, but…"

"Don't worry about money," Mitch cut in. "I'll pay you every week. Just make sure it's strong."

Jay smiled. "Done."

The upper floor of the building became their headquarters. It was enormous, more than six thousand square feet, with two executive bedrooms, attached baths, couches lined against the walls, and wide carpeted areas where people eventually passed out and slept. Most nights the crowd stayed until noon the next day. Some stayed through Saturday, waiting for the next round to begin.

Mitch bought extra mattresses and leaned them against the walls. Food was whatever was easiest. Usually pizza. Sometimes fast food if somebody was willing to drive.

Week after week, the same cycle repeated itself.

Alcohol. Music. Drugs. Late mornings.

For nearly three months, Mitch barely left the building.

Mr. Callaghan's friends began to notice his own absence from the usual weekend gatherings.

"It's been a while since you hosted one of your parties," one of them remarked.

Mr. Callaghan smiled and lied with ease. "I've been busy training Mitch this summer. We'll start again once school begins."

He never told them the truth.

Mitch had already taken over the floor.

Even so, Mr. Callaghan kept his professional relationship with Mr. Moreland intact. The legal work continued. No threats. No pressure. Not yet.

For a while, that gave Liz and Mr. Moreland a cautious kind of relief. Their strategy of delaying seemed to be holding.

But Liz did not trust the quiet.

Without telling many people, she started looking for part-time work of her own. A gas station. A convenience store. Anything that could serve as a backup if the Callaghans suddenly pulled their support.

Mr. Moreland told her to wait.

"Let's see what happens first," he said. "We don't need to panic yet."

Liz nodded, but the unease never left her.

She knew one thing too well to believe in easy peace.

Men like Mr. Callaghan did not forget rejection.

And sons like Mitch did not forgive it.

Chapter 12:
The Calm Before the Final

When the new school year began, Jordan and Tiffney made a quiet decision. Publicly, they would keep their distance. Both families agreed it was the safest approach. No extra attention. No rumors they could not control. No reason to provoke trouble before it found them.

It did not take long for the halls to fill in the silence with their own story.

Jordan and Tiffney had broken up.

Mitch heard the rumor almost immediately, and for the first time in months, he smiled. To him, it meant one thing only. His father's pressure was finally working.

Jordan, meanwhile, cared about only one thing.

Basketball.

He trained three to four hours every weekday after school and seven to eight hours on weekends. His coach pushed just as hard. The rest of the team followed. They lived with a single goal in mind.

Win the state championship.

By the time the tournament arrived, Jordan's name had spread far beyond Pemiscot County. Coaches from across Missouri watched him closely. Some asked Caruthersville for scrimmages, not out of courtesy, but because they wanted to study him. They wanted to know how he moved, how he responded under pressure, and whether he could be contained at all.

Everyone understood who stood in the way.

St. Louis High School.

A dynasty.

They had dominated the state for years, drawing top talent from across the city. Their reputation alone was enough to attract elite players willing to relocate just to wear the jersey. Some people called it unfair. St. Louis called it winning.

Jordan himself had once received an offer to transfer there.

He refused.

He chose loyalty instead. Challenge instead. The harder road.

From the opening game of the tournament, it was obvious that Caruthersville was not the same team people remembered from earlier years. Their passes were sharper. Their defense was tighter. Their timing was better in every part of the game. Jordan had taken his own play to another level, and the team had risen with him.

Round after round, they advanced without much trouble.

Then one number started making people pay close attention.

Caruthersville was winning by twenty points or more every game.

An assistant coach from St. Louis attended nearly every one of Jordan's matchups, notebook in hand. St. Louis did not fear many teams, but it feared disruption. And Jordan had become exactly that.

Caruthersville pushed through to the Final Four.

Whenever she could, Tiffney watched from the stands, often beside Jordan's mother and younger sister, who would be joining the high school the following year and was already turning heads as an athlete in her own right. Liz came to most of the games too, making a point of staying close and driving Tiffney home afterward.

Caruthersville secured its spot in the championship with another dominant win.

Then they waited.

The semifinal between St. Louis and Poplar Bluff was tighter than anyone expected. Poplar Bluff led at halftime and for a while looked capable of pulling off the upset. But experience carried St. Louis through. They took control in the second half and won by five.

So the final was set.

The same matchup as the year before.

Only this time, everything felt different.

St. Louis was chasing a fifth straight championship, and their confidence had tipped into arrogance. So certain were they of winning that they had already recorded celebratory segments for local television before the game had even been played.

Most of the state quietly rooted against them.

People wanted change.

They wanted Jordan and Caruthersville to end the monopoly.

Inside the St. Louis locker room, the real concern had narrowed to one name.

Jordan.

Film of his games played again and again. His average of more than fifty points per game was impossible to ignore. The coaches reduced their strategy to one simple command.

"Stop Jordan."

Everything else came after that.

They assigned three defenders to him, their tallest, strongest, and most aggressive players. They were willing to risk fouls. They were willing to play rough. If the officials let it go, so would they.

Jordan's coach expected all of it.

The answer he had prepared was different.

Three-point shooting.

All season long, Jordan had practiced quietly from well beyond the arc, over and over, without drawing much attention to it. In earlier games, he had held back, following instructions and keeping that part of his game in reserve.

Now it was time.

If Jordan could stretch the floor and force St. Louis outward, their whole defensive system would start to crack.

The championship would not be won by strength alone.

It would be won by precision, patience, and timing.

Chapter 13:
The Championship Game

The wait was finally over.

The arena pulsed with noise as the final minutes before tipoff disappeared. Banners hung high above the court, cameras flashed from every direction, and thousands of voices blended into one restless roar. This was the state championship, the game every player had imagined, the one every town in Missouri would talk about by morning.

Inside the locker room, Caruthersville's coach stood in front of his team with a calm that seemed to steady the air around him.

"Do not get intimidated," he said. "Not by the crowd. Not by their name. This game is going to come down to nerves. The team that stays calm, the team that stays mentally strong, will win."

He tapped the whiteboard with one finger.

"They're going to play rough. They'll do everything they can to trap Jordan in the paint. So move the ball. If he's outside the arc, get it to him. If the lane opens, attack the basket yourselves. Trust what we worked on."

The team answered together.

"Yes, Coach."

A whistle pierced the noise outside.

The game began.

St. Louis scored first, feeding off the energy in the arena, but Caruthersville answered immediately. The pace was fast from the opening possession, physical and intense, just as everyone expected. Each time Jordan stepped into the lane, St. Louis collapsed on him. Elbows. Hands. Bodies. They crowded him from every side.

Jordan adjusted.

He drifted outside the arc.

Swish.

Three points.

The warning whistles started coming early as St. Louis got more aggressive, but the game stayed tight. Caruthersville missed a few shots in a row, and their coach quickly called timeout.

"Relax," he told them. "Do not rush. Do not panic. Stay with the plan."

By halftime, Caruthersville led by two.

58 to 56.

The St. Louis coaches still looked confident. Their team had built its reputation on second-half dominance. Older players. Deeper legs. More experience. They believed the pressure would eventually break Caruthersville down.

"We've got them where we want them," the St. Louis head coach said. "They'll run out of gas."

Inside Caruthersville's locker room, the message was different.

"We have to get more aggressive," their coach said. "They're going to come after us even harder in the second half. This is the moment we've been preparing for. Help Jordan get free, especially beyond the arc."

He looked around the room, making sure every player was with him.

"This is how we make history."

The second half opened with St. Louis tying the game. Their bench jumped up, shouting, and the crowd sensed momentum starting to shift.

Then Jordan caught the ball on the wing.

A defender came hard at him.

Jordan released from a difficult angle.

Three points.

The arena went quiet.

What followed stunned nearly everyone in the building.

St. Louis missed shot after shot, seven straight possessions unraveling in front of them. Their offense lost rhythm. Their confidence started to crack. Jordan, meanwhile, caught fire.

A three.

Then another.

Then another.

In less than five minutes, the run was devastating.

21 to 2.

The scoreboard read 79 to 58.

St. Louis called timeout. Their head coach was furious.

"What are you doing?" he shouted. "Stop trying to answer him with hero ball. Play your game. Shut Jordan down."

But the game was already slipping away.

Caruthersville stayed composed and kept executing. Jordan mixed patience with precision, and when St. Louis started fouling out of frustration, he made them pay there too. Free throws stretched the lead even further.

Soon the margin reached twenty-five.

Some fans started leaving their seats.

Another timeout followed. Another speech, but this one had a different tone.

"Finish with some dignity," the St. Louis assistant coach said quietly. "We've lost control of this game."

With four minutes left, Caruthersville's coach gathered his players once more.

"We're almost there," he said. "Slow it down now. Control the clock. Let them rush. We won't."

Jordan nodded.

From that point on, he played with complete control. Short passes. Smart movement. No wasted energy. St. Louis fouled again and again, hoping to disrupt the rhythm, but it only added more points to the board.

A desperate three from St. Louis finally dropped, pulling scattered cheers from what remained of the crowd.

Jordan answered immediately.

Three points.

Then St. Louis missed badly on the next possession. Jordan held the ball, waited, let the clock run down, and just before it expired, rose and released.

Another three.

The lead hit thirty.

By then, much of the arena had already emptied.

When the final whistle blew, the scoreboard read 110 to 75.

Caruthersville High School were state champions.

Jordan had scored sixty-five points.

The court erupted. Players mobbed one another, then lifted their coach, and after that they lifted Jordan. Cameras rushed in from every angle. Reporters pushed closer, fighting for position.

When Jordan finally spoke, he did it the way he always did, without ego.

"This was a team win," he said. "Our coach prepared us well. We stayed calm, trusted the plan, and followed through. St. Louis is a great team, but today we played better."

Then he paused and added, "This win belongs to Pemiscot County. To our parents. To everybody who believed in us."

By evening, the story had spread across the state.

A Diamond in the Rough, the headlines said.

The next day, the principal dismissed school early. The town celebrated like it had been waiting for this moment its whole life. Radio stations replayed the highlights over and over. Newspapers ran Jordan's photograph across their front pages.

For Jordan's parents, the pride of that moment washed over years of quiet struggle.

For Tiffney and her family, hope no longer felt distant.

And for Caruthersville High School, a small school most people had never taken seriously, history had finally been made.

But while the town celebrated, anger was gathering somewhere else.

And Mitch had watched every second of it.

Chapter 14:
Seeds of Resentment

All across Pemiscot County, people celebrated the first state basketball title in school history. Church bells rang. Local radio replayed the game highlights on a loop. Jordan's name turned up in diners, gas stations, barber shops, and school hallways. For most people, it was a moment of pride they would remember for years.

For Mitch, it was unbearable.

While the county celebrated, Mr. Callaghan sat in his private office overlooking the river, a glass of bourbon resting untouched in his hand. Across from him sat Riley, his advisor, fixer, and shadow for nearly fifty years.

Riley had been tied to the Callaghan family since childhood. His parents died in an accident at one of the family's rice mills, an incident buried quickly because outdated machinery and ignored safety violations would have raised dangerous questions. To keep the matter quiet, Mr. Callaghan's father took Riley in and raised him alongside his own son.

From the beginning, Riley's loyalty bordered on unnatural.

He and Mr. Callaghan went to school together. Riley fought his battles, covered for his mistakes, and absorbed blame that should have belonged elsewhere. When both boys dropped out after eighth grade, it was Riley, not Mr. Callaghan, who took on the discipline, pressure, and hard lessons of becoming useful.

Mr. Callaghan had never possessed much instinct for business.

Riley did.

Mr. Callaghan's father saw that long before anyone else did. Before he died, he formally made Riley his son's advisor and extracted a promise from him, something close to an oath, that he would never walk away.

Riley never did.

Over the years, he perfected two things. He knew exactly when to agree, and he knew exactly how to flatter power. He never criticized openly. Never crossed personal lines. He reassured, guided, and quietly managed disaster while making Mr. Callaghan feel like the smartest man in the room.

For decades, it worked.

Until now.

Mr. Callaghan finally broke the silence.

"I'm worried about Mitch," he said, still looking out the window. "He doesn't listen anymore. He's always with those friends of his."

Riley nodded. "That worries me too," he said. "Especially the drugs."

Mr. Callaghan let out a tired breath. "We drank. We chased women. But we never touched that poison."

"Exactly," Riley replied. "College is not the issue. He doesn't need college. He just needs to stay alive and functional long enough to inherit what's waiting for him."

Mr. Callaghan turned toward him. "He'll get through high school. That part is taken care of."

A faint smile touched Riley's mouth. "Yes. I already spoke to the principal."

That seemed to relax Mr. Callaghan, but only a little.

"What worries me more," Riley continued, "is Mitch's mind. He cannot stand losing. And now he has lost something he cannot buy."

Mr. Callaghan's jaw tightened.

"Jordan."

Riley let the name hang in the room.

"Everybody's talking about that boy," Mr. Callaghan said bitterly. "A nobody, and suddenly he's a hero."

Riley answered carefully. "Public admiration does not last. Power does."

Mr. Callaghan finally lifted his glass.

"You think this ends with basketball?"

Riley met his eyes. "No," he said. "I think this is where it starts."

Outside, the county was still celebrating.

Inside that office, something else was taking shape. Resentment. Slow, controlled, dangerous.

And Mitch was close enough to feel it.

Mr. Callaghan leaned back, irritation flaring again.

"Now this Black kid is a hero," he said coldly. "The whole county is praising him after one championship. It's driving Mitch crazy."

Riley listened without interrupting.

"Mitch believes Jordan turned Tiffney against him," Mr. Callaghan went on. "I don't believe that myself. But jealousy doesn't need facts."

Riley nodded slowly. "That's why we need to be careful. Not just here in Pemiscot County, but across the whole Bootheel. People are proud right now. This victory belongs to them."

Then, after a pause, he said, "We should hold a public celebration at the high school."

Mr. Callaghan looked at him. "For what?"

"For all of it," Riley said smoothly. "A big one. Ten thousand dollars for the coach. Ten thousand for Jordan as Man of the Match. Two thousand for every team member. Another ten thousand for sports development."

Mr. Callaghan did the math quickly. "That's fifty thousand."

"A small price," Riley replied. "It buys goodwill. Not just here. Across Missouri."

Mr. Callaghan considered it for a moment, then nodded. "Fine. Do it."

Riley allowed himself a small smile. "And don't worry about Mitch. When the time comes, I'll deal with Jordan. And Tiffney."

Then, more quietly, he added, "But first, we need to cut off whoever's supplying Mitch."

Mr. Callaghan relaxed a little. "Take care of it."

Almost as an afterthought, he muttered, "It's been a while since I've enjoyed younger company."

Riley did not react. "The ceremony should be next Friday," he said. "Exams are coming up. The timing will be good."

The announcement went out the next morning during school prayer. A celebration would be held Friday at one o'clock. Free snacks. Drinks. Media coverage. Sponsored by Mr. Callaghan and his son, Mitch.

Local radio stations, television crews, and newspapers had already been paid to attend. Invitations went out to parents, alumni, and community leaders. Mr. Callaghan's brothers, the congressman and the state senator, confirmed they would be there. Even the governor of Missouri was invited. He could not come on such short notice, but he promised to visit later in the summer.

Riley was pleased.

Political capital was being gathered.

By the time the ceremony began, the gymnasium was packed. More people were standing than sitting. The principal took the podium and praised Mr. Callaghan's "continued generosity" and the family's "commitment to education."

The applause was thunderous.

Then the awards began.

Ten thousand dollars for the coach.

A standing ovation.

Then, as planned, the principal called Mitch forward.

"Our brilliant student," he said proudly, "will now present the Man of the Match award."

It had all been arranged in advance by Riley and the principal.

Mitch walked forward wearing a broad, practiced smile and handed the envelope to Jordan.

The applause that followed was deafening.

Jordan thanked Mitch and Mr. Callaghan politely, and nothing more. One by one, the rest of the team received two thousand dollars each. Then Mr. Callaghan announced another ten-thousand-dollar donation, this time to expand girls' sports programs.

The crowd erupted again.

On camera, it looked perfect.

A generous family. A united community. A county celebrating its champions.

But behind the smiling faces, Riley and Mr. Callaghan were not studying the athletes. Their eyes moved through the room for other reasons entirely, lingering where they should not have lingered.

By evening, the celebration dominated the headlines.

Community pride. Generosity. Unity. Progress.

Mr. Callaghan and Riley were satisfied.

Jordan's parents felt grateful.

And that night, for the first time, Jordan's family invited Tiffney's parents to dinner at their modest home.

It was a small, quiet moment of happiness.

The kind that comes just before something breaks.

Chapter 15: Preparing for the Target

Jordan and Tiffney entered tenth grade with a clear sense of purpose.

Final exams took up most of their time, but neither of them lost focus. When the results came in, everyone moved on to eleventh grade, and, as usual, Mitch once again earned perfect scores in every subject. By then, no one even bothered to question it. It had become one of those things people accepted without comment, whether they believed it or not.

Tiffney returned to the law firm in Kennett, Missouri, where she had worked the year before. This time, she came back with more confidence and a stronger sense of direction. Mr. Smith had already seen how dependable she was, how quickly she learned, and how easily she handled Spanish-speaking clients. He raised her hourly pay and trusted her with more responsibility.

That meant more to Tiffney than the paycheck itself.

What mattered most was that she was earning respect. Not because of who her family knew, not because of favors, but because she was proving herself.

Jordan's summer looked nothing like hers.

His life revolved around training. Basketball remained at the center of everything, but he pushed himself far beyond the court. Track, swimming, weightlifting, boxing, and rifle shooting filled his days. Whatever he tried, he seemed to excel at, but what drove him was not praise. It was discipline. He wanted to sharpen every part of himself.

The team trained with that same seriousness.

They were no longer the surprise story. They were the defending state champions, which meant every school in Missouri would be studying them. Each player had received two thousand dollars in prize money, and the recognition from their title had spread far beyond their county. Still, the coach made it clear that success had made them more vulnerable, not less.

"Everybody knows our game now," he warned them. "Every school we face will build its defense around stopping Jordan."

Then he looked at the whole team and said, "We cannot rely on one man anymore. We need a second option. And a third."

Jordan agreed immediately.

"If they shut me down," he said, "somebody else has to be ready. I'll help every one of you get there."

From that point on, the work changed. Training became less about talent and more about endurance, flexibility, and adapting under pressure. Running, swimming, and strength work were folded into the daily routine. The goal was simple.

Outlast everyone.

Six hours a day. No excuses.

They knew St. Louis would come back stronger, angrier, and much better prepared. If Caruthersville wanted to win again, talent alone would not be enough.

They would have to evolve.

And while Jordan was training to defend what he had earned, other forces, quieter and far uglier, were already beginning to move against him.

Mitch's summer moved in the opposite direction.

While Jordan was building himself with discipline, Mitch sank deeper into indulgence. The parties got bigger, louder, and more reckless. He drank harder, used more drugs, and surrounded himself with the same mix of wealthy classmates and hangers-on who never seemed to run out of appetite for what his money could provide. Free alcohol. Free drugs. Free rides. Nobody asked questions as long as the night kept going.

Riley was paying attention.

True to his word, he had started watching Mitch and the people around him more closely. Riley had his own standards, if they could be called that. Alcohol and women were one thing. Illegal drugs were something else. To him, they were not indulgences. They were liabilities.

To find out where the drugs were coming from, Riley hired a discreet IT company to install hidden cameras throughout the upper party floor. Officially, it was done for security.

Unofficially, it served two purposes.

The first was to identify whoever was supplying Mitch.

The second was darker. It gave Mr. Callaghan a private record of the girls who passed through that space.

When Riley explained the plan, Mr. Callaghan laughed.

"You really do have a talent for criminal thinking," he said.

Riley only smiled. "I do what is necessary."

Within a week, he had what he wanted.

The cocaine was coming from a former student, recently graduated but still deeply tied to Mitch's circle. Riley brought the footage to Mr. Callaghan and laid it out without drama.

"I found him," he said. "I'll handle it. I just need your permission."

Mr. Callaghan did not hesitate.

"You know what to do."

And Riley did.

He contacted one of his old associates, a man who handled certain problems quietly and permanently. Riley gave him a photograph and an envelope.

"It'll be clean," the man said.

A few days later, the news spread.

Mitch's friend was dead.

Mitch was shaken, but not by grief.

What he felt was fear. More than that, panic.

He was not mourning the loss of a friend. He was terrified of losing access to what that friend had been bringing him.

He asked questions. No one had answers. The rumor going around was that it had been a drug dispute, maybe over money, maybe over the wrong people.

Riley waited until the shock had settled in before making his move.

He stopped by the party house as though he had simply decided to check in.

"Just seeing how you're doing," he said warmly. "You all right?"

Mitch looked rattled. "Someone killed my friend."

Riley frowned. "Drugs?"

"Cocaine."

Riley sighed, just enough to sound disappointed rather than surprised.

"That's what happens in that world. Dealers don't forgive mistakes."

Then he lowered his voice a little.

"You haven't been messing with that stuff, have you?"

Mitch hesitated.

Then he confessed.

"I need help, Uncle Riley. Please don't tell my dad."

Riley leaned in, speaking with almost fatherly concern.

"Promise me you'll stop. I know a doctor who can help with withdrawals. Family physician. Discreet."

Mitch nodded quickly. "I promise."

Riley made the call.

The next day, Mitch met the doctor, a trusted physician with emergency room experience and ethics flexible enough to match the money coming his way. He prescribed Methadone and gave Mitch a Narcan nasal spray, just in case.

Later that evening, Riley visited the clinic after hours.

The doctor nodded toward him. "Your OxyContin and Viagra were delivered. The pharmacist took care of it."

Riley set an envelope on the desk. "Five thousand. For helping with Mitch."

The doctor smiled. "As always, confidential."

But Mitch was already deciding what he wanted for himself.

He hated the Methadone.

The very next day, he went back and demanded OxyContin instead. Stronger. Cleaner. Better.

"I'll pay you directly," Mitch said, sliding a thousand dollars across the desk. "Nobody else needs to know."

The doctor accepted.

Doctor-patient confidentiality had a way of stretching when cash was involved.

Summer moved quickly after that.

Jordan kept training.

Tiffney kept building her future.

And Mitch drifted further into alcohol, OxyContin, sex, and isolation. He spoke less and less to his parents. He moved through his days with the confidence of someone who believed he still had control.

He did not.

And Riley, who missed very little, knew exactly when the trap would tighten.

Chapter 16: Eyes Watching

Jordan's junior year passed faster than anyone expected.

Basketball still dominated his life, but this season felt different from the last. The goal was not just to win now. It was to defend something they had already claimed. And with that came a different kind of pressure, along with a level of attention none of them had seen before.

At games, new faces began to appear.

They did not wear school colors. They did not cheer. They sat quietly, took notes, and left as soon as the game ended. According to the coach, they were recruiting consultants, some independent, some working directly with top college basketball programs across the country.

Their job was simple.

Find elite talent.

Jordan noticed them too. He did his best to ignore it and keep playing the way he always had, but he understood what it meant. Every possession mattered now. Every choice. Every mistake. What happened on that court could follow him far beyond high school.

At home, his younger sister had just started high school.

Like Jordan, she had natural athletic ability, but what stood out even more was her discipline. The girls' basketball team had never been especially strong, yet she threw herself into it with the same determination Jordan brought to everything. She pushed the other girls, helped organize practices, and raised the team's level almost immediately.

She was confident, driven, and strikingly pretty.

Jordan was proud of her. He recognized the same fire in her that had carried him this far.

Tiffney, meanwhile, had narrowed her focus almost entirely to academics.

She worked tirelessly to keep her grades high because she understood exactly what was at stake. Scholarships would decide her future. Pre-law programs, recommendations, financial aid, every detail mattered. Her work at the law firm continued to strengthen her résumé, and Mr. Smith's support was becoming more valuable with each passing month.

She was doing everything right.

Mitch was doing the opposite.

Cocaine had faded from his routine, but only because OxyContin had taken its place. It was easier to hide, easier to manage, and far more dangerous than he understood. The family physician warned him more than once to request refills early so he would not hit withdrawal.

Mitch ignored the warnings.

He just paid more cash.

Before long, he was not only taking the pills himself. He was handing them out to girlfriends and using them like favors, like gifts, like currency. The doctor looked the other way. Money made it easy to overlook things that should never have been overlooked.

Jordan was rising.

Tiffney was steadily building a future.

Mitch was sinking deeper into dependence.

And around all of them, different sets of eyes were beginning to settle on the same story. On the court. In offices. In places where decisions were made quietly.

It was no longer just about basketball.

It was becoming something much more dangerous.

A few weeks into the semester, Riley reached out to Mr. Moreland again.

The reason for the message was obvious.

Tiffney.

Mr. Moreland and Liz were both surprised. They had started to believe the matter had faded on its own. Months had gone by without direct pressure, without follow-up meetings, without any open reminder that the Callaghans were still waiting.

For a while, it had almost seemed buried.

But it wasn't.

Mr. Moreland returned Riley's call that evening.

"Let's wait until next year," he said carefully. "Tiffney needs to focus on school right now. We don't want anything distracting her."

Riley listened without interrupting.

"She isn't seeing anyone at school," Mr. Moreland added. "So there's no reason for you or Mr. Callaghan to worry."

There was a pause.

Then Riley thanked him politely and ended the call without argument.

But he was not satisfied.

He set the phone down slowly, his expression giving away nothing. He understood better than most people that silence did not mean surrender. It usually meant people were adjusting, buying time, looking for another way through.

Delays could be useful.

Patience, when used properly, could be a weapon.

Mr. Moreland believed the danger had passed.

Riley knew it had not.

The proposal was still there.

It had simply been postponed.

Chapter 17:
No Longer an Underdog

When the basketball tournament began, Jordan's team did exactly what everyone expected them to do.

They dominated.

Game after game, the pattern held. They played with control, discipline, and confidence, winning decisively without looking rattled. The girls' team had a strong season too, reaching the quarterfinals before falling short of the Final Four. Even so, it was a milestone year for that program, and much of that progress could be traced back to the culture Jordan's sister had helped create.

Jordan's team moved smoothly into the Final Four.

Then the announcement came.

Their semifinal opponent would be St. Louis High School.

For the first time in nearly two decades, one of the giants of the tournament was in danger of falling short of the final. The impact of that reality was immediate. The St. Louis players knew what was at stake. Their dynasty, built on reputation, recruiting, and a long habit of getting its way, was facing a real threat.

Even their head coach and assistant coach looked unsettled.

Losing in the semifinal would not just be a defeat.

It would be humiliation.

The game itself lived up to everything people expected. St. Louis played much better than it had the year before. Their ball movement was sharper, their defense tighter, and their physical pressure more relentless.

It still was not enough.

Jordan's team was simply stronger.

From the opening quarter, Caruthersville controlled the game with a steady lead of around ten points. Jordan managed the pace beautifully, creating space for his teammates when they needed it and scoring whenever the moment demanded it. The game never truly felt out of their hands.

By the time the buzzer sounded, the scoreboard made the difference clear.

Jordan's team had won by seventeen points.

For St. Louis, it was a public embarrassment.

For much of Missouri, it felt like relief.

Schools that had spent years living under the shadow of St. Louis's dominance celebrated quietly in their own corners of the state. The championship game would now be between two small-town teams, and Jordan and his teammates took pride in that. It meant more than a win. It meant that power and reputation were not enough on their own.

The final had a very different energy.

It was calm. Controlled. Focused.

Before the game, the coach kept his instructions simple.

"Play your natural game. Stay relaxed."

The team answered together.

"Yes, Coach."

Both teams played hard, but the difference between them became obvious before long.

Jordan.

At that point, people were no longer talking about him as just a great high school player. The comparisons had started to stretch higher. Some said his skill already looked beyond the college level. Some said his future was bigger than any high school gym could hold.

Jordan's team won the final by fifteen points.

Back-to-back state champions.

This victory did not feel chaotic the way the first one had. There was no desperation in it, no shock. Pemiscot County had expected this one. The team carried itself that way too. Jordan hugged players from the other side after the game. The coaches shook hands with real respect.

There was no arrogance in the win.

Only certainty.

When the team returned home, the principal addressed the school with unmistakable pride.

"Congratulations to our coach and our players," he said. "You've made history. Two state championships in a row."

The applause thundered through the room.

Jordan smiled.

But somewhere beyond the cheers, beyond the celebration and the praise, other eyes were still watching.

Winning once had made him a story.

Winning twice changed everything.

Jordan was no longer an underdog.

He was a target.

Chapter 18:
Senior Year Shadows

As the school year wound down, Jordan, Tiffney, and the rest of their classmates turned their attention to final exams. For most students, it was the usual kind of pressure that came at the end of every year. For Jordan and Tiffney, it felt different. The future they had talked about for so long no longer seemed far away. It felt close enough to reach, but fragile enough to lose.

Mitch, meanwhile, was becoming more unstable by the week.

OxyContin no longer gave him the rush cocaine once had. His tolerance had climbed, his moods had darkened, and even the family physician had begun to show concern. Eventually, the doctor cut back Mitch's prescription and warned him that the level of overuse could not keep being ignored.

Then the letter arrived.

Both the physician and the pharmacy received formal notices from the Bureau of Drug and Narcotics Division, a Missouri state agency based in Jefferson City. The request was precise. They wanted prescription records for ten patients who had been receiving controlled substances from the same doctor and the same pharmacy.

Mitch's name was on the list.

So was Riley's.

The physician panicked and contacted Riley immediately.

"I need your help," he said. "We should meet in person."

Riley remained calm. "Bring me a copy of the letter," he said. "I'll deal with it."

Then, almost casually, he added, "Viagra isn't doing much anymore. Do you have something stronger?"

The physician nodded. "Levitra. It lasts longer. I'd also like to check testosterone levels. At your age, that's common."

Riley smiled faintly. "The medication isn't for me. It's for Mr. Callaghan. We'll need his blood work done."

"No problem," the doctor replied. "Everything will remain confidential."

The arrangements were made quickly. A nurse would come to Mr. Callaghan's office the following afternoon.

As for the BNDD inquiry, Riley was not especially worried. He intended to bring in Mr. Callaghan's brother, the state senator, and make sure the matter disappeared quietly. Some investigations were never meant to survive long enough to become public.

Exams ended, and everyone moved up to twelfth grade.

Senior year.

For Jordan, the pressure was now greater than ever. By October or November, college recruiters would begin finalizing scholarship offers. His future depended on which programs came after him and how strong those programs really were. College was the immediate goal.

But the dream went beyond college.

He wanted the NBA.

Tiffney's future rested on different things, though they were no less important. Her GPA, her recommendations, the reputation of the programs she could reach, all of it mattered. If she stayed focused, the path toward law school was there.

Summer arrived.

Jordan went back to training with the same relentless discipline that had carried him this far. Tiffney started working full-time at Mr. Smith's law firm. Mitch drifted further into pills, parties, and the kind of denial that made him think he was still in control.

Just before the new school year began, the Morelands invited Jordan and his parents over for dinner.

It was meant to be simple.

Mr. Moreland asked Jordan about his plans, and Jordan answered honestly. He talked about college, scholarships, and how uncertain everything still felt.

"I want to play in the NBA," he said quietly. "But a lot depends on where I go and what I'm able to do once I get there."

Mr. Moreland nodded. "It's a good goal," he said. "I hope you make it."

No one said aloud what everyone at the table already understood. Jordan and Tiffney cared deeply for each other. Once college entered the picture, that relationship would become harder to hide. For now, distance was still part of the strategy.

It was a form of protection.

At one point, Jordan mentioned that Tiffney would one day make a strong criminal attorney. His parents smiled, even if they did not fully understand the title. They understood something even better.

They understood success.

The evening ended warmly. But as Jordan's family left around 9:30 that night, a neighbor watched from across the street. Her daughter, who was in Jordan's sister's class, frowned in confusion.

"Why is Jordan's family here?" she whispered. "I thought he and Tiffney broke up. Everybody knows she's supposed to marry Mitch."

Then, with the careless cruelty people often reveal when they think they are only speaking in private, the girl added, "That Black family doesn't belong here."

Something about it felt wrong.

And for the first time, the whispers began moving faster than the truth.

Chapter 19:
Rumors and Ultimatums

When school resumed after the holiday break, the halls filled with new faces. The ninth graders moved carefully, their heads down, their voices low, the way freshmen always did when they were still learning the shape of the place. Seniors noticed them right away. They always did.

One afternoon at lunch, Jordan's sister, Lakesha, was stopped by Tiffney's neighbor, a girl known more for spreading gossip than for knowing what she was talking about.

"My dad saw your family at Tiffney's house last week," she said with a smirk. "What were you all doing there?"

Lakesha answered without losing her composure. "Tiffney's parents invited us for dinner. Jordan won the championship."

The girl lifted an eyebrow. "Really? How many families get invited over like that? Are they together again?"

"No," Lakesha said firmly. "They broke up a long time ago. Our parents are just friends."

The girl did not look convinced.

Later that day, Lakesha found Tiffney and told her what had happened. Tiffney let out a groan.

"She's ridiculous," she said. "She lives on gossip."

But even as she said it, the concern stayed with her.

"Be ready," Lakesha told her quietly. "If she's talking, Mitch is going to hear about it."

She was right.

Within a week, the rumor had spread through the school. Jordan's family had eaten dinner at Tiffney's house, and from that simple fact came a flood of whispers.

They're back together.

The breakup was fake.

Mitch heard all of it.

He cornered Tiffney in the hallway. "Are you seeing him again?"

Tiffney did not hesitate. "No. It's not true. Somebody's lying."

The next day, Riley called Mr. Moreland.

"It's nonsense," Mr. Moreland said firmly. "We invited Jordan's family over for dinner, nothing more. We wished each other well. That's all."

Riley's tone changed.

"I need a final answer this month," he said. "We expect to announce the engagement within the next month or two."

Mr. Moreland hesitated. "Give me six months."

"One month," Riley snapped. "Stop playing games."

Then he hung up.

Mitch had been listening nearby.

"I told you," he said angrily. "They're stalling."

Riley raised a hand. "One month," he said. "Let me handle it."

That evening, Mr. Moreland sat down with Liz and Tiffney.

"They want an answer," he said quietly. "One month."

Tiffney did not flinch. "Then tell them the truth. I'm not ready. I need at least another year. I'm a minor. They can't force this."

Liz nodded. "Use the law," she said. "That's the only thing they respect."

A month later, Mr. Moreland called Riley.

"She isn't ready," he said calmly. "Legally, we cannot force a minor into an engagement. That would put all of us in legal danger."

Riley exploded.

"You've been playing games with us for years," he said. "Now you'd better be ready for what comes next."

His voice dropped, colder now.

"I've been holding Mitch back. I won't do it anymore."

There was a brief silence.

"One week," Riley said. "Change your answer, or deal with the consequences."

Then he ended the call.

Mr. Moreland passed the message on to Liz, Tiffney, and Jordan.

For the first time, patience gave way to fear.

They knew better than to run to the police. Complaints in Pemiscot County had a way of disappearing when they crossed the wrong family. Warnings did not stay warnings for long. They often came back as punishment.

So all they could do was wait.

And hope.

But in Pemiscot County, hope had never carried as much weight as power.

Chapter 20: The Scholarship

In the second week of October, Jordan got a message from his basketball coach asking him to come to the principal's office. As he walked down the hallway, his thoughts immediately turned dark. With everything that had been happening, he feared the meeting might have something to do with Mitch.

Instead, the moment he stepped inside, both the coach and the principal stood up smiling.

"Congratulations, Jordan," the coach said, reaching out to shake his hand.

The principal followed, gripping Jordan's hand firmly before pulling him into a brief hug. "This is a proud day," he said. "For you, for this school, and for everyone who has watched you work."

The coach's face was full of pride.

"You've been selected by one of the top-ranked basketball colleges in the country," he said. "They've offered you a full scholarship."

Jordan stood still, almost unable to process the words.

"All expenses are covered," the principal added. "Tuition, housing, meals, everything. Neither you nor your parents will have to pay a cent."

The coach nodded. "More than half of their basketball players go on to the NBA. And even if that doesn't happen, this school opens doors in every direction. With your talent and discipline, I can see you playing in the NBA within four years."

Jordan's eyes filled.

"Thank you," he said quietly. "I won't let you down. I'll give everything I have. For this school. For this county. For this state. For America."

The coach smiled. "You've already earned this."

"And hopefully," the principal said with a grin, "you'll help us win one more state championship before you leave."

Overwhelmed, Jordan stepped back into the hallway and immediately spotted his sister, Lakesha, sitting with one of her classmates, Jarred, a polite, soft-spoken boy from a small town a few miles from Haiti. Jordan had met him before and liked him.

He stopped in front of them and asked, "Are you two dating?"

Lakesha smiled shyly. "Yes. We like each other."

Jordan laughed, then blurted out, "I just got a full scholarship from one of the top basketball colleges in the country."

Both of them jumped to their feet.

"That's incredible," Jarred said.

"We're so proud of you," Lakesha said. "I'm telling Tiffney right now."

In a school as small as Caruthersville High, news never stayed contained for long. Within hours, almost everyone knew Jordan had received a full scholarship to one of the best basketball programs in the country.

Students congratulated him in the halls. Teachers stopped him to shake his hand. Staff members smiled when they saw him. Jordan had always been well liked, and moments like this made it obvious why. He was gifted, yes, but he was also humble, respectful, and hardworking.

Almost everyone was happy for him.

Almost.

Mitch and a small circle of his closest friends were the only ones who stayed silent, their jealousy growing sharper by the hour.

Tiffney heard the news from Lakesha, and when she did, a deep calm settled over her. Jordan had earned this with discipline, sacrifice, and relentless work. There was nothing accidental about it. He deserved every bit of it.

"Give him a hug and a kiss from me," she said with a smile. "I'll give him the real one this weekend."

Lakesha laughed. "Message delivered."

Before the final bell, she found Jordan surrounded by teammates, all of them congratulating him at once. She pushed through the crowd, hugged him tightly, and kissed him on the cheek.

"That one's from Tiffney," she teased. "She says the real kiss comes this weekend."

Jordan laughed. "You're impossible."

That evening, Jordan's parents could hardly contain their pride. For the first time, they allowed themselves to believe that their son's future might truly be limitless.

Tiffney's parents were just as happy. They understood that this was not just an award. It was the kind of moment that could change a life forever.

But while celebration filled one home after another that night, somewhere else resentment was hardening into something more dangerous.

The scholarship was not just Jordan's triumph.

For Mitch, it was the breaking point.

Chapter 21: The Trap

The next morning at school, Tiffney found Lakesha near the lockers, glancing around before she stepped closer.

"Tell Jordan I took tomorrow off from the law firm," she said in a low voice. "It's Saturday, and I'm taking him out to dinner in Cape Girardeau. Tell him to be ready by three. I'll pick him up from his house."

Lakesha smiled immediately. "He'll probably be ready before noon."

Neither of them noticed Mitch standing farther down the hallway, watching.

By then, Mitch and his friends had already pieced it together. Lakesha was the one carrying messages between Jordan and Tiffney. One of Jordan's neighbors had fallen in with Mitch's circle, and Mitch had already made his instructions clear.

"Watch them," he had said. "Every move."

So when Jordan canceled basketball practice after one o'clock the next day, word reached Mitch almost at once. And from Mitch, it went straight to Riley.

In a small town, secrets did not stay buried. They barely survived the hour.

Tiffney was supposed to arrive at Jordan's house around three, but she got there early, a little before two. At 2:05, Mitch's informant called.

"Tiffney's car is at Jordan's house."

At 2:30, another call came.

"They just left."

Mitch's voice turned cold. "Follow them. I want to know exactly where they're going."

A few minutes later, the next update came in.

"They're heading north on Highway 55."

Mitch smiled, then picked up the phone and called Riley.

"Cape Girardeau," he said. "Or maybe Sikeston."

Jordan and Tiffney, meanwhile, felt lighter than they had in weeks. For the first time in a long while, they were alone without pressure pressing in from every side. The air between them felt easy again.

As they approached the Warren exit, Tiffney suddenly pulled off to the side of the road.

Jordan looked over at her, puzzled. "Why are we stopping?"

She leaned across the console and kissed him deeply.

"That's why," she whispered.

They both laughed, their hearts unburdened for the moment, never realizing they were already being followed.

A few seconds later, she started the car again and merged back onto Highway 55 North.

About ten minutes later, just past the Portageville exit, they saw flashing lights ahead.

Then more behind them.

Then everywhere.

Police cars, too many to count.

Tiffney's hands tightened on the wheel. "They must be after someone else."

Still, she slowed and pulled over.

Every police vehicle stopped.

In an instant, they were surrounded.

Highway 55 was shut down.

Two officers approached with guns drawn.

"Out of the vehicle!" one of them shouted. "Hands over your heads!"

Jordan moved first, calm and controlled, doing exactly what he was told. Tiffney froze for half a second before panic overtook her.

"What's happening?" she cried. "What did we do?"

Then the Caruthersville police chief stepped forward, his face hard and expressionless.

"We received information that Jordan has been transporting cocaine to Sikeston and Cape Girardeau," he said flatly.

More vehicles kept arriving, sheriff's units, local police, state officers. Nearly twenty in all.

"We're searching the vehicle," the chief said. He held out his hand. "Keys."

Tiffney's fingers shook so badly she almost dropped them before handing them over.

Jordan was handcuffed and shoved into a large black SUV. Tiffney was pulled away from him and placed in a separate patrol car.

A few minutes later, an officer shouted from the rear of the vehicle.

"Sir, we found it."

A sealed bag of cocaine.

The chief nodded once. "Don't touch anything. DEA is on the way."

Ten minutes later, a DEA agent arrived. The chief briefed him quickly, like this was just another routine stop.

"We've been watching this kid for a year," he said. "Remember that young man who was killed last year? He was connected."

He pointed toward the SUV where Jordan sat.

"Seventeen years old," the chief said. "We're charging him as an adult. We need to make an example out of him."

The DEA agent said nothing.

About an hour later, Tiffney was released.

The chief stepped close enough that she could smell coffee and tobacco on his breath.

"You're lucky," he said. "We're not charging you. Otherwise, you'd be looking at eight to ten years for conspiracy."

Tiffney broke into sobs. "Sir, this is a mistake. Jordan doesn't do drugs. He's a state champion. He just got a full scholarship. We were only going to dinner. We were celebrating."

The chief's voice turned colder.

"The cocaine was in your trunk," he said. "Jordan put it there while he was at your house."

Then he leaned even closer.

"You and your father should be thanking Mr. Callaghan, Riley, and Mitch. If not for them, you'd be sitting in jail right now."

For a second, her knees nearly gave way.

He straightened and looked at her as though she disgusted him.

"If you're not gone in five minutes, I'll arrest you too."

Tiffney drove home alone.

She cried the whole way.

Not for herself.

For Jordan.

Because what had begun as nothing more than a dinner invitation had just torn his life open.

And somewhere behind it all, powerful men were smiling to themselves, knowing the trap had closed exactly the way they intended.

Chapter 22: The Price of Power

Tiffney knew it before she even walked through the front door.

It was Mitch. It was Riley. And it was Mr. Callaghan.

They had put the drugs in her car.

Her parents looked up the moment she came in. Her mother was the first to speak.

"You're back already? Did you change your plans?"

Then she saw Tiffney's face.

Mr. Moreland stood up at once. "Why are you crying?"

Tiffney barely made it to the couch before she collapsed into tears.

"It's my fault," she sobbed. "I asked Jordan to go to dinner in Cape Girardeau. They knew everything. They knew we were on Highway 55. They were waiting for us."

Mr. Moreland's face changed. His daughter was not someone who cried easily. Whatever had happened, it was serious.

"Sit down," he said, though his own voice had gone tight. "Start at the beginning. Tell us everything."

Through tears, broken breaths, and trembling hands, Tiffney told them all of it. The police cars. The roadblock. The search. The cocaine in her trunk. The DEA agent. The chief's words.

"It was them," she cried. "Riley, Mitch, and Mr. Callaghan. I know it was. I know it. The chief kept telling me that you and I should be grateful to them for not charging me. He said otherwise I'd be in prison for eight or ten years for drug conspiracy."

Her mother covered her mouth.

Mr. Moreland closed his eyes for a long moment before he asked the only question that mattered now.

"Where is Jordan?"

"I don't know," Tiffney whispered. "They arrested him before they even searched my car. They shoved him into a black SUV and drove off with the DEA agent."

Mr. Moreland nodded slowly, grimly, already thinking ahead.

"They found the drugs in your car," he said. "Legally, they could have arrested you too. Mr. Callaghan has money, influence, political reach. They can make almost anything happen."

Tiffney grabbed his arm.

"Please," she begged. "Find him. Represent him. This is my fault. If he goes to prison, his life is over. His scholarship, his future, everything. I can't live with that."

"Stop," her father said, more sharply than he meant to. Then his voice softened. "You are not to blame. Let me find out what I can."

He went straight to the Caruthersville Police Department.

"I'm representing Jordan," he said as soon as he was shown in. "I need to know where he is."

The police chief looked at him for a long, unreadable moment.

"New Madrid County Jail," he said at last.

Then his voice dropped.

"Off the record, stay away from this case. Nobody can protect that boy. The evidence is strong. If you care about your family, leave this state."

Mr. Moreland held his gaze. "Thank you."

At the New Madrid County Jail, Jordan's first question was not about himself.

"How's Tiffney?" he asked immediately. "Is she in jail?"

"She's safe," Mr. Moreland said. "She's home."

Jordan let out a breath, as if that alone mattered more than the handcuffs, the cell, or anything else around him.

Then he looked up again.

"Do you believe them?" he asked. "That I was transporting cocaine? They told me they've been watching me for a year."

"We know you're innocent," Mr. Moreland said. "This was arranged. Mr. Callaghan, Riley, and Mitch are behind it. Law enforcement in Pemiscot, Butler, New Madrid, Sikeston, all around this area, too many of them answer to the same power."

He slid a document across the table.

"Sign this. Appoint me as your attorney. I'll review everything they claim to have, and I'll meet with the DEA agent in Cape Girardeau."

Jordan signed without even glancing down.

"Thank you," he said quietly. Then, after a pause, "Did Tiffney tell you about the scholarship?"

Mr. Moreland's expression shifted.

"Yes," he said softly. "And I'm going to fight for you. But you need to understand something. These are dangerous people."

Jordan looked at him, bewildered and wounded all at once.

"Why?" he asked. "What did I do to them?"

Mr. Moreland exhaled.

"Mitch hates you for two reasons," he said. "First, because Tiffney chose you over him. She rejected everything he thought his name and money should have guaranteed. Second, because you took the attention he believes belongs to him. The championships. The praise. The spotlight."

He paused.

"Mitch has been spoiled his entire life. He cannot accept rejection. And his father will crush anyone he thinks has humiliated his son."

Jordan looked down, his fists tightening slowly.

"Stay strong," Mr. Moreland said. "I'll come back next week."

When he left, the truth remained hanging between them, too heavy to ignore.

In Pemiscot County, justice did not belong to the innocent.

It belonged to the people who could afford to shape it.

Chapter 23:
Evidence Without Truth

From the jail, Mr. Moreland went straight to meet the DEA agent and formally introduced himself as Jordan's attorney.

"I'm representing Jordan," he said. "I need to understand exactly what charges you're bringing against him."

The DEA agent looked at him for a moment, then opened a file.

"He's being charged as a cocaine distributor," he said. "The Caruthersville police have been monitoring him since last year, after the murder of a young man who had recently graduated from high school. That individual was involved in cocaine distribution and had ties to Jordan."

Mr. Moreland frowned.

"Do you honestly believe that?" he asked. "The Jordan I know is one of the finest student-athletes this school has ever produced. He won two straight state championships. He just received a full scholarship from one of the top colleges in the country. How does somebody like that suddenly become a drug dealer?"

The agent's face did not move.

"I know about his athletic background," he said. "But we have substantial evidence."

He slid the file across the desk.

"The man who placed the cocaine in your daughter's car has confessed," he continued. "He says he worked for Jordan for nearly a year. You and your daughter may not have known anything about Jordan's operation."

Mr. Moreland went still.

The agent flipped to a series of photographs.

"These were taken by Caruthersville police," he said. "This man was photographed opening your daughter's trunk and placing the cocaine inside. Our informant tipped us off. We followed him. Then we followed your daughter and Jordan on Highway 55 North."

He turned another page.

"Jordan was supposed to deliver one packet in Sikeston and another in Cape Girardeau."

Mr. Moreland leaned forward. "That makes no sense. My daughter asked Jordan to go to Cape Girardeau for dinner. It wasn't even his idea."

The agent's tone hardened immediately.

"I strongly advise you not to repeat that statement, especially in court. If you do, we'll arrest your daughter as well. We are not concerned with whose idea the trip was. We are concerned with evidence."

He leaned back, as if the matter were obvious.

"We have the informant's call records. We have the photographs. We have the confession. We found the cocaine in your daughter's trunk with Jordan present. Your daughter wasn't charged only because we found nothing tying her directly to the alleged operation, and because Jordan's supposed partner says he never dealt with her."

Mr. Moreland held his voice steady.

"Can I meet the man who claims he put the drugs in her trunk?"

"If he agrees, yes."

"What's the worst-case outcome for Jordan?"

The agent answered without hesitation.

"If he fights the case, ten to fifteen years. If he cooperates and takes a plea, two to three."

Mr. Moreland swallowed.

"I've never handled a criminal case," he admitted. "Would it help to bring in a criminal defense attorney?"

The agent gave him a thin look.

"They'll charge you at least twenty-five thousand dollars. And honestly, it won't change much. This will end in a plea deal. Nobody beats the government."

Mr. Moreland left the office shaken.

In his heart, he knew exactly what had happened. But his heart did not matter here.

Power mattered. Mr. Callaghan. Riley. Mitch.

Together, they had ruined a young man whose future had burned brighter than almost anyone else in that county.

Later, Mr. Moreland met the man who had supposedly planted the drugs. The story never changed. Not once. Same words. Same tone. Same rehearsed certainty. The man insisted he had supplied Jordan with cocaine for more than a year.

Mr. Moreland spent less than twenty minutes with him.

That was enough.

The man had been prepared.

It was a perfect setup.

When Mr. Moreland returned to Jordan, he laid everything in front of him. He showed him the photograph of the man placing the drugs in Tiffney's trunk.

Jordan stared at the image as though it belonged to somebody else's life.

"I've never seen this man before," he said. "Not once. This is the first time I've ever seen his face."

Mr. Moreland nodded slowly.

"I know. Mr. Callaghan, Riley, and Mitch framed you. But the evidence they've built is heavy."

Jordan looked up sharply.

"What do you mean you can't protect me?" he asked. "What evidence do they really have?"

"Enough to put you in prison," Mr. Moreland said. "Maybe two years. Maybe fifteen. It depends on whether you take a deal."

"But they're lying," Jordan said. His voice shook now. "There's no proof I sold drugs. No money trail. No transactions."

"You're right," Mr. Moreland said. "And we believe you. But they found cocaine in your girlfriend's car. If we fight too hard, they will charge Tiffney too."

Jordan went silent.

For a few moments he just stared at the table between them.

Then, very quietly, he asked, "What about my basketball career?"

Mr. Moreland did not answer.

Jordan's voice broke when he asked again.

"What about my basketball career?"

Mr. Moreland swallowed hard.

"I don't have an answer for that, son."

Jordan lowered his head.

"They're powerful," Mr. Moreland said after a moment. "And right now, they're winning. All we can do is pray."

Then he saw the tears gathering in Jordan's eyes, not just the tears of fear, but something deeper and harder to look at.

The tears of a dream being stolen in front of him.

And in that moment, the truth became almost unbearable in its clarity.

Justice had nothing to do with innocence.

It had everything to do with who controlled the system.

Chapter 24:
When Truth Is Powerless

The arrest of Jordan rippled through Pemiscot County like a shockwave no one could ignore. By the end of the day, people were talking in schools, in churches, in grocery stores and coffee shops. The story moved fast, but the disbelief moved faster. No one who truly knew Jordan could make sense of it. Not his teachers, who had watched him grow. Not his coaches, who had trained him. Not the students who had seen him earn everything he had.

But there was something else everyone understood, even if no one said it out loud.

Jordan was the boy Mitch hated.

And Jordan was the boy Tiffney loved.

Mitch, the only son of Mr. Callaghan, had grown up believing that certain things were his by right. Attention. Respect. Control. And when Jordan came along and took all of that without asking permission, Mitch had never forgiven him. Around town, people whispered the same thing in different ways. This was personal. This was revenge. But the official story was something else entirely.

According to the DEA, the evidence was strong.

There were witnesses.

There were photographs.

There was cocaine.

And in the eyes of the law, that was enough.

Mr. Moreland came home late that evening, his shoulders heavy, his face drawn. He had not eaten all day. He had barely noticed the hours passing. Since leaving the jail, his thoughts had not moved far from Jordan, and the weight of it all sat on him like something he could not shake loose.

As he stepped inside, questions followed him.

Why did God give so much power to men who used it this way?

Why create boys like Jordan, honest, gifted, disciplined, only to let them be broken by the very system that claimed to protect them?

Jordan's dream had never been complicated. He wanted to play in the NBA. He wanted to lift his family out of poverty. He wanted to live with dignity. That was all.

Now he was sitting in a cell.

And no one could tell him how to get his future back.

Liz and Tiffney had been waiting all day. The moment Mr. Moreland walked through the door, they knew the answer was written on his face before he said a single word. When he finally spoke, he told them everything. Every detail. Every conversation. Every dead end.

By the time he finished, both women were in tears.

Tiffney's grief came out in waves, sharp and angry, while Liz sat still, her silence heavier than any words. What had happened to Jordan was no longer just about one boy. It was something much larger, something uglier, something people had lived with for years but rarely faced this directly.

A system that claimed fairness.

A system that promised equality.

A system that delivered something else entirely.

Jordan had done nothing wrong.

But in this world, that had never been enough.

The next morning, when Tiffney finally spoke, her voice was quiet but steady.

"What are we going to do now?"

Mr. Moreland took a long breath before answering. "Tomorrow," he said slowly, "I'm going to meet Riley. I'll ask him to let Jordan go."

The following afternoon, he walked into Riley's office right on time. The room felt cold, controlled. Riley sat behind his desk as though nothing unusual had happened, as though Jordan's life had not been turned upside down.

"Riley," Mr. Moreland began, his voice unsteady despite his effort to control it, "Jordan is innocent. Whatever happened between Mitch and my daughter should not destroy that boy's life. Please… if it's money you want, take it. Just let him go."

Riley didn't react. Not even a flicker.

"There are only three ways this ends," he said, his tone flat and final.

Mr. Moreland felt his chest tighten.

"First, Tiffney agrees to marry Mitch. Second, she publicly distances herself from Jordan and stays silent at school. Third, Jordan and his family leave Missouri. Permanently."

He leaned back in his chair as if he had just outlined a simple business deal.

"You have one month," he added. "After that, there will be no mercy."

Mr. Moreland left that office feeling smaller than he had in years.

That evening, he waited for Tiffney to come home. When she walked in around 3:30, exhaustion clung to her. The looks at school, the whispers, the weight of everything had already worn her down.

He told her what Riley had said.

For a moment, there was silence.

Then, without hesitation, she spoke.

"I'll do it."

Both of her parents froze.

"If marrying Mitch will free Jordan… I'll do it," she continued, her voice soft but unwavering. "If leaving Missouri will save his future, I'll accept that too. He's innocent. This happened because of me."

Tears ran down her face, but her eyes never wavered.

"I'll give up my dreams so he can keep his."

Liz covered her mouth, stunned.

Mr. Moreland felt something break inside him, something deep and painful, and yet at the same time, a strange, fierce pride rose alongside it.

Tiffney was only seventeen.

And she was ready to give up everything.

For love.

Chapter 25: Truth Has a Price

Tiffney began to dread going to school.

The hallways felt different now. Every glance lingered too long. Every whisper seemed to follow her. Even when no one spoke directly to her, she could feel the questions hanging in the air.

Did Jordan really do it?

Was it all a lie?

Did he destroy his own future?

She refused to stay silent.

"He's innocent," she told anyone who would listen. "Jordan has never touched drugs. Someone set him up. This is revenge."

Her voice carried further than she expected. Eventually, it reached the local media. When she spoke to reporters, she did not soften her words.

"How does the best basketball player in Missouri suddenly become a drug dealer?" she asked. "Where is the money? He never even had a bank account."

Most outlets chose to stay quiet. They all understood the same thing. Power in Pemiscot County was not something you challenged lightly.

But one paper was different.

The Southeast Missouri News had built its reputation on refusing to look away. It was family-owned, independent, and, more importantly, unafraid. Its editor, Rick, had spent his life watching systems bend to protect the powerful.

"This place doesn't run on justice," he often said. "It runs on influence."

When Tiffney told her father that a journalist named Shirley wanted to meet her, fear settled in his chest.

"Do not accuse Mitch or the Callaghans directly," he warned her. "We don't have proof. Just tell your story. Nothing more."

That night, he repeated Riley's ultimatum again, each word heavier than the last. Tiffney listened without interrupting. Liz's anger burned quietly beside her.

"They're monsters," Liz said.

Tiffney's answer came without hesitation.

"I'll do it," she said again. "If it saves Jordan."

The next day, Mr. Moreland went back to the jail.

Jordan looked up the moment he saw him.

"Is Tiffney okay?" he asked.

"She's safe," Mr. Moreland said. "That's what matters right now."

When he explained Riley's terms, Jordan's eyes filled immediately.

"Tell her no," he said, his voice breaking. "I don't care about basketball anymore. I care about her. If she gives up school or marries Mitch, I'll confess to everything. I'll take the blame. I'll go to prison. She has to become what she's meant to be."

He pressed his hands against the glass, as if trying to hold onto something slipping away.

In that moment, Mr. Moreland understood something he hadn't fully seen before.

These two were stronger than anyone with power over them.

Stronger than Mitch.

Stronger than Riley.

Stronger, even, than the system trying to crush them.

When he later visited Jordan's family, he told them everything as gently as he could.

"Jordan is holding up," he said. "You'll be able to see him next week. I'll take you."

For the first time since the arrest, something like hope returned to their faces.

Later, Jordan's father pulled him aside.

"Is there any chance he gets out?"

Mr. Moreland hesitated, then told him the truth. Riley's demand. Tiffney's willingness to sacrifice herself. Jordan's refusal to accept it.

Jordan's father shook his head firmly.

"I don't want my son saved like that," he said. "That girl deserves a future. She should not be trapped in a life like that."

When Mr. Moreland returned home and shared everything, Liz listened in silence before speaking.

"Thank God they love each other this much," she said softly. "But I agree. Tiffney must never marry Mitch."

Her voice trembled, anger just beneath the surface.

"Everyone here knows what that family is. Mitch would destroy her, just like his father destroyed his own wife."

Mr. Moreland nodded slowly.

"He married for land, not love," he said. "And Mitch is already worse than him."

Liz took Tiffney's hand.

"If you go into that house," she said quietly, "you will never be free."

And for the first time, all three of them understood what they were really facing.

This was no longer just about saving Jordan.

It was about saving Tiffney too.

Chapter 26

Tiffney chose to meet Shirley in Poplar Bluff instead of Steel. She did not want the meeting anywhere near home. In a place like that, information traveled too easily, and Mitch's reach seemed to extend further than it should.

They met in a small office above a printing press. The walls were lined with old headlines, faded clippings, stories that had survived long enough to matter.

Shirley switched on her recorder and gave her a steady look.

"Start from the beginning."

Tiffney took a breath, steadying herself.

"It was my first week of ninth grade," she said. "I was walking between classes when someone came up behind me and slapped me. I turned around, and he was laughing. He said his name like I was supposed to recognize it. Like it meant something."

Shirley leaned forward slightly. "Did you know who he was?"

"I had heard of him," Tiffney said. "Everyone had. They said he was powerful. That being around him made things easier. But I had never spoken to him before that moment."

"And after?"

"He sent people to me," she said. "Boys. Girls. They told me to apologize. Told me to join his group. Or things would get difficult."

"Did you report it?"

"I told the principal. He said he would handle it. Then he asked me not to tell anyone."

Shirley's expression tightened. "And Jordan?"

"I met him a few days later," Tiffney said, her voice softening. "He was sitting alone in the cafeteria. Quiet. Polite. Nothing like Mitch. We started talking. About school. About basketball. We were just friends."

"And Mitch noticed."

"In a place like that," she said, "everyone notices everything."

She went on, step by step, telling the story as it had unfolded. Mitch's anger. His father's involvement. The pressure on her family. The delays. The second championship. The dinner. The rumor.

Then her voice trembled.

"Jordan had just gotten his scholarship. I wanted to celebrate. I asked him to dinner. They followed us. Someone put cocaine in my trunk while my car was parked outside his house."

Shirley's voice dropped. "And then they arrested him."

"They arrested him before they even searched the car," Tiffney said. "The man they say did it claims he worked for Jordan. But Jordan has never even seen him. There's nothing. No money. No proof. Just what they planted."

Shirley was silent for a moment, then asked quietly, "Did Riley offer you anything?"

Tiffney hesitated, then nodded.

"They said they would drop everything," she whispered, "if I left school, married Mitch, and Jordan's family left Missouri."

Shirley's eyes hardened.

"That's extortion."

"I can't prove it," Tiffney said. "But it's true."

Shirley reached over and turned off the recorder.

"I'll take care of this," she said. "I won't use your name. Not your father's either. But the story will come out."

She handed her a card.

"Read Sunday's paper."

Tiffney held the card tightly in her hand.

"Thank you," she said.

Chapter 27

Tiffney sat at the kitchen table across from her parents, the stack of opened mail still scattered between them. Her hands rested in her lap, but there was tension in every part of her body.

"I told Shirley about Riley's offer," she said quietly. "She promised she wouldn't use your name or mine. If Riley confronts us, I'll say the rumor could have come from Mitch or one of his friends. They were bound to be angry anyway. We already refused them."

Mr. Moreland nodded, his face drawn. "We have to assume they'll come after us no matter what now."

Then he reached for the pile of envelopes and slid them toward her.

"These came today," he said. "From colleges."

Tiffney looked at them for a moment before touching them, as if she were afraid they might disappear if she moved too fast. Her fingers trembled when she opened the first one.

Harvard.

Then Duke.

Then Princeton.

Each letter offered her a full scholarship.

For a second, she could not speak. She only covered her mouth with one hand and stared down at the pages, her eyes filling. These were not just schools. They were the places she had imagined in private, the kind of future she had allowed herself to dream about when everything felt uncertain. Elite pre-law programs. A way forward. A life that belonged to her.

Liz's eyes brimmed over first.

"My baby," she whispered. "You did it."

Mr. Moreland came around the table and pulled Tiffney into his arms. "You earned this," he said, his voice breaking a little. "Every bit of it."

Tiffney drew a long breath and tried to steady herself. "We need to visit them as soon as possible," she said. "I need to decide."

"I agree," her father said. "You and your mother should go. I'll stay here and keep working on Jordan's case."

The next morning, Tiffney met with her academic coordinator. He congratulated her warmly, and when she asked for time away to visit the schools, he approved it without hesitation.

"Take whatever time you need," he told her. "This is your future."

Tiffney glanced toward the door before lowering her voice. "Please keep this confidential."

He gave a quick nod. "Of course."

Within a few hours, she had contacted all three universities, and each one invited her for an early visit. For the first time since Jordan's arrest, something fragile and unfamiliar stirred inside her.

Hope.

That same Sunday, the new edition of the *Southeast Missouri News* landed across the region like an explosion. By breakfast, copies were already being passed from hand to hand in diners, barbershops, and church parking lots. Shirley's story was on the front page, and it hit with the force of something people had half-suspected but never expected to see in print.

The article reported that a rumor had spread through Caruthersville High and beyond: Mr. Callaghan and Riley had allegedly offered a private deal. All charges against Jordan would disappear if Tiffney agreed to marry Mitch, quit high school, and give up her dream of becoming a lawyer. Jordan and his family, in turn, would be forced to leave Missouri. In exchange, he would walk free.

Shirley ended the piece with a question that chilled anyone who read it.

Would Tiffney sacrifice her future to save the boy she loved?

Or would Mitch Callaghan finally get what he wanted?

By mid-morning, Riley stood in Mr. Callaghan's office holding the paper, his jaw tight. Mr. Callaghan read the article slowly, one line at a time, his expression darkening with every paragraph.

"That woman wrote this carefully," he said at last, his voice cold and measured. "She knows exactly how to make us look like monsters."

Riley gave a small nod. "She didn't name anyone directly, but she made it credible. That's enough."

Mr. Callaghan slammed his fist onto the desk so hard the bourbon glass beside him rattled.

"How did this get out?"

He snatched up the phone and dialed Mitch. When Mitch answered, his father didn't bother with greetings.

"Did you tell anyone about the deal?"

There was a pause on the other end. Then Mitch said, uncertainly, "I don't remember. Maybe I said something. Why?"

Mr. Callaghan's face twisted with rage. "You stupid fool. It's on the front page of a newspaper."

Mitch exploded immediately.

"I'll kill that bitch."

"Don't you dare do anything," Mr. Callaghan snapped. "You stay out of this. Riley and I will handle it."

He hung up hard and turned back toward Riley, still seething.

"You should never have let Mitch know about the arrangement."

Riley let out a slow breath. "That mistake is already made. From this point on, he stays out of everything."

Outside that office, the storm was already moving. Only this time, it was not hidden behind closed doors. It was public.

Riley moved toward the window, the newspaper still folded in his hand. "We need to deal with the publisher," he said. "Rick. His daughter wrote the story. Their paper and printing press are in Poplar Bluff."

Mr. Callaghan leaned back in his chair, though the anger had not left his face. "I know Rick. Honest man. Too honest for this part of the world. His daughter learned it from him."

"That's the problem," Riley said. "Nobody likes them. They go after police, sheriffs, politicians, judges, everybody."

"I never cared before," Mr. Callaghan muttered. "Not until now."

Riley looked at him carefully. "This isn't the sort of man you can buy."

A thin smile touched Mr. Callaghan's mouth. "Everyone has a price."

"Not Rick."

Mr. Callaghan waved him off. "I'll be in Poplar Bluff in a few days anyway. We're finalizing that cinema purchase. I'll handle him."

Riley hesitated, then said, "His daughter is older, if that matters. In her forties. Divorced. One child. Lives with her parents."

"Then forget her," Mr. Callaghan said, almost under his breath.

The article sent aftershocks through southeast Missouri. Police chiefs, sheriffs, and DEA agents were furious, but the public reaction moved in the opposite direction. For the first time, people began questioning Jordan's arrest openly. In small towns and coffee shops, the same sentence kept surfacing again and again.

This boy was framed.

Mr. Moreland bought several copies of the paper that morning and carried them with him to New Madrid County Jail. Jordan's parents, his sisters, and his younger brother were already there when he arrived. Without a word, he handed Jordan one of the newspapers.

"They're finally talking," he said.

Jordan read in silence, his hands trembling slightly as he turned the pages. When he finished, Mr. Moreland told him the rest.

"Tiffney got full scholarships," he said. "Harvard, Duke, Princeton. She and Liz are visiting them now."

Jordan looked up sharply, disbelief and pride crossing his face all at once.

"And she's made her decision," Mr. Moreland added. "She's staying in school. She's going to law school. She is not marrying Mitch."

Jordan closed his eyes, and for the first time since the arrest, something like relief moved across his face.

"Thank God."

Mr. Moreland sat down across from him. "This case is going to take time. The holidays are coming. Judges will be gone. Everything will slow down. But this article matters. It changes things. We'll keep fighting."

Jordan gave a faint nod. "I already prepared myself for the worst," he said quietly. "People like Mitch and his father don't stop easily."

After the visit, Mr. Moreland drove Jordan's family back to Haiti. They thanked him over and over again, not in grand words, but in the quiet, exhausted way people thank the last person still standing beside them when everyone else has stepped back.

He was the only man in that county willing to stand between a powerful family and a boy who had done nothing wrong.

Chapter 28:
The Price of Integrity

A few days later, Riley and Mr. Callaghan were in Poplar Bluff for a business meeting involving the old cinema. They had nearly finished for the day when Mr. Callaghan turned in the back seat and said, almost casually, "We're stopping at the newspaper office."

Riley stiffened at once. "Sir, that's not a good idea."

Mr. Callaghan barely looked at him. "Everything is for sale."

"Not Rick."

Mr. Callaghan smiled with quiet arrogance. "Everyone has a price. You'll see."

Riley said nothing after that. He drove the black bulletproof SUV down Highway 53 toward Kennett, though he already knew how this would go. The newspaper office stood alone, weather-beaten and stubborn, a low brick building with rusted gutters, cracked pavement, and a faded sign that read *Southeast Missouri News*.

"This place hasn't changed in twenty years," Riley muttered.

Rick owned the building outright. Inside were two cramped offices, a narrow kitchen, and an old press in the back that still shook the walls when it ran. Rick handled editing and proofreading. His wife, Martha, ran the press. Their daughter, Shirley, did most of the reporting. Their grandson, Matthew, only twelve years old, already spoke of becoming a journalist someday, one who would write for people nobody else defended.

Security cameras covered the lot from every angle.

"That's Rick's car," Riley said. "He's here."

Mr. Callaghan picked up his briefcase and stepped out. "Wait here."

The parking lot was full of potholes, and he crossed it carefully before ringing the front bell. No one answered at first. Then Martha appeared on the monitor inside, studied him for a second, and came to the door.

"Can I help you?"

"I'm here to see Rick."

She led him inside without expression and opened Rick's office door. "Someone to see you."

Rick looked up from behind his desk, glasses low on his nose, a pencil still in one hand. "Sorry," he said flatly. "I was working."

Martha returned to the printing room. Mr. Callaghan stepped inside smiling, polished and composed.

"Mr. Rick," he said, "my name is J.D. Callaghan. I enjoy reading your paper. Your daughter's work too. You both have courage. You expose real problems."

Rick did not offer him a chair.

"What do you want?"

Mr. Callaghan let his gaze drift around the office. The worn furniture. The cracked walls. The old press humming in the background. He made a show of taking it all in.

"It's a shame," he said, almost softly. "Work like yours matters. Yet people like you still have to struggle this much. No one seems to appreciate what you do."

Rick's eyes narrowed. "Get to the point."

Mr. Callaghan set the briefcase on the desk and opened it.

It was filled with cash.

"This," he said, "is just a small token of appreciation. The beginning of a long friendship."

Rick stood slowly.

"Are you trying to bribe me?"

Mr. Callaghan lifted a hand as if correcting him. "Not a bribe. A thank-you."

Rick stared at him for a long moment. Then he smiled, though there was nothing warm in it.

"Come closer," he said. "Tell me again."

Mr. Callaghan took a step forward. "We can help each other. This money is only—"

He never finished.

Rick's hand came across so fast that Mr. Callaghan didn't even see it. The slap cracked through the room like a gunshot. He stumbled sideways, one hand flying to his ear, his face flooded with shock.

"My hearing…" he gasped.

Rick leaned toward him, voice low and hard.

"I know exactly who you are. And I know exactly what you came here to do."

Mr. Callaghan's face turned crimson. "You just made the biggest mistake of your life. You have no idea what the name J.D. Callaghan means in this region."

Rick didn't so much as blink.

"When you walked into my office, you told me your name. Believe me, I already knew who you were. I didn't forget. I chose how to answer."

He pointed at the open briefcase.

"You came into my office with dirty money and tried to buy me. Call it whatever you want. It was a bribe. I took a second to decide what kind of answer a man like you deserved, and then I realized something. Money wouldn't teach you anything. Humiliation might."

Mr. Callaghan stared at him, breathing hard, one hand still pressed to his ear.

"Yes, I slapped you," Rick said. "Maybe it lands me in trouble. Maybe it doesn't. But there's no proof. And you will never tell anyone Rick slapped J.D. Callaghan. That would embarrass you more than it could ever hurt me."

He took one step closer.

"So here's my advice. Let what happened in this room stay in this room. And never come back here with a briefcase full of cash thinking you can buy my silence."

Mr. Callaghan shook with rage.

"I will never forget this."

Rick gave a small nod. "That was the point."

Mr. Callaghan turned and walked out, the sting of the slap still ringing through the left side of his face.

Riley had been watching from the SUV. The moment Mr. Callaghan stepped back outside, he knew something had gone wrong. His posture was rigid. His jaw was locked. He was gripping the briefcase far too tightly.

Riley opened the rear door. "Is everything all right?"

Mr. Callaghan slid into the back seat without answering at first. Then, in a low voice that trembled with fury, he said, "Take me to the Poplar Bluff police chief. Now."

Riley drove a short distance, then pulled the SUV onto the shoulder and stopped.

"Sir," he said carefully, turning around in his seat, "before we do anything else, you need to tell me what happened. If we act on emotion now, we'll destroy ourselves."

Mr. Callaghan was still pressing his hand to his ear.

"He hit me," he said. "Rick slapped me. I can't hear out of my left ear."

Riley shut his eyes for a moment. He had warned him. He had known.

"I told you not to go in there. Rick doesn't bend. He doesn't scare. He doesn't sell out."

Mr. Callaghan's voice rose. "I want him destroyed. Him and his whole family."

Riley turned sharply. "Never say that again. Not to me. Not to anybody. If anything happens to them now, everyone will know where it came from. That paper already has people watching them."

Mr. Callaghan was breathing hard, his anger looking almost feverish.

"We do not kill journalists," Riley said quietly. "We erase them another way. We use the system."

That, at least, Mr. Callaghan understood.

So they drove to the Poplar Bluff police department instead.

The chief greeted them warmly, almost eagerly.

"It's an honor to see you both."

Riley placed the briefcase on the desk. "Mr. Callaghan appreciates your service to the community."

The chief smiled as he opened it.

"Anything you need."

Riley slid the Sunday edition of the newspaper across the desk.

"This man and his family are becoming a problem," he said. "We need their business handled."

The chief studied the page, then nodded slowly. "They've been a headache for a long time."

Riley leaned forward.

"Quietly."

The chief smiled again, this time without warmth.

"Of course."

Chapter 29:
Time Bought with Silence

Tiffney and Liz came back from the college visits exhausted, but for the first time in weeks, there was something lighter in the house.

They had seen Harvard. They had seen Duke. They had seen Howard. Each campus had its own beauty, its own promise, its own way of making the future feel real. But Howard stayed with them in a way the others did not. Its pre-law program, its history, its diversity, the sense that generations of people had walked those halls determined to fight for justice, all of it settled deep in Tiffney's heart. By the time they returned home, she already knew.

Howard felt like home.

Mr. Moreland agreed the moment they told him.

"It's the right place for you," he said. "I don't even need to think about it. Howard fits you."

Back at school, no one asked many questions about her brief absence. Tiffney had told her friends she needed time away because of everything happening with Jordan, and that explanation was enough. In a small town, people already knew more than they should, and what they didn't know, they invented.

That evening, Mr. Moreland handed her Shirley's Sunday article. Tiffney read it slowly, carefully, every line making her pulse beat harder. Shirley had done something remarkable. She had written with precision, with enough restraint to protect them and enough force to shake the region. The phrase *sources within the high school* did exactly what it needed to do. It shielded both Tiffney and her father while still putting the story into the world.

And in doing so, it tightened the net around Mitch, Riley, and Mr. Callaghan. Too many people already suspected too much. Now suspicion had found words.

At school, whispers multiplied. Stories about Mitch had lived in the shadows for years. His pills. His girls. His temper. His money. His power. Jordan's arrest had not created those stories. It had only dragged them into daylight.

More than a month passed like that, tense and uncertain, until Riley finally called again.

"Have you decided?" he demanded.

Mr. Moreland kept his voice even.

"Let's talk in January or February. Everyone is overwhelmed right now. Emotions are too high."

Riley snapped without hesitation.

"If there's no deal by the end of January, the offer disappears."

But by then Mr. Moreland was no longer trying to negotiate. He was buying time, day by day, week by week. Every delay mattered. Every day Tiffney remained in school was a day he had managed to protect something.

When he visited Jordan, he told him everything. About Howard. About Shirley's article. About the way public opinion was beginning to shift. Jordan listened quietly, and when Mr. Moreland finished, something softened in his face for the first time in weeks.

"She deserves that life," he said, almost to himself.

Mr. Moreland leaned forward.

"Your family is our family now," he told him. "We're not going to abandon them."

Jordan nodded, though the heaviness in his eyes did not lift.

"If I lose basketball," he said, his voice low, "then at least she doesn't lose her future. But please... don't tell her I said that."

Outside the jail, the truth was spreading in ways Mr. Callaghan could no longer fully control. And for the first time in years, his power no longer felt absolute.

The blow came one week before Christmas.

Police units from four counties, Butler, Dunklin, Pemiscot, and New Madrid, descended on the *Southeast Missouri News* building in Poplar Bluff. More than fifty patrol cars flooded Highway 53 and blocked the roads around the little newspaper office until it looked less like a workplace and more like a crime scene. The Poplar Bluff police chief led the raid himself.

Rick and his wife, Martha, were inside when armed officers forced their way in. They were questioned for hours before being released, but by then the real damage had already been done. Every computer had been seized. The printing press had been shut down. The entire building was sealed off.

The warrant accused the paper of publishing provocative material meant to turn the public against law enforcement, the courts, and elected officials. It claimed the paper had spread misinformation and threatened public order. The language was polished, official, and false.

Rick was handed a court order before he left. He, Martha, and Shirley were required to appear in court within thirty days. They were advised to retain counsel immediately.

For the first time in more than fifty years, the loudest independent newspaper in southeast Missouri had been silenced.

The reaction was immediate. Civil rights groups condemned the raid. Journalists condemned it. Ordinary people who had never trusted men like Rick suddenly realized what his paper had been protecting. But Shirley went even further. She took the story where the authorities could not control it.

On Facebook, she posted the version of events they never wanted told.

She uploaded photographs from the paper's security cameras. In them, Mr. Callaghan stood in their parking lot holding a briefcase. She explained that he had come offering money, trying to buy their silence about Jordan, Mitch, and the corruption twisting through the case. Rick had refused. Mr. Callaghan had threatened him.

Then, only days later, the raid happened.

She did not need to spell anything out.

Everyone understood.

Rick met with a local attorney soon after, and the man did not soften what he had to say.

"This is bigger than Poplar Bluff," the attorney told him. "Four counties are involved. We have to demand discovery from every department that touched this. Then we answer the judge. The hearing probably won't happen until late January or February."

He paused, then looked Rick squarely in the face.

"They're going to try to bleed you out financially before this even gets heard. And they may come after Shirley's social media next."

Rick frowned.

"Can they do that?"

The attorney gave a tired nod.

"Yes. If they pressure Facebook hard enough, they may be able to freeze her account. She needs backups. Another account. A YouTube channel. Somewhere the story can keep living."

Rick leaned back, thinking.

"And worst case?"

The lawyer hesitated before answering.

"If this goes badly, prison is possible. They can manufacture what they need if they decide to. Look at Jordan. Everybody knows he was framed. It didn't stop them."

Rick did not look away.

"Truth scares power," he said quietly. "That's why they're this afraid of us."

And for the first time in decades, southeast Missouri was watching in real time what happened when somebody told the truth too clearly.

Chapter 30:
The Sound of Consequences

Mr. Callaghan was pacing when Riley came in with the latest news.

"The raid worked," Riley said. "Rick's paper is finished."

Mr. Callaghan stopped, turned, and glared at him.

"That isn't what I asked. Why isn't he in jail?"

Riley kept his tone measured.

"The police have to move carefully. But they'll get there. Don't worry."

Mr. Callaghan frowned and took a step closer.

"I can't hear you properly."

Riley studied him.

"What do you mean?"

"My left ear," Mr. Callaghan snapped. "It hasn't been right since that day."

Riley's expression shifted.

"The ear Rick hit?"

Mr. Callaghan flinched, as if the memory itself offended him.

"Yes. Since then it's been ringing. Constantly. Like static."

Riley made a call at once.

Dr. Moore arrived that evening carrying a small case of equipment. He examined Mr. Callaghan's ears in silence, then frowned.

"There's a rupture in the tympanic membrane of the left ear," he said at last. "That's what's causing the ringing. Tinnitus."

Mr. Callaghan scowled.

"Fix it."

Dr. Moore hesitated.

"This kind of damage usually comes from trauma. A hard blow. It doesn't always heal well."

Riley let out a short, humorless laugh.

"Rick never looked dangerous. Apparently his hands are."

The doctor stiffened.

"Rick? The publisher?"

Riley stepped closer, lowering his voice.

"You'll keep this to yourself. Your BNDD issue is still buried, Doctor. We can always unbury it."

Dr. Moore swallowed.

"I understand."

Mr. Callaghan slammed a hand against the arm of his chair.

"What can you do?"

"I need an MRI first, just to rule out anything deeper. I can prescribe medication, but tinnitus is often permanent."

Riley's smile turned cold.

"So Rick managed to take something from him money couldn't replace."

The doctor gathered his equipment, then paused at the door.

"Stay away from Rick. If you damage the other ear, you could lose your hearing completely."

Riley's face went hard.

"Get out."

When the doctor left, Mr. Callaghan sat there clenching his fist, the ringing in his ear now more than just an injury. It had become a reminder, a constant echo of a man he had failed to buy, failed to intimidate, and failed to control.

That, more than anything, made Rick dangerous.

During the first week of January, Rick's attorney filed a formal discovery request, demanding all evidence the government claimed to have against him and his paper. Days passed. Nothing came back. He called the prosecutor. Still nothing.

So he notified the court that the state was withholding discovery and preventing the defense from preparing. That, too, disappeared into silence.

Then the truth emerged, plain and ugly.

The judge presiding over the case was married to Mr. Callaghan's sister.

Rick's attorney immediately filed a motion asking that the case be moved to Poplar Bluff, where Rick lived and where his paper had operated for more than half a century.

The request was denied without explanation.

Instead, the government moved the case to Kennett, deep inside Callaghan territory.

At that point, any illusion of fairness was gone. This was not a prosecution anymore. It was a warning.

Rick was not being tried.

He was being buried.

Chapter 31: The Deal Is Over

In the first week of February, Riley called Mr. Moreland one last time.

"This is your final chance," he said.

Mr. Moreland did not hesitate.

"My daughter is not ready. She's emotionally shattered. She's seeing a counselor now, and I will not push her. If I do, I'm afraid she could hurt herself."

Riley's voice turned flat and icy.

"You and your family have been playing games with us for years. The deal is over. Be ready for the consequences. I can't control Mitch anymore."

The line went dead, but the threat stayed behind.

Starting next week, you'll receive no legal work from us, or from anyone connected to us.

Mr. Moreland had known this moment was coming.

That night, he told Liz and Tiffney everything.

"You have to be careful now," he told his daughter. "Never be alone at school. Not for a second. Mitch is dangerous."

Tiffney nodded.

"I know. I carry pepper spray."

In mid-February, Rick's attorney finally received part of the state's so-called evidence. It was a pathetic collection of ten handwritten letters, each supposedly from a different county, each accusing Rick's paper of inciting hatred against police, courts, and government. Each demanded the newspaper be shut down. All of them were dated three or four months before the raid.

Rick sat across from his attorney as the man spread the letters across the desk.

"They're fake," the attorney said quietly. "Every one of them."

Rick stared at the pages, disgust settling over him.

"How do they even get people to write garbage like this?"

The attorney sighed.

"That part is easy. Most of these people probably have something hanging over them. DUI charges. Drug cases. Probation problems. The police or the DEA offer them a bargain. Testify, cooperate, say what we need, and your own troubles disappear."

Rick's fists tightened slowly.

"So they'll lie in court."

"Yes," the attorney said. "And the judge is related to Callaghan. They don't need real evidence."

Rick looked back down at the papers.

"There's not a single article listed here. Nothing we actually printed."

"That won't stop them. But if we can get back into the building and recover your archives, we can show a jury what was really published."

Rick let out a slow breath.

"We had digital copies. The police took every computer."

The attorney leaned forward.

"Then I'll file a motion. We ask the court for supervised access to the building so we can retrieve the archives."

Rick nodded.

"Do it."

The emergency motion was filed that very morning.

That same night, the newspaper building burned to the ground.

By the time the fire department arrived, there was almost nothing left to save. The press was gone. The archives were gone. The offices were gone. By dawn, all that remained was ash, twisted metal, and the official explanation.

Electrical failure.

Rick's attorney called him as soon as the report came in.

"They'll probably claim you did it yourself," he said quietly. "They'll say you knew the records were gone, so you burned the place down."

Rick's jaw set.

"The safest move now may be to discuss settlement," the attorney continued. "We'll see what they want. But fighting the government head-on is nearly impossible."

He paused, and when he spoke again, bitterness edged every word.

"We're raised on freedom of speech and equal justice. But when power feels threatened, the law becomes a weapon. Truth stops mattering."

Rick stood in silence for a moment, staring at the wall.

"So this is America," he said at last.

The attorney did not try to soften it.

"The government has unlimited money, unlimited manpower, and unlimited influence. They can create witnesses. Invent evidence. Rewrite the story until it sounds official. When they decide to destroy someone, they don't need to be right. They just need to be stronger."

Rick looked at him.

"They're a mafia."

The lawyer gave a tired nod.

"With badges."

Rick's voice hardened.

"I always knew the system was unfair. But I never imagined it was this rotten. If they can do this to me, a white publisher, imagine what they do to Black families, to poor people, to anyone without power."

He stood a little straighter then, as if the truth of it had settled something inside him.

"Everything I ever wrote was true," he said. "And now they've proved it."

He lifted his head.

"Whatever comes next, I won't beg. I won't lie. I'll face it."

Chapter 32:
The Walls Begin to Close

Mr. Callaghan wasted no time.

Within days, every business tied to him cut off Mr. Moreland's law firm. The phone calls dried up first. Then the court referrals disappeared. Longtime clients began pulling away without explanation, though none was needed. In towns where everyone knew everyone else, the warning moved quickly and quietly: stay away from the Morelands.

It took less than a month for the damage to show.

Liz took a job at a gas station. Mr. Moreland kept telling himself it was temporary, but neither of them truly believed that. The income that had once sustained their home had been severed almost overnight. Late at night, after the house went quiet, he began searching for towns in Tennessee and Arkansas. Dyersburg. Small river communities. Places far enough away that Callaghan's reach might finally thin out. Once Tiffney left for law school, he meant to move all of them.

At school, the cruelty became more open.

Mitch and his friends hovered like scavengers, always nearby, always waiting for the right moment to strike. Whenever Tiffney or Lakesha passed, the insults came fast and loud enough for everyone around them to hear.

"Well, look who it is," one of them called out. "The drug dealer's girlfriend."

Another voice followed. "No, that one's the dealer's sister."

Then Mitch himself, with that lazy, poisoned smile. "What's the matter, Tiffney? No cocaine for us today? Or are you selling something else now?"

Tiffney kept her eyes forward. Lakesha's hands tightened into fists, but neither of them answered. They both knew what Mitch was capable of, and by then silence had become its own form of survival.

Lakesha had already made her decision. As soon as the school year ended, she was leaving. She would transfer somewhere else, anywhere else. She refused to spend another year in a place that had turned her brother into a criminal in the public eye and called it justice.

Jordan, meanwhile, sat in his cell waiting for March to come. The trial hung over him like weather you could feel before it arrived, slow, heavy, and impossible to outrun.

Then another blow landed.

Jordan's mother got a call from her sister in Sikeston. She had been sick for weeks, worn down and frightened, and now the doctors suspected a mass in her uterus. She had three young children. The oldest was the same age as Jordan's younger brother, who was supposed to start first grade in the fall.

Jordan's mother didn't hesitate. She packed a bag and started spending her days at her sister's house, cooking meals, cleaning up, watching the children while her brother-in-law worked. She had always been the baby sister, the one others protected. Now she was the one being asked to hold everything together.

And Jordan, sitting behind bars, could do nothing for her except pray.

As if losing his own life were not enough, suffering had begun spilling into the lives of everyone he loved.

One afternoon, not long after that, Tiffney was sitting in the cafeteria waiting for her last class when a teacher approached her table. His voice was casual, almost offhand.

"Jordan's basketball coach wants to see you," he said. "He said it's important."

Tiffney looked up, uneasy.

"In his office?"

The teacher nodded. "That's what he said."

She hesitated for a second, then rose from her seat. "All right. I'll go."

From across the room, Lakesha saw her leaving and felt something tighten inside her. It was not a thought so much as a feeling, sharp and immediate. Something was wrong.

Tiffney crossed toward the gym and knocked on the coach's office door beside the court. There was no answer.

She frowned and stepped farther into the gym.

Then Mitch appeared.

He came from the far side of the court with two older boys beside him, all three walking toward her with the easy confidence of people who believed nothing could touch them. Mitch was smiling before he even spoke.

"You didn't think you could keep avoiding me forever, did you?"

Tiffney felt her stomach drop. "Where's the coach?"

Mitch laughed.

"The teacher works for me," he said. "This whole thing was a setup."

She turned instinctively, ready to run, but Mitch lunged and caught her before she could get clear. Tiffney fought immediately. She tore a small spray canister from her purse and aimed for his face. Most of it missed, but she got close enough to scratch him hard along the cheek. Her nails cut skin. Blood surfaced at once.

Mitch roared and grabbed a fistful of her hair.

At that exact moment, Lakesha came running into the gym, shouting for help. She barely made it onto the court before the two older boys rushed her. They forced her down hard, pinning her while she struggled beneath them.

"Hold her," Mitch barked. "I'll deal with Tiffney."

Tiffney fought with everything she had. She kicked out wildly and caught Mitch in the face, but he came at her again, stronger now, angrier. For one terrible instant, it seemed certain the situation was about to turn into something even worse.

Then a voice split the gym.

"Stop!"

The basketball coach came charging in.

He crossed the court at a run and shoved Mitch away from Tiffney with enough force to send him stumbling backward. The two older boys released Lakesha at once. Startled, all three of them bolted for the exit. Mitch followed, wiping blood from his face as he ran.

Lakesha collapsed, shaking so hard she could barely sit up. Tiffney was still standing, but only just.

The coach grabbed the nearest phone and called 911 immediately.

As he helped both girls toward the principal's office, the principal himself appeared at a distance. He saw their faces, saw their condition, and in that instant understood enough to know what had happened. But instead of coming forward, he stopped.

"I have an emergency," he muttered to his secretary. "I have to leave."

Then he turned around and walked out.

Within minutes, an ambulance arrived. Tiffney and Lakesha were taken to the hospital for examination, treatment, and an official report. The coach promised to follow.

"I'll be right behind you," he told the paramedics. "I'll give my statement there."

At the emergency room, Dr. Moore was on duty when a nurse hurried in to brief him.

"Two teenage girls just came in by ambulance," she said. "They were attacked at the high school. They said Mitch and his friends tried to rape them, but the basketball coach intervened."

Dr. Moore turned toward the security monitor, and the moment he saw Tiffney, something in his expression changed. He knew exactly who she was. And that meant he knew exactly what this was.

His voice remained calm.

"Get their vitals. Put them in gowns. I'll be there shortly."

As soon as the nurse left, he pulled out his phone and called Riley.

"They're here," he said quietly. Then he gave him the names of the paramedics who had brought them in.

Riley's answer came back cold and immediate.

"Blame it on the coach. I'll handle the rest."

At that moment, the receptionist stepped into view.

"Doctor, the basketball coach is here asking about the girls."

Dr. Moore slipped the phone away and straightened his coat. "Send him in."

When the coach entered, his face was full of worry.

"Doctor, are they all right?"

"They're stable," Dr. Moore said smoothly. "You did the right thing bringing them here. Tiffney's father is already on his way."

The coach exhaled.

"Because this could become a sensitive legal matter," Dr. Moore continued, "I need you to write down exactly what you witnessed. Every detail."

The coach nodded and did it at once. He wrote out everything: Mitch, the two boys, the attack, the struggle, the girls fighting back, his intervention, their escape. When he finished, Dr. Moore took the paper and glanced over it.

"Thank you," he said. "The police will be informed. Those boys will be arrested."

For the first time since he arrived, the coach seemed to believe the worst was over.

"Good," he said quietly. "They should be."

Dr. Moore smiled.

But behind that smile, the next stage of the trap had already begun.

The moment the coach left the exam room, Dr. Moore picked up the phone again.

"He's gone," he said softly. "You can take care of him now. I'll handle things here."

Then he returned to the girls.

The nurse had already photographed Tiffney's and Lakesha's injuries. Dr. Moore ordered lab work and documented their condition, but when he opened their files, he did not record the truth. Instead, he wrote a different story, one clean enough to pass as official.

Then he called the local police.

"There's been an incident at the high school," he said calmly. "Two girls were assaulted. According to the victims, the basketball coach summoned one of them to his office by sending a teacher as a messenger. When the girls arrived, the coach attempted to rape Tiffney. They fought back and screamed for help."

He paused, then continued.

"Two students, friends of Mitch Callaghan, heard the screaming and rushed in. They restrained the coach and brought the girls here for treatment. The coach fled before police arrived."

The nurse stared at him, horrified, but said nothing.

A moment later, she spoke in a near whisper. "Doctor, the police are here in the waiting area. Also, two boys want to see you."

Dr. Moore did not look surprised.

"Send them to my office."

The two boys, Mitch's friends, entered with nervous grins and restless hands. Dr. Moore closed the door behind them.

"Listen carefully," he said. "You two saved those girls from the basketball coach. You brought them here. The coach ran after writing a statement. That is all you tell the police."

He leaned in, voice hard now.

"You do not mention Mitch. You do not mention anything else. Do you understand me?"

The boys exchanged a glance, then nodded.

"Yeah," one of them said. "We got it."

"Good. Wait here. The officers will come to you."

Next, Dr. Moore called Mr. Moreland.

"Tiffney and another girl are in the ER," he said in a calm, reassuring tone. "They have minor injuries. They're stable. The police are involved. You can come now."

Then he hung up.

Everything was moving exactly as Riley wanted.

The truth was already being erased.

A few minutes later, Dr. Moore called for the investigating officer.

When the man entered, notebook in hand, Dr. Moore repeated the story as if he were reading from a script he had always known.

"As I explained on the phone, there was an attempted assault at the high school. One girl was summoned to the basketball coach's office through a teacher. Once she arrived, the coach tried to rape her. The girls resisted and screamed for help."

He slid two typed statements across the desk.

"These are their written accounts. Their injuries and psychological distress have also been documented."

The investigator skimmed the pages. "They're minors?"

"Yes," Dr. Moore replied. "They're both in shock. I've given them mild anti-anxiety medication."

At that moment, the two boys came in.

The investigator turned to them. "Tell me what happened."

One of them answered quickly, too quickly.

"We're friends with Mitch. He was out hunting, so he asked us to keep an eye on Tiffney. We heard screaming, ran into the gym, and saw the basketball coach trying to rape the girls. We pulled him off them and brought them here."

"And the coach?" the officer asked.

"He ran," the second boy said. "But not before writing something."

Dr. Moore produced another paper.

"He left this before fleeing."

The officer took it and nodded.

"Thank you, boys. You did the right thing."

After dismissing them, he turned back to Dr. Moore.

"Can I talk to the girls?"

"I wouldn't recommend it tonight," Dr. Moore said at once. "They're sedated, traumatized, and under medical care. We already have written statements and physical findings. For their mental health, it's better not to question them again right now."

The investigator hesitated, then accepted it.

"All right. We'll follow up later."

And just like that, the lie became official.

It had signatures. It had paperwork. It had medical language and police notes and silence in all the right places. Which meant the truth, for the moment, no longer existed in any record that mattered.

Mr. Moreland arrived at the hospital just after midnight. Dr. Moore met him near the nurses' station, composed, rehearsed, and entirely in control.

"The basketball coach attempted to rape your daughter and another girl named Lakesha," he said. "Fortunately, two young men intervened and saved them."

Mr. Moreland stared at him.

"Where is the coach?"

"That is now a police matter," Dr. Moore replied. "He fled the scene. I can't say more than that."

"Can I see the girls?"

"Yes. But don't ask them about the attack. They've been through severe emotional and physical trauma."

When Mr. Moreland entered the room, Tiffney and Lakesha were sitting side by side in gowns, pale and shaken. The instant they saw him, both girls rushed to him and held on tightly.

Dr. Moore handed him a small bag of ointment.

"Use this on the scratches. There are no serious physical injuries. The police are searching for the suspect. You may take them home."

Then, lowering his voice, he added, "Do not discuss the case with anyone until the suspect is found. This is extremely sensitive."

After dropping Lakesha at her home, Mr. Moreland drove Tiffney back to Steel. Liz was waiting at the door, frantic with worry. The moment she saw her daughter, relief flooded her face.

"Thank God you're all right."

Still trembling, Tiffney told them everything. All of it. Mitch. His two friends. The setup. The gym. The coach charging in to save them.

"It was Mitch," she said. "He and those two boys trapped us. The coach came in with a baseball bat. He hit Mitch and the others and saved us. I scratched Mitch's face. I made him bleed."

Mr. Moreland's stomach tightened.

"Did they take anything from under your fingernails? DNA?"

"I think so," Tiffney said. "Dr. Moore seemed nice."

"Did the police question you?"

She shook her head. "No. Not once."

Liz looked stricken.

"That's not normal."

Mr. Moreland forced himself to stay steady.

"Let's eat something. We'll talk again in the morning."

But morning came with a horror none of them were prepared for.

Mr. Moreland was standing in front of the television when the local news broke the story.

HIGH SCHOOL BASKETBALL COACH DEAD IN CRASH – POLICE SAY HE WAS THE ASSAILANT

The reporter's voice continued over images of flashing patrol lights and a wrecked vehicle.

"Authorities say the coach attempted to rape two teenage girls. Friends of Mitch Callaghan intervened and saved them. The coach fled and later died in what police believe may have been a suicide."

Mr. Moreland felt sick.

When Tiffney came downstairs, he turned toward her slowly.

"They're saying the coach attacked you," he said. "They're saying he's dead. That he killed himself."

Tiffney went still.

"That's a lie," she whispered. "He saved us. He stopped Mitch. He saved us."

Liz pressed a hand to her mouth.

"Oh my God…"

At that moment, Tiffney's phone rang. It was Lakesha, crying so hard she could barely get the words out.

"They're saying the coach did it," she sobbed. "But it was Mitch. We know it was."

Tiffney closed her eyes.

"They killed him," she said quietly. "They had to. He knew the truth."

Mr. Moreland stared at the television, and in that moment something cold and terrible settled over him.

The story had already been written.

And the truth was already dead.

Tiffney turned to Lakesha, her hands still shaking.

"Do you have the coach's home number?"

Lakesha nodded. "Jordan used to keep everybody's numbers. Let me check."

A moment later, she found it and handed the phone to Mr. Moreland. He dialed.

A woman answered after a few rings, her voice already thin with grief.

"Yes?"

"This is Mr. Moreland. My daughter is Tiffney. I'm so sorry about your husband. He saved my daughter and Jordan's sister yesterday."

There was a long pause. Then the woman began to cry.

"He told me that when he got home around six," she said. "He said Mitch and his friends had tried to rape two girls. One was Jordan's sister and the other was his girlfriend. He was angry, but he kept saying he got there in time."

Her voice trembled more with every word.

"At eight o'clock, a police investigator called and told him to come to the station right away. He left immediately. He never came back."

Mr. Moreland closed his eyes.

"I called the Caruthersville and Haiti police around ten," she continued. "They told me nobody had called him. They said they were 'looking for him.' I stayed up all night."

Her voice cracked completely then.

"At four in the morning, a patrol car came to the house. They said they found his car in a ditch. They called it an accident. Then maybe suicide. I told them he would never kill himself. Somebody killed him."

A few seconds passed before she spoke again.

"Then they told me he had tried to rape two girls," she said, sounding half-broken and half-disbelieving. "They said two senior boys saved the girls and that he confessed in the ER to Dr. Moore before running. None of it makes sense. None of it."

Mr. Moreland spoke carefully, but there was iron in his voice now.

"Your husband was a good man. He saved those girls. Mitch Callaghan, his father, and Riley are behind this. They're the same people who framed Jordan. The same people behind what happened to the newspaper in Poplar Bluff. The police and Dr. Moore are part of it."

Silence met him on the other end.

"Please," he said. "Don't believe their story."

After he hung up, he turned back to Tiffney.

"You are not going back to that school," he said. "Not another day. This town is no longer safe for you. You and your mother need to leave for a while. Dyersburg. Memphis. Anywhere. Just go."

Tiffney nodded, tears sliding down her face.

"I'll tell Lakesha too."

Then, after a moment, she said quietly, "The history teacher who sent me to the gym... and the principal... they work for Callaghan. It was planned from the beginning. Every part of it."

Mr. Moreland looked at his daughter for a long time.

"They tried to kill the truth," he said. "They failed."

Then his voice lowered.

"But now we survive."

Chapter 33:
The Truth Begins to Surface

Tiffney called Lakesha early that morning, before the house had fully settled into the day.

"Do not go to school," she said the moment Lakesha answered. Her voice was low, urgent. "And if the police come to talk to you, do not say anything to them by yourself. Tell them you will only give a statement in front of my father. They'll twist whatever we say if we let them."

Lakesha agreed at once. She was frightened already, and Tiffney could hear it in her breathing. After what had happened the day before, neither of them trusted anyone in authority anymore. In their world, uniforms, titles, and official voices no longer meant safety. They meant danger dressed up as procedure.

Since Mr. Callaghan had stripped all business away from his law firm, Mr. Moreland had found himself with something he had not had in years.

Time.

And now he was using it for the most important fight of his life.

He started with the police investigator. When he stepped into the office, he kept his tone calm and controlled, though anger was pressing hard beneath the surface.

"I represent Tiffney and Lakesha," he said. "I want to see everything you have."

The investigator handed over Dr. Moore's emergency room report along with the written statements from Mitch's two friends. Mr. Moreland read through them carefully, line by line, his face growing tighter the longer he looked.

Then he lifted his eyes.

"Did you interview either of the girls?"

The investigator shifted in his chair. "No. Dr. Moore told me they were sedated and emotionally unstable. He said they had already given statements."

Mr. Moreland let that sit for a second.

"And did you ever speak to the coach?"

"No," the investigator admitted. "I was told he confessed to Dr. Moore and ran."

Mr. Moreland leaned forward slightly, his voice still quiet, but sharper now.

"So let me understand this. You accused a man of attempted rape without ever speaking to the victims or to the man you were accusing."

The investigator hesitated. He looked uncomfortable, but he didn't answer.

Mr. Moreland kept going.

"Let's assume, for the sake of argument, that the coach was guilty. Why would a guilty man bring both girls to the emergency room himself? Why not run the moment he had the chance?"

The investigator said nothing.

"Did you confirm with the hospital staff who actually brought the girls in?"

A beat passed.

"No," he admitted. "Dr. Moore introduced me to the two boys and said they were the ones who brought everyone in."

Mr. Moreland sat back, studying him.

"Does it make any sense to you," he asked, "that two teenage boys overpowered a trained, athletic basketball coach and somehow dragged everyone to the hospital instead of going to the police?"

The investigator swallowed.

"I didn't think about that."

"No," Mr. Moreland said, rising to his feet. "You didn't."

Then he buttoned his coat and added, "Meet me at the emergency room in two hours. We'll find out what actually happened."

From there, Mr. Moreland went straight to Dr. Moore's clinic. The doctor's car was parked outside, but when he stepped in and asked for him, the nurse gave him a practiced little smile and said the doctor was out. Two hours later, he went to the ER and waited.

The investigator never came.

Mr. Moreland called once. Then again. No answer.

That told him enough.

So he did what good lawyers do when officials stop being honest. He went to the people who had actually been there.

He found the ER receptionist and approached her carefully.

"Do you remember who brought the two girls in yesterday?"

She nodded without hesitation.

"Yes. The basketball coach brought them."

Mr. Moreland took out his recorder, held it where she could see it, and asked, "You're certain?"

"Absolutely," she said. "I know him well. My son played on his team. We even spoke before he left. So when I heard later that he was the one being accused, I couldn't believe it. It didn't make sense."

Mr. Moreland kept his voice even.

"And the two boys?"

"They came later," she said. "At least an hour after the girls arrived. The coach was already gone by then."

That was it.

That was the fracture in the lie.

When the investigator later tried to raise those doubts with his chief, the answer he got was short and cold.

"If you want to keep your job, you stick to the story. And you stay away from Mr. Moreland."

The same warning went to Dr. Moore.

By evening, Mr. Moreland had gone to the coach's house. He sat across from the widow and told her what the receptionist had said, that her husband had brought the girls to the hospital himself, that the two boys had shown up much later, and that the official story was already beginning to crack.

Tears filled her eyes before he even finished.

"I knew it," she whispered. "He would never hurt anyone. Never."

Mr. Moreland nodded slowly.

"The police, Dr. Moore, and people inside that school are all working for Callaghan," he said. "Your husband died because he told the truth."

By then, the war was no longer hidden behind favors and rumors and quiet threats.

Now it was open.

And now it was personal.

Chapter 34: The Lines Are Drawn

Once Mr. Moreland formally took on representation for both Tiffney and Lakesha, he moved fast. Within hours, he filed an FIR at the Haiti Police Station naming Mitch Callaghan, J. D. Callaghan, Riley, and Mitch's two friends. By evening, he had also filed criminal charges against all five at the local courthouse.

At nearly the same time, Mitch was sitting inside Dr. Moore's clinic, his face swollen and raw. The scratch Tiffney had left across his cheek was deep enough to cut into the skin in jagged lines, and Dr. Moore was leaning in close, applying antibiotic cream before wrapping fresh bandages across it.

Mitch stared at his reflection in a metal cabinet and seethed.

"That stupid bitch did this to me," he snarled. "I swear to God, I'll wipe her out."

He turned toward Dr. Moore, eyes burning.

"You should've killed both of them while they were in the ER."

Riley stepped between them so sharply that even Mitch seemed startled.

"Enough," Riley snapped. "Stop talking like an idiot. We're in a clinic, not some bar."

Then he looked to Dr. Moore.

"How long will that take to heal?"

Dr. Moore adjusted his glasses and examined the wound again before answering.

"It's deep. I can't stitch it. The skin is too irregular and torn. It'll have to heal naturally. With regular dressing changes and antibiotic cream, I'd say one to two months."

Riley nodded as if that answer pleased him.

"Good. Then you're not going to school during that time."

Mitch gave a bitter laugh.

"I wasn't planning to. Everybody would keep asking questions."

Riley allowed himself the faintest smirk.

"I'll handle that. I'll tell the principal you got hurt while deer hunting."

Then, almost casually, he added, "Tiffney's out of school too. I'm hearing she's severely depressed. Supposedly seeing a psychologist because of suicidal thoughts."

Mitch leaned back in the chair and laughed in a way that made the room feel colder.

"I don't care if she's depressed," he said. "I don't care if she kills herself."

Riley didn't smile.

"That kind of talk creates problems," he said flatly. "From now on, you do exactly what I tell you. We're past stupidity. We're in a war now."

Mitch said nothing after that. He sank back into the reclining chair, his wounded face throbbing, his silence heavy with something uglier than pain.

Hatred.

Chapter 35:
The Weight of Power

Later that day, Dr. Moore stood with Riley inside his private office, the door shut tight behind them. His voice, for once, carried a hint of strain.

"What are we going to do about this case?" he asked. "Mr. Moreland filed charges against Mitch and those two boys for attempted rape. I changed what I could, especially the lab results and the material from under the girl's fingernails, but if this starts getting out of hand, it won't be enough."

Riley remained calm, almost bored.

"Don't worry. The Pemiscot County police chief is ours. So is the magistrate judge. That case is going nowhere."

Dr. Moore hesitated.

"And the ambulance crew? The ER nurses?"

Riley gave him a thin, knowing smile.

"They know better than to talk. Everyone saw what happened to the newspaper in Poplar Bluff. After that fire, nobody in this region is brave enough to stand against us."

That evening, Mr. Moreland sat across from Jordan in the jail's interview room and told him what had happened. He did not dramatize it. He didn't need to.

"Mitch and his friends tried to rape Tiffney and Lakesha at school," he said quietly. "The basketball coach stopped them. Later that night, someone killed him. Most likely Mr. Callaghan. Then they turned around and pinned the whole thing on the coach."

Jordan lowered his head. His fists tightened slowly, knuckles whitening against the table.

"And Dr. Moore?"

"He's their family doctor," Mr. Moreland said. "He falsified the hospital records."

Jordan sat still for a moment. When he finally spoke, his voice was low and frayed at the edges.

"So this is what kind of country we live in," he said. "The rich do whatever they want, and everybody else helps them do it. The police. The courts. The doctors. All of them."

He looked up, but there was no anger in his face anymore. Just exhaustion. Something deeper than exhaustion.

"What is a poor kid like me supposed to do? Where do people like us go?"

His voice broke then.

"I used to believe God was watching. But after all this..." He looked away. "I don't know anymore."

Mr. Moreland leaned forward, resting his arms on the table.

"I feel that same pain," he said. "I do. But night doesn't last forever. Morning always comes. Right now they're winning, yes. But history turns. It always does."

Then he told Jordan something else.

"The newspaper office in Poplar Bluff was shut down in December. After that, someone burned it to the ground. Rick and Shirley were the ones who wrote about your case. Their hearing will probably happen in March or April."

Jordan nodded slowly, absorbing it.

"And Tiffney?" he asked after a moment.

"She and Lakesha are on medical leave. The principal approved it. They only need to return for exams. Both are seeing psychiatrists now. We need that trauma documented."

Jordan let out a long breath.

"That's good."

Then he hesitated before speaking again.

"My mom's decided to move to Sikeston. My aunt is sick, and she needs help with the kids. After school ends, the whole family's leaving."

Mr. Moreland nodded.

"That makes sense. Once Tiffney starts college, we're planning to move too. Tennessee, probably. Dyersburg or somewhere near there. I already have a Tennessee law license. We need to get somewhere safe."

For a while, neither of them said anything more.

Two families.

Two futures.

And both of them caught inside a system built to crush anyone who stood in the way of power.

Chapter 36:
The Price of Silence

Rick's court hearing was set for the end of March, and with every passing day the reality of it grew harder to ignore. His attorney had been in regular contact with the government prosecutor, pressing for details, trying to find some opening, some weakness, some reason to believe the case was still winnable. But every update he brought back was worse than the last.

At one meeting, he set his file down, looked at Rick for a long moment, and said, "Without physical evidence, we have almost nothing. The fire took everything. Every newspaper, every file, every computer. There's nothing left for us to build a defense around. The government, meanwhile, has ten witnesses who signed complaints against your paper. On top of that, they have police chiefs, sheriffs, church leaders, businessmen, and politicians lined up to testify. Mr. Callaghan himself is prepared to speak."

Rick stared at the table in silence before finally asking, "And what do we have?"

The attorney did not dress it up. "Nothing," he said. "I reached out to your friends, old readers, other journalists, anyone I thought might stand beside you. No one will do it. They're scared."

Rick closed his eyes for a moment, then leaned back in his chair as if the weight of the answer had settled physically into his bones. The attorney kept going, because there was no point pretending this was easier than it was.

"There are really only two paths left," he said. "We take a settlement, or we go to trial. If we go to trial and want a serious chance, we'd need a specialist out of St. Louis. Just bringing someone like that in would cost at least a hundred thousand dollars. And if we lose, you, Martha, and Shirley go to prison. On top of that, you'll be financially ruined."

Rick let out a slow breath. "I don't have that kind of money. My house might be worth thirty thousand. The paper is gone. The business is gone." He looked up, tired and hollowed out. "Let me talk to my family."

That evening, he sat with Martha and Shirley at the kitchen table. Even Ethan, Shirley's teenage son, stayed quiet and listened, sensing from the adults' faces that this was not a conversation meant for children, even though he was old enough to understand more than they wished he did. No one argued for heroics. No one spoke about pride. They all understood the same thing. Rick and Martha were old enough now that prison would not just be punishment. It would be the destruction of whatever remained of their lives.

So they agreed to settle.

Two days later, they met again in the attorney's office. The government's proposal was waiting for them, and it was every bit as ruthless as Rick's lawyer had feared. If they accepted it, Rick, Martha, and Shirley would be permanently banned from publishing, printing, journalism, and any kind of media work. They would be barred from suing any government agency. They would not be allowed to work for any news organization or on social media platforms in any professional capacity. In exchange, the criminal charges would disappear.

Rick's attorney looked at the proposal, then at the government lawyer across from him, and his voice hardened. "This is excessive. Lifetime punishment without a conviction is not justice."

He leaned forward, not raising his voice, but making sure every word landed. "My client also has evidence that Mr. Callaghan brought Rick a briefcase full of cash. Later, that same briefcase ended up in a police chief's office."

The government attorney stiffened almost imperceptibly. Then he said, "Be very careful. If that accusation reaches the wrong people, your clients could be arrested before the day is over."

The warning was obvious, and it worked exactly as intended. Negotiation began in earnest after that. Rick's attorney pushed back where he could. Lifetime became ten years. Ten years became seven. By the end of the day, that was where it settled.

Seven years.

No journalism. No publishing. No printing. No media work of any kind.

After seven years, they would be free to work again. There would be no prison, no fines, no additional charges. It was a settlement designed to bury them without bars, and everyone in the room knew it.

Rick, Martha, and Shirley signed anyway.

The government had gotten what it really wanted.

Silence.

Chapter 37:
The First Crack

Mr. Moreland, meanwhile, had formally filed charges against Mitch Callaghan and his two friends for the attempted rape of Tiffney and Lakesha. The paperwork was complete. There was nothing left to do but wait and see whether the court would act like a court or like everything else in Pemiscot County.

Then, one evening, the basketball coach's widow called.

Her voice was shaking so badly that for the first few seconds Mr. Moreland could barely make out what she was saying.

"Someone called me," she said. "A man. He said he saw my husband's accident. He wouldn't leave his name, but he said a white Ford F-250 hit my husband's car and forced it off the road. He said he's been living with the guilt ever since."

Mr. Moreland straightened at once. "Did he leave a number?"

"Yes."

"Give it to me."

He called immediately. The man answered, nervous from the first word.

"I was behind them," the witness said. "That truck was moving fast. It hit the coach's car from the side. Hard. The car lost control and rolled off the road." His voice faltered. "I didn't stop. I should have, but I was scared. I've regretted it every day since."

Mr. Moreland took down his name, his address, his contact information, and when the call ended, he sat in silence for several seconds.

So it hadn't been suicide.

It had been murder.

And if the coach had been murdered, then the rest of the story fell into place with brutal clarity. He had not been the attacker. He had been removed because he was a witness.

Mr. Moreland filed a motion with the court immediately, presenting the existence of the new witness. He knew full well what would happen next. Somebody inside that courthouse would leak it. Somebody always did.

Within a week, the police investigator finally called and asked to meet.

When they sat down together, the man looked uneasy even before he spoke. "I hear you found a witness."

"I did," Mr. Moreland replied. "A man who saw the truck hit the coach's car. We know the vehicle type. We're tracing the owner."

Then he leaned forward and lowered his voice just enough to make the words personal.

"You're still young. You still have a future. You do not want to be the man left holding the bag for Callaghan and Riley when this story collapses. And it will collapse. When it does, everybody who helped build the lie is going down with it."

The investigator said nothing for a long moment. Finally, he looked away and said quietly, "Give me a couple of days."

After Mr. Moreland left, the investigator went straight to his superior and told him what had happened.

"We have a witness," he said nervously. "He saw the truck that hit the coach's car. Moreland is close to identifying the owner."

The senior officer barely reacted.

"Relax," he said. "The judge is with us. And if this starts getting ugly, we settle."

Two days later, the court responded.

A hearing was scheduled for two weeks out.

For the first time in months, Mr. Moreland felt something he had almost forgotten how to feel.

Hope.

And if this crack widened, Jordan's case would be next.

The senior police officer wasted no time carrying the new witness information to the Pemiscot County police chief. Once the office door was shut, he laid it out bluntly.

"This changes everything. The witness saw the F-250 hit the coach's car. He even got the plate."

The chief's face tightened. He reached for the phone and called Riley.

"We have a problem," he said the moment Riley answered. "There's now an eyewitness to the crash. The pickup that hit the coach has been identified. And Mitch can't testify anyway. His face is still scarred."

There was silence on the line for a moment before Riley spoke.

"There is no scenario where Mitch gets near a witness stand," he said. "Not looking like that. He looks guilty just standing still."

"The truck has to disappear," the chief said. "And we should settle this before it spreads. Pay the coach's family. Pay the girls' families. Moreland can talk them into it."

Riley exhaled sharply, the sound full of irritation rather than surprise.

"I'll handle the truck. You handle the settlement. I'm getting tired of cleaning up Mitch's mess."

Within the hour, the chief had summoned the government prosecutor. When the prosecutor arrived, the chief did not waste time.

"This case is falling apart," he said. "The coach didn't do it. We have a witness to the crash. We need to drop the charges against him and settle the rape case quietly."

The prosecutor leaned back in his chair, considering.

"How much do you think the families will want?"

"That's between you and Moreland," the chief replied. "Riley already agreed to settle."

The prosecutor nodded slowly.

"I'll meet with him tomorrow."

The chief's eyes narrowed. "And make sure he understands this. If he doesn't take the deal, he loses everything anyway."

A thin smile crossed the prosecutor's face.

"I know exactly what you mean."

Chapter 38:
The Price of Silence

The government prosecutor called Mr. Moreland late the next afternoon.

"Are you available tomorrow?" he asked. "Ten o'clock or one?"

"Ten," Moreland said.

The next morning, the prosecutor got straight to the point.

"We're prepared to drop all charges against the basketball coach," he said. "In exchange, you drop the rape charges against Mitch Callaghan and the two boys."

Mr. Moreland did not blink.

"You think I don't see what this is?"

The prosecutor leaned forward. "You don't have a case. The ambulance technicians and the ER physician will testify that no rape occurred. They'll say the girls made the whole thing up. We also have proof that Mitch was deer hunting that afternoon."

A faint, humorless smile touched Mr. Moreland's face.

"And I have a witness who saw the pickup truck ram the coach's car," he said. "It was murder. I know the truck. I know the owner. And Mitch is still walking around with scratches on his face from Tiffney's nails."

The prosecutor's expression hardened.

"Even if the truck belongs to Callaghan, that doesn't prove Mitch was driving it. His father already filed a stolen vehicle report."

"How convenient," Moreland said.

The prosecutor sighed, then shifted tactics.

"How much money do you want?"

Mr. Moreland paused, letting the number settle in his own mind before he said it.

"Ten million for the coach's family. Five million each for Tiffney and Lakesha. And all charges against Jordan dropped."

The prosecutor shook his head almost immediately.

"I might be able to get the money," he said. "Jordan is different. The DEA won't agree to dismiss that case."

"Then the Callaghan name gets dragged through open court," Moreland said quietly. "And this turns into something none of you can control."

That evening, he sat down with Tiffney and Lakesha and told them the truth. Dr. Moore had already corrupted the physical evidence. The ambulance crew had lied. The truck was now officially listed as stolen. Every door that should have opened onto justice had instead opened onto another lie.

"We can fight," he told them. "But the system is built against us. They control the judge, the police, the witnesses. If this goes to a jury, they can destroy you."

The room went still.

Then Tiffney spoke.

"We take the money," she said softly. "And we leave."

Lakesha nodded.

Later, Mr. Moreland met Jordan's parents and laid it out for them as well. They agreed. The system had already taken Jordan. They would not let it take the girls too.

Two days later, Callaghan's attorney made the counteroffer.

"Six million for the coach's family. Three million each for the girls. All charges against the coach disappear. The rape case disappears with them."

"And Jordan?" Moreland asked.

"The DEA won't dismiss his case," the attorney said. "But they won't recommend prison either. The judge will decide."

Mr. Moreland's eyes hardened at once.

"Then Mitch's friends stay charged."

The attorney frowned. "I'll speak to my client."

So the war did not end. It only shifted.

The price of silence had now been named.

Later, in the county jail's small visiting room, Mr. Moreland sat across from Jordan and his family and spoke as gently as he could.

"I wish I could prove everything Mitch did," he said. "But the truth means very little when the system has already chosen its side."

Jordan listened without interrupting, his jaw drawn tight.

"Money isn't justice," Moreland continued. "But it can protect your family. It can protect Tiffney's. Right now, that is the best I can do."

Jordan nodded. "I trust you. Whatever you decide, we'll accept it."

Then Mr. Moreland said the hardest part.

"We have to talk about your case. If we take this to a jury, you are almost certainly looking at fifteen to twenty years. If we take a plea, it may be eight to ten. Possibly less with good behavior."

Jordan swallowed hard.

"A plea means I admit I sold drugs."

"Yes," Moreland said. "It means accepting a lie so you can survive what the truth would cost."

Silence filled the room.

"If you go to trial without witnesses or evidence, they will bury you," Moreland said. "Either way, you become a felon. But with a plea, there is at least a path back to life."

Jordan closed his eyes for a long time. When he opened them again, the decision was already there.

"Then I'll follow your advice," he said quietly.

That afternoon, Moreland met again with Callaghan's attorney.

"I'll drop the charges against Mitch and his friends," he said, "if you submit a written request asking the judge for leniency in Jordan's case. No prison recommendation. He's young. First offense."

The attorney gave a slow nod.

"I'll try."

That evening, Moreland returned to Jordan's family and explained what that might mean.

"Six to eight years," he said. "With good behavior, he could be out in less than five."

Relief moved through the room, but it was the kind that comes wrapped in grief. No one mistook it for justice. It was only survival.

Liz and Tiffney sat listening in silence. Then Tiffney's hands began to shake.

"They destroyed him," she whispered. "They took everything. His future. His dream. All because Mitch wanted something that was never his."

Tears ran down her face. Liz pulled her close and held her while Moreland sat across from them, exhausted by the ugliness of what he had to say next.

"This is the world we live in," he said softly. "But maybe your generation will change it."

Tiffney lifted her head. Her eyes were wet, but there was fire in them now.

"I will."

Chapter 39:
The Price of Mercy

One week later, Mr. Callaghan's attorney contacted Mr. Moreland and asked him to come to his office. The government prosecutor would be there as well. When Moreland arrived, both men were already waiting for him, seated with the kind of calm that came from knowing most of the hard bargaining had been done behind closed doors.

The prosecutor slid a folder across the desk. "We've agreed in writing that the government will not seek a prison sentence," he said. "We will also formally ask the judge to consider Jordan's age and the fact that this is his first offense."

Mr. Moreland said nothing at first. He opened the folder and read every page carefully, line by line, not trusting a single sentence until he had weighed it himself. Across from him, Callaghan's attorney waited with folded hands, then finally added, "We'll hold a conference call in one week. Once the final language is approved, we'll notify both courts."

One case would stay in Pemiscot County, where the rape allegations would be resolved. The drug charges, however, would be handled in Cape Girardeau District Court. Even the separation of the cases carried its own kind of strategy. Nothing about any of this was accidental.

When Moreland returned to the jail, he went through every page with Jordan, translating each legal phrase into plain language until Jordan understood exactly what he was agreeing to and exactly what would be taken from him in return. Jordan listened without interrupting, his face still, his eyes darker than they had once been. When the time came, he signed.

Tiffney and Lakesha signed the civil settlement tied to the rape case. The coach's widow signed after them. Her hands trembled as she held the pen, but when she finished, some of the strain seemed to ease from her face.

"No amount of money will bring him back," she said quietly, looking down at the paper as if she could barely stand to see it. "But at least my children will be safe now."

The courtroom in Pemiscot County was packed on the day the matter was formally closed. Tiffney, Lakesha, and the coach's widow sat beside Mr. Moreland. Across the aisle sat Mitch and his two friends with their attorney, while Riley took a seat just behind them. Mitch kept his head lowered, as though he were tired, though everyone understood he was hiding the healing scar on his face.

The judge reviewed the agreements and then looked directly at Mitch. "Do you agree to compensate the victims as stated in this settlement?"

Mitch gave a stiff little nod.

Checks were handed over to Mr. Moreland. The judge raised his gavel, brought it down once, and said, "The case is dismissed."

No one moved for a moment. No one even seemed to breathe. The room had all the weight of justice, all the ritual of law, but everyone sitting there knew what had really happened. Justice had not been served. It had been bought.

Three weeks later, Jordan stood in federal court to enter his plea. Tiffney and Liz were not there. Mr. Moreland had refused to let them come.

"I won't give Mitch the satisfaction," he had told them. "He doesn't get to see what this costs you."

The judge leaned forward and fixed Jordan with a long, searching look. "Do you understand that by pleading guilty, you waive your right to appeal?"

"Yes, Your Honor."

"And no one has forced you to do this?"

"No, Your Honor."

Mr. Moreland rose then. He kept his voice steady, but there was force beneath it.

"Your Honor, Jordan is eighteen years old. He led his high school to two state championships. Without him, that team fell apart. He earned a full scholarship to one of the top basketball colleges in the country. He made a terrible mistake, yes, but he is still a young man with a future."

The prosecutor, keeping to the written agreement, asked for leniency. Then the courtroom went quiet. The judge sat for a long time before speaking, as if he wanted the weight of the next words to feel unavoidable.

"The evidence before the court shows that drugs were found in the trunk of Jordan's girlfriend's car," he said slowly. "A single witness claims Jordan instructed him, but there are no financial records, no communication records, and no evidence of profit or distribution beyond that statement."

Then he looked directly at Jordan.

"Even so, the law requires a sentence."

He paused again, and in that pause Jordan already felt something inside him falling.

"Eight years in federal custody," the judge said. "Five years' probation to follow."

Jordan's heart dropped so sharply it almost felt physical.

"You will receive credit for time served," the judge continued. "Seventy-eight months remain."

At Mr. Moreland's request, the judge allowed Jordan thirty minutes with his family and his attorney before he was returned to county custody. His transfer to the low-security federal prison camp in Greenville, Missouri, had already been arranged. The machinery of the system was moving efficiently now. Once the sentence was spoken, everything else followed as though it had been waiting all along.

Mr. Moreland was not satisfied. He knew the number could have been worse, but that did not make it fair.

"It's obvious the judge was under pressure," he said quietly once they were alone. "Everybody in that courtroom knows the reach of the Callaghan family. One brother in Congress. Another in the state senate. Influence like that doesn't stop at the courthouse door."

He shook his head and looked at Jordan with a tired kind of anger. "This entire case was a setup. The DEA and the prosecution cornered us into a plea, knowing the judge would still be expected to hand down seven or eight years. That's how these courts actually work when powerful people are involved. Instructions come down from above, and everyone else pretends they're just following the law."

Then his voice softened.

"You lost that college. You lost the path you thought was opening in front of you. Maybe, for now, you even lost your shot at the NBA. But listen to me. If you keep training in prison, if you stay disciplined, this is not the end of your life. When you come out, you can still go to college. You can still chase something better than what they wanted for you."

Jordan nodded slowly. His eyes were burning, but the fire in them had not gone out.

"I will," he said. "I'll work every day. I won't let them take all of it from me."

His parents held him then, and his mother spoke through tears.

"We're moving to Sikeston. We'll be closer to you."

Mr. Moreland stood back and watched them, but his thoughts were elsewhere too. He could not stop thinking about how deeply corrupted the system had become, about how prosecutors, DEA agents, police officers, and courts had stopped acting like separate parts of justice and started moving like one machine built to create the result it wanted. Evidence could be bent. Facts could be rearranged. Lies could be made to sound official simply because the right people said them in the right order.

Even the judges knew.

They knew, and still they followed the pattern. Orders did not always need to be spoken openly when power had already made its wishes clear. In Jordan's case, there was no money trail. No history of dealing. No criminal past. No proof he had ever sold so much as a single gram of drugs. By any honest standard, the case was paper-thin.

Yet everyone in that courtroom understood what had really happened. This was not justice.

It was revenge.

A wealthy tyrant had turned the law into a weapon because his son could not bear rejection. And so a gifted eighteen-year-old, who should have been stepping onto a college basketball court, was instead marched toward a prison bus.

Not because he was guilty.

Because he was powerless.

And because he was Black.

A few days later, Tiffney met Jordan in prison. The visit room was cold and plain, but she spoke to him as if the walls around them did not get to decide the shape of his future.

"I'll call that college," she said. "And if not them, then another. You are not finished."

Liz sat beside her and nodded. "You still have a future."

Jordan believed them, or at least he wanted to. In a place like that, hope was no small thing. It was a discipline of its own.

Back in Pemiscot County, eight years did not feel like enough to Mitch.

Chapter 40:
The Cost of Power

Mitch was furious. To him, the sentence was an insult. To his father, it felt like a costly failure. Mr. Callaghan sat in his office staring out through tinted glass at the city skyline while Riley stood nearby.

"We lost eighteen million dollars," Mr. Callaghan said coldly. "Legal fees. Settlements. Damage control. And on top of that, our reputation took a hit."

Riley gave a small nod. "We used every political channel available to us. The judge was expected to land somewhere between eight and ten years. He did exactly that."

Then, for the first time in a long while, something close to honesty slipped into his tone.

"In truth," he said, "even that was too much. The boy didn't deserve it."

Mr. Callaghan turned sharply, surprised enough to show it.

Before he could answer, Mitch stormed into the room. The scar on his face had faded, but not enough to disappear.

"I hate that girl," he snapped. "Instead of trying to rape her, I should have killed her. I should have killed both of them. That idiot Dr. Moore should have finished the job."

Mr. Callaghan slammed his fist on the desk.

"Enough."

Mitch stopped cold.

"You are lucky you are not in prison for attempted rape and for the coach's murder," Mr. Callaghan said. "We barely got you out of this. This cost us millions and nearly destroyed this family."

Mitch looked away, breathing hard.

"High school is over," his father continued. "No more girls. No more drugs. No more parties. You're going to learn the business. You're going to grow up."

Mitch scoffed, turned, and walked toward the door without answering. Riley watched him leave, then looked back at Mr. Callaghan.

"What are we going to do with that psycho?" Mr. Callaghan muttered. "When is he ever going to mature?"

Riley answered calmly. "He's eighteen. Dangerous, yes. But still manageable. I'll handle him."

Mr. Callaghan nodded once. "Make sure he stays away from Tiffney and her family. If he touches them again, everything we built will collapse."

Riley's smile was thin and unreadable. "Don't worry. I won't let that happen."

That same evening, Mrs. Callaghan went to see her son. She had already heard the news about Jordan's sentence, but what unsettled her more were the whispers that trailed behind it, about Jordan, about Tiffney, and most of all about Mitch's role in everything.

When she stepped into his room, Mitch barely looked up.

"Congratulations," she said quietly. "Jordan has been sentenced."

"Thanks, Mom," he muttered. "But I'm not happy."

She frowned. "Why not?"

"Because he only got eight years." His expression twisted. "I hate that bitch."

"Tiffney?"

Mitch nodded.

"Did you love her?"

He hesitated. "I used to. Now I hate her."

Then he turned his face slightly and traced the faint line on his cheek.

"See this scar? She did that."

Mrs. Callaghan pulled him into her arms at once.

"Why didn't you tell me?" she whispered. "I should have gone to her parents myself. I should have protected you."

His voice cracked in a way she had not heard since he was little.

"I'm sorry, Mom. I should have come to you. Not Dad. Not Riley."

She stroked his hair in silence, and when he finally looked up, his face had changed.

"Mom," he said, "I need to tell you something."

And then he told her everything.

How Jordan had been set up. How the evidence had been planted. How the trap had been built step by step. Mrs. Callaghan pulled back and stared at him, stunned.

"So you planned this?"

"No," Mitch said quickly, almost desperately. "Dad and Riley did it. I just... I agreed."

The color drained from her face.

"I always knew," she said quietly.

Mitch froze. "Knew what?"

"After your uncle died in that fire, I knew."

He stared at her. "Uncle died?"

She nodded once. Tears had already started to form.

"They killed him. It was planned. That fire was no accident."

Mitch said nothing.

"That was the day I stopped caring about myself," she said.

He looked at her differently then, as if he were seeing not just his mother, but a woman who had been living beside something terrible for years.

"Then why did you stay married to Dad?"

She laughed, but there was no joy in it.

"It was never love. I'm fifteen years younger than him. It was an arranged marriage."

Then she told him about the land, the inheritance, the betrayal, and the truth that came out after her own father died. She told him how she had discovered she owned nothing, that her brother had everything, and that J.D. and his father had only ever wanted her because they believed she came with land.

"When they found out I had nothing to offer them," she said, "I became useless."

The room went quiet.

She took both of his hands in hers.

"You're eighteen. You still have a chance to walk away. Leave the drugs. Leave the crimes. Leave them. Go to college. Live."

Mitch hugged her hard, but when he pulled back, there was something defeated in his face.

"It's too late, Mom. I'm already too deep."

He reached the doorway, then stopped and turned back.

"One more thing. Why don't my aunts and uncles get along? I know they all helped me in Jordan's case, but we don't feel like a family. Is it the land?"

Mrs. Callaghan closed her eyes.

"Yes," she said. "It always comes back to the land."

She sat down again and explained. Their grandfather had owned fifty thousand acres, meant to be divided among his sons and daughters. But after his sudden death, the will gave everything to Mitch's father.

Mitch's stomach tightened.

"So they think Dad did something."

"They don't just think it," she said softly. "They believe it."

Then she told him what had lived in whispers for years, that his grandfather may have been murdered, that the will may have been changed, and that Riley and his father had always been at the center of the suspicion.

"That explains everything," Mitch murmured.

"But then why did they still help me?"

Mrs. Callaghan gave him a weary, sad smile.

"Because the Callaghan name still matters. To the outside world, they are one powerful family. No matter how much they hate one another, they close ranks when the family is threatened."

She rose and touched his arm.

"Greed broke them apart. Reputation keeps them together."

Mitch nodded slowly. "I understand now."

He picked up his jacket and left. Mrs. Callaghan watched him go, knowing every answer she had given him had pulled him deeper into a truth he was never meant to carry.

Later that same evening, Riley called Mr. Moreland.

"It would be better if you moved out of Pemiscot County," he said quietly. "This place isn't safe anymore. Mitch is unstable. He could hurt Tiffney."

Mr. Moreland's voice hardened. "Are you threatening us?"

"No. I'm warning you. Mr. Callaghan and I do not want anything to happen to your daughter. Please. Leave the county. Leave the state if you can."

After he hung up, Mr. Moreland told Liz and Tiffney what Riley had said. Neither of them hesitated.

"We need to leave," Liz said at once.

That night they sat together at the kitchen table and went through their finances. Mr. Moreland laid it out plainly.

"We have three million dollars. That is more than enough to start over."

Tiffney shook her head. "I won't need more than three or four hundred thousand for college over the next seven years."

"That money is yours," Liz said firmly. "It's your future."

Mr. Moreland nodded. "Liz and I will each take one million. You take one million too."

Tiffney thought for a moment, then answered.

"I'll take one million. But half of it is for Jordan. Five hundred thousand for my education, and five hundred thousand for him when he gets out."

Her parents exchanged a glance, then nodded.

"We should move near a major city," she added. "Somewhere near an airport. If I end up at Harvard, I'll need easy flights."

Mr. Moreland had already been researching.

"I found a place. Farmington, Missouri. It's about an hour from St. Louis and forty-five minutes from Greenville Prison. You could fly in and out of St. Louis. It's also close to Sikeston, where Jordan's family is moving."

For the first time that evening, Tiffney smiled faintly.

"Perfect."

The next day, all three of them drove to Farmington. They found a modest three-bedroom house, quiet, safe, close enough to town to be practical but far enough from their old life to feel like something new. Mr. Moreland planned to use part of it as a law office so he could keep expenses low and start rebuilding without needing much.

They signed a five-year lease.

"This will be our home until Jordan comes back," Tiffney said softly.

That afternoon, Mr. Moreland called a real estate broker in Steel and put their old house on the market. There was still a mortgage on it, so the best he could hope for was around one hundred thousand dollars in equity. The broker promised to list it the next morning.

Then Moreland called three moving companies. One agreed to take the job within five days.

Before the day ended, one final call came from the county jail.

"Jordan has been transferred to Greenville Prison Camp," the officer told him.

Mr. Moreland closed his eyes for a moment before thanking him.

When he hung up, the room was quiet.

The past was not gone, not really. It had taken too much for that.

But it was behind them now.

And for the first time in a long time, they were moving toward something instead of only running away.

Chapter 41: Jordan Arrives at Greenville Prison Camp

The transport bus rolled through the tall iron gates just after sunrise. Jordan sat near the back, his wrists loosely cuffed in front of him, staring through the narrow window as cold Missouri air moved across the fog-covered fields beyond the fence. A weathered sign came into view as the bus slowed.

Greenville Federal Prison Camp.

It did not look like a prison the way he had imagined it all those nights in county jail. There were no towering walls, no sniper towers, no dark concrete fortress swallowing men whole. Instead, it looked almost like a neglected college campus, low concrete buildings, open yards, and inmates in orange uniforms moving under the constant watch of correctional officers.

But Jordan knew better.

Freedom did not live here.

The bus jerked to a stop. The doors hissed open.

"Move!" a guard barked.

Jordan stepped down onto the pavement carrying nothing but a small plastic bag. Inside it were his court papers, a toothbrush, and a folded photograph of Tiffney, the one Mr. Moreland had slipped into his pocket during their last meeting.

Inside intake, the air smelled of disinfectant and sweat. Everything happened quickly and without dignity. He was fingerprinted, photographed, ordered out of his clothes, searched, processed, and handed a thin mattress, a gray uniform, and prison boots that fit badly enough to hurt.

"You're Camp D-12," the officer said, handing him a bunk number without looking at him. "Lights out at ten. Work assignment tomorrow."

Jordan nodded once.

As he was led across the yard, some of the men glanced at him with passing curiosity. Others looked longer, colder, as if already deciding what kind of man he might be. One tall inmate with tattoos winding up his neck leaned toward the man beside him and muttered, "Fresh meat."

Jordan kept walking.

His bunk sat inside a long open dorm filled with rows of metal beds, thin mattresses, and lockers barely large enough for shoes and soap. It felt less like a room and more like a storage space for broken men. He sat on the edge of the bed, reached into the plastic bag, and unfolded the photo.

Tiffney was smiling in it, soft and bright, her face still full of the hope and future both of them had once believed in.

"I'll come back," he whispered. "I promise."

Later that afternoon, a guard began calling out work assignments. Jordan sat half-listening until he heard his own name.

"Jordan Walker. Gym maintenance."

He looked up at once.

The gym.

Something in his chest stirred for the first time since the sentencing. He followed the officer through a side building and into an old basketball court, worn and imperfect but still alive. The hardwood was cracked in places. The hoops were slightly crooked. But it was a court.

A man in his late forties stood there holding a clipboard.

"I'm Coach Alvarez," he said. "You play?"

"Yes, sir."

"High school?"

"Two-time state champion."

Coach Alvarez lifted an eyebrow, not impressed so much as interested. "We'll see what you've got tomorrow."

For the first time since his arrest, Jordan felt something he had not allowed himself to feel in months.

Hope.

That night, after the camp quieted and the last sounds faded into the usual prison hush, Jordan lay on his thin mattress staring at the ceiling above him. He was fenced in. Labeled a criminal. Separated from the girl he loved. But there was a basketball court inside these walls.

And as long as there was a court, he was not finished.

Not even close.

Chapter 42: The First Call

It took a full week before Jordan's phone privileges were approved. By then, he had learned the rhythm of Greenville, the morning counts, the meal lines, the way tension never fully disappeared even during the quietest hours. Still, none of that mattered as much as the one thing he had been waiting for.

That first phone call.

When his name was finally called, his hands trembled as he picked up the receiver. The first number he dialed was Mr. Moreland's.

The line clicked.

"Jordan?" Mr. Moreland said.

"Yes, sir. It's me."

Relief moved through both of them at once, so clear Jordan could hear it in the older man's voice. Mr. Moreland told him they had fully moved into Farmington and that the old office number from Steel had been transferred. It was a small detail, but it comforted Jordan more than he expected. Even after everything, the people he trusted were still standing, still building, still refusing to collapse.

"I'm okay," Jordan said. "Better here than county jail. They've got a basketball court. I already started practicing."

Mr. Moreland chuckled softly. "I knew you would."

Then he passed the phone to Tiffney.

When her voice came through the line, it felt like sunlight after a long winter.

"How are you?" she asked. "I miss you so much."

"I miss you too," Jordan said. "I already mailed you the visiting forms. You should get them soon. Please fill them out for my family too."

"Don't worry about money," she said quickly. "I'll send whatever you need."

Jordan explained how the prison system worked, how she could put funds on his account through the Bureau of Prisons system, how commissary limits worked, and how even simple things like decent shoes, hygiene items, and extra food all depended on having money available.

"I'll send it today," she said.

"Thank you. Commissary is in three days."

Their time disappeared too quickly.

"Love you," Tiffney whispered.

"Love you too."

Then the line went dead.

The visiting forms did not arrive right away. With the move to Farmington and the address change, the mail was delayed. So Tiffney drove all the way to Haiti to check Jordan's family mailbox herself. The forms were there. She filled them out carefully that same day and mailed them to the prison counselor. Then she sat with Jordan's parents, who were already making plans to move to Sikeston.

"Make sure you get a landline in the new house," she told Lakesha. "Jordan's going to need a number he can call."

Lakesha nodded. "We're getting a bigger place this time. Four or five bedrooms. We finally can."

Tiffney drove back that same night. She did not want to stay in Pemiscot County one minute longer than necessary.

Two days later, her own copy of the forms arrived at the new address. She filled them out too and sent them in. For the next week, Jordan checked with the prison counselor every morning, trying not to seem too eager, though he knew he failed at that every time.

Then, one afternoon, he finally got the answer.

"They approved everyone," he told Tiffney over the phone. "You. My parents. My sisters."

Tiffney smiled through tears.

"I'll come first," she said. "Then I'll bring your family."

"Visiting hours are Saturdays and Sundays, ten-thirty to two-thirty."

"I'll be there this Saturday."

"I've got everything I need now," Jordan said. "Thank you."

After the call ended, Tiffney sat for a long time staring at her phone. For the first time since Jordan had been taken away, something good was no longer just a memory or a promise.

It was coming.

Saturday arrived faster than she expected. Tiffney barely slept the night before. Every time she closed her eyes, old memories came back, the cafeteria, the basketball court, the easy laughter they used to share before everything had been ripped apart. Now she was going to see him again, but not in a school hallway or over dinner in Cape Girardeau.

She would see him in prison.

Mr. Moreland drove her to Greenville just after sunrise. Neither of them spoke much on the way. The silence was not awkward. It was heavy. Every mile seemed to carry its own grief.

When the prison finally came into view, Tiffney's chest tightened. Tall fences wrapped in coils of razor wire surrounded low, flat buildings. Guards watched from towers. It was not the kind of place anyone could walk into and still pretend life had not changed.

Inside the visitor processing area, she handed over her identification, removed her jacket, and stepped through the metal detector. Every sound made her flinch. She kept telling herself to stay calm, to stay strong, but this place made strength feel thin and fragile.

After what felt far longer than it probably was, a guard called her name.

"Visiting Room C."

She followed him down a long hallway.

Then she saw Jordan.

He was standing near a table wearing a plain prison uniform. He looked thinner than before, but when he saw her, his whole face changed. That smile, the one that had always made the world feel safer than it was, was still there.

"Tiffney."

"Jordan."

They moved toward each other and held on tight, forgetting for one brief second where they were. A guard cleared his throat sharply, reminding them of the rules, but even then neither of them let go right away.

When they finally sat down, their hands stayed close, still touching.

"How are you?" she asked softly.

"I'm okay. It's better than county jail. Most of the men here are low-level offenders. No gangs. No real violence."

She studied his face, and the first thing she noticed was not the uniform, or the prison, or the weight he had lost.

"Your eyes look tired."

"I sleep fine," he said. "I just think about you all the time."

Tears rose in her eyes instantly. "I'm sorry."

He tightened his hold on her hands. "Don't say that. None of this was ever your fault."

They talked about everything they could fit into that short window of borrowed time, the move to Farmington, his family's plans for Sikeston, her classes, and the basketball court inside the camp.

"They have a gym," he said with a faint grin. "I play every day. I'm not letting my dream die in here."

"I knew you wouldn't."

A guard's voice broke through the room.

"Five minutes."

Jordan's smile dimmed. "I hate this part."

"I'll come again," she said. "Next time I'll bring your parents."

"Tell them I love them."

"I will."

When the final call came, they stood slowly, as if moving too quickly would make the goodbye more real.

"I'm proud of you," Tiffney said. "You're stronger than anyone I know."

"And I'm still yours," he answered. "Prison doesn't get to change that."

They held each other again, longer this time. When she finally turned to leave, she looked back once more and saw him still standing there, still watching her go, the way he always had.

She didn't cry until she reached the parking lot.

And even then, the tears were not only sorrow.

For the first time in months, they carried hope.

Soon after that, Tiffney called Lakesha at the family's new home number and told her she would arrive around eight-thirty in the morning so they could leave together by nine for Greenville. That Sunday became something none of them had expected prison to allow.

It became something close to joy.

Jordan was waiting when they arrived. The moment he saw his parents, his younger brother, and both sisters, a brightness came over his face that no fence, no sentence, and no prison uniform could hide. For a few precious hours, the room felt less like a prison visiting hall and more like a family gathering interrupted by hard chairs and guards.

They laughed. They talked. Jordan teased his younger brother and sisters, telling them to keep practicing basketball and never let go of their own dreams. He explained the routine at the camp, the early counts, the work schedule, the meals.

"The food's not great," he said with a smile, "but at least they give us fruit every day."

Tiffney laughed. "Don't you dare come home overweight."

Everyone laughed with her.

After that, Tiffney and Jordan's family visited whenever they could, usually every other week, and sometimes every week when her schedule allowed it. She had about two months before leaving for college, and she meant to use every one of them. When she could not make the trip, Jordan's father went instead. With the Cadillac Escalade he had bought, the drive was easier now, longer in miles than in comfort, but still manageable.

The previous eight months had been filled with fear, injustice, and grief almost beyond bearing. But now, inside the same life that had stripped so much away, Jordan began to feel something he had nearly forgotten how to trust.

Hope.

Chapter 43:
Dreams That Refuse to Die

Rick and his wife had settled into a quiet kind of retirement in their small home in Poplar Bluff. The bitterness had not disappeared, not really. It still lingered whenever Rick thought about Mr. Callaghan, the police department, and the slow, deliberate destruction of the newspaper he had built with his own hands. But there was nothing left for him to do. The settlement he had signed with the government had closed that chapter of his life and sealed it shut.

Now they lived on Social Security, which covered the basics and little more. Shirley worked full-time at an insurance company and brought in a steady paycheck. Her son, Ethan, was still in high school, and already talking about journalism the way other boys talked about sports or cars. He wanted the same life his mother and grandfather had once loved, and despite everything that had been done to that family, the desire to tell the truth had survived.

Tiffney's first year of college was going well. More than well, in fact. She was thriving. Her grades were strong, her focus sharper than ever, and she had thrown herself into her future with the same determination that had carried her through everything else. She spoke with Jordan at least three times a week on the phone she had bought specifically so she could stay in close touch with him and with both families. Mr. Moreland's law practice remained slow, but money was no longer an immediate fear. After selling their old house, they had managed to keep about one hundred thousand dollars in savings. Jordan's family had settled comfortably in Sikeston, closer to his aunt, and for the first time in a long while their lives felt somewhat steady.

At Greenville Prison Camp, Jordan had thrown himself into basketball with the intensity of a man trying to keep one part of himself alive. He was the youngest inmate at the facility, and that alone made him stand out. His roommate, Bunker, had taken to him quickly. He was kind in a quiet, practical way, and protective without making a show of it. It did not take him long to decide that Jordan was innocent, one more young man broken by a system that served money before truth.

One of Jordan's closest new friends was Kremer, a man from Jackson, Tennessee. Kremer had once been a major drug distributor across several states, and he talked about his past with the calm of someone who had already paid for every mistake in it. His life had gone off the rails when he was sixteen. He had been expelled from school and thrown out by his parents, not because of any crime, but because he had crossed paths with a rich and powerful boy who wanted the same girl. Once he ended up on the street, the drug trade found him before anything better could. After that, there had been no easy way back.

When Jordan told him his own story, Kremer's face darkened with anger. But when he heard that Tiffney was still waiting for him, something softer entered his expression.

"You're lucky," Kremer said. "I lost my girl, my school, and my family all at once. When somebody pushes you into this kind of life, most people never find their way out. They just keep sinking."

He still had seven years left on his sentence.

"We might get out around the same time," he said one day, almost casually.

Jordan admitted to him then how much anger still lived inside him, how often he imagined getting revenge on Mitch, on the Callaghans, on Dr. Moore, on the police, even on the judge.

Kremer shook his head.

"That anger will eat you alive," he said. "You've got something better than revenge. You've got a reason to build a life when this is over. Hold on to that. Basketball matters, sure. But it's not the only thing you've got. I'll help you figure out the rest when the time comes."

Outside the prison walls, Mitch Callaghan was sinking deeper into the same darkness he had always fed. The parties had returned. So had the drinking, the drugs, and the cruelty. He had no real interest in business, none in discipline, and certainly none in becoming the kind of man his father kept pretending he could be. His life revolved around appetite and destruction. While Jordan was trying to rebuild himself behind bars, Mitch was rotting in plain sight, slowly stripping away whatever little humanity he still had.

Time passed that way, quietly but never without consequence.

Tiffney graduated from college with honors and was accepted into Harvard Law School on a full scholarship. The news filled both families with pride. Against every threat, every injustice, every effort to break her spirit, she had done exactly what she promised she would do. She had kept moving forward. She had protected her future without abandoning the man she loved.

During those four years, plenty of men asked her out. Some were polite. Some were persistent. Some assumed they only needed time. She refused them all. Whenever anyone asked why, she only smiled and said she already had someone in her life. Her heart had long since made its choice.

Inside Greenville, Jordan was changing too. He trained relentlessly, adding strength, endurance, and discipline to the talent he had always carried. He was no longer just a gifted high school athlete trapped in the wrong place. His body now carried the power and control of a grown man who had learned how to sharpen himself under pressure. Kremer became more than a friend. He became a mentor.

He taught Jordan HVAC and plumbing, the kind of work that could feed a man when dreams alone could not. Jordan worked in maintenance around the camp, earning seventy-five dollars a month while learning furnace repair, pipe fitting, and basic electrical work. He also took computer and IT classes, helped by a former roommate who had worked in technology before prison. He was not simply waiting for release anymore.

He was preparing for it.

Back in Farmington, Mr. Moreland's law practice slowly began to recover. He and Liz still refused to touch the million dollars they had set aside. In their minds, that money belonged to Tiffney, no matter how often she argued otherwise.

"Buy a house," she told them more than once. "Buy a better car. Live a little."

But they would not do it. Liz always said the same thing.

"That money is your future."

Meanwhile, Ethan, Rick's grandson, had entered college and already found part-time work at a local newspaper. The editor there had noticed his sharp instincts almost immediately. The boy had courage, a strong eye for weak arguments, and none of the caution that makes ordinary writing safe and forgettable. Journalism, for better or worse, was already in his blood.

Shirley waited patiently for the end of her seven-year ban. When it was finally over, she intended to go back to journalism stronger than before, louder than before, and impossible to bury in silence again.

In one way or another, they were all waiting.

Waiting for justice.

Waiting for freedom.

Waiting for Jordan.

And when the waiting ended, none of them intended to be weak enough to break.

Chapter 44:
The Man Who Knows

Jordan had been watching the man for days before he finally asked about him. There was something unusual about him, something hard to place at first. He was tall and thin, with long, unkempt hair and a beard streaked with gray. One of his eyes had an almost unsettling sharpness to it, as if it saw more than it should. While most of the inmates avoided work whenever they could, this man never seemed to stop moving. He cleaned toilets, scrubbed bathrooms, swept the campgrounds, hauled trash, and handled nearly every maintenance job in the place.

Eventually Jordan asked Kremer.

"That's Jack," Kremer said. "He's doing life for murder. Been inside more than twenty-five years. He's got less than three or four left now."

"Where's he from?" Jordan asked.

"Southeast Missouri," Kremer said. "You ought to talk to him. He's been here so long the camp counselor put him in charge of most of the work crews. Cleaning, trash, gym, all of it. This place runs smoother because of him."

Jack always looked tired, worn down in the way only decades of confinement can wear a man down. But there was also something kind about him, something quiet and steady that did not fit with the story his sentence told.

One afternoon Jordan saw him sitting just outside the camp fence feeding stray cats. They swarmed around him like they knew him well, rubbing against his legs, waiting patiently as he tossed them bits of food from a paper sack.

Jordan walked over.

"I heard you're from southeast Missouri," he said. "So am I."

Jack looked up at him for a long moment, then patted the bench beside him.

"Sit."

Jordan sat.

For a while Jack said nothing. He only fed the cats. Then, without looking at him, he asked, "How long did you get?"

"Eight years."

"For what?"

"Selling drugs. Cocaine. But I didn't do it. I was framed."

That got Jack's full attention.

"By who?"

Jordan swallowed once before answering.

"A rich man. John Dillon Callaghan. His son too. Mitch."

Jack's hand stopped in midair.

"I never touched drugs in my life," Jordan went on. "They planted cocaine in my girlfriend's car and pinned it on me."

Jack slowly looked up.

"Why?"

"There was a girl in our class. Tiffney. Mitch wanted her. She hated him. She loved me. That made them angry. The police, the DEA, even the judge, they all went along with it."

Jack stood up so suddenly that the cats scattered.

"What did you say his name was?"

"John Dillon Callaghan. People call him J.D. Callaghan. He's rich. Powerful."

Jack stared at him with an expression that had gone beyond anger into something darker and older.

"I know that son of a bitch," he said. "He's the reason I'm in this place."

Jordan said nothing.

"J.D. Callaghan is my brother-in-law," Jack continued. "My sister is Mrs. Callaghan. My father owned fifty thousand acres of some of the best farmland in southeast Missouri. He had two children, my sister and me. She was older. I was five years younger."

He sat back down slowly and picked up another scrap of food for the cats.

"When my father made his will, my sister told him she didn't want anything. So he left everything to me. The land. The money. The house. All of it."

Jordan stared at him.

"Callaghan's father didn't know that. He approached my father with a proposal for an arranged marriage between J.D. and my sister. She was fifteen years younger than the man they wanted her to marry. She wasn't happy about it, but my father was sick, and she didn't refuse him."

His voice darkened.

"Six months after the wedding, my father died."

He turned and looked directly at Jordan.

"And then Callaghan's father found out about the will."

Silence stretched between them.

"That's when J.D. and Riley decided I had to go," Jack said. "If I died, everything would pass to my sister. Which meant everything would end up in J.D.'s hands."

Jordan felt cold all over.

"Callaghan asked his father to help get rid of me. The old man refused. He said the land ought to be divided among his three sons and two daughters. Riley didn't like that. So they killed him."

Jordan stared at him.

"They staged it. Then they brought in lawyers and financial advisers and produced a new will. A fake will. It left everything to J.D. His brothers and sisters knew it was a lie, but they couldn't prove it."

Jack gave a hard, bitter laugh.

"That's why the Callaghan family hates each other."

Then his face changed again.

"After that, I was the last obstacle."

He looked out past the fence as though he could still see the place where it all happened.

"It was deer-hunting season. My best friend was staying with me. He knew they were trying to kill me. He knew if I died, the land would be stolen."

He stopped, swallowed, and went on.

"At four in the morning, the house caught fire. Kerosene was everywhere. We knew right away it was arson. We barely made it out. We were burning alive."

Jordan listened without moving.

"My friend saved me," Jack said. "At the door, he grabbed the gold family chain from my neck and told me, 'If you live, pretend to be me. Let them think you're dead. That's the only way you survive.'"

His voice cracked then, just slightly.

"Then he ran back into the flames."

Tears burned in his eye, though he blinked them back.

"I was too badly burned to stop him. Seventy percent of my body was on fire. I blacked out."

He took a long breath before speaking again.

"When I woke up, I was in a Memphis hospital. I spent almost a year fighting to stay alive."

Then the bitterness returned.

"When I finally recovered, I learned that J.D. and Riley had accused me of starting the fire and killing my 'friend.' My gold chain was found near his body. They thought that proved I was dead."

Jordan's voice dropped to a whisper.

"So they won."

"They thought they did," Jack said. "The land was transferred into my sister's name. J.D. was celebrating."

Then he gave Jordan a sharp look.

"But knowing J.D. and Riley, they would force her to sign it all over eventually. Men like that always get what they want."

Jordan leaned toward him.

"Did you ever tell anyone you survived? That you're really Jack?"

Jack shook his head.

"No. Nobody would've believed me. And even if they had, J.D. and Riley would've killed me in the hospital or out on the street. My friend didn't die so I could waste the chance he gave me. He died so I could live as him."

He looked down at his hands.

"My real name isn't Jack," he said quietly. "Every legal record in here says Jonathan. You're the first person I've told. But after hearing what they did to you, after finding out we were both ruined by the same people, I couldn't keep quiet."

Jordan nodded slowly.

"You can trust me. I'm younger than you, sure. But prison changes people. The last few years changed me. I won't betray you. What do you want from me?"

Jack studied him for a long moment.

"I'll be eligible for parole in less than three years. You'll be out in three or four. When we're both free, I want to go after them. Not with violence. With truth. I have secrets. I have documents. I have things I never trusted anybody with."

"Then why me?"

"Because I'm getting old," Jack said. "And you're not. I've got the mind for it. You've got the strength. We work together."

Jordan did not hesitate.

"They killed their own father. They ruined innocent lives. We've got the same enemy."

Jack nodded once.

"You don't owe me anything. You can walk away whenever you want."

"I won't," Jordan said.

For the first time, a real smile crossed Jack's harsh, tired face.

"Good. Then we do this smart. No recklessness."

He hesitated before speaking again.

"There's one thing I want."

"What?"

"I want to see my sister. Just once. Can you find a way to reach her, quietly?"

Jordan thought about it.

"Yes. But not yet. It'll be safer after I'm released."

Jack let out a long breath.

"You're right."

Then both men fell silent. Around them, the stray cats circled and settled, and the prison yard went on pretending to be ordinary. But on that bench, something larger than hope had begun to take shape.

It was a purpose. And it was dangerous.

Chapter 45:
The Long Game Begins

Jordan, Jack, and Kremer had begun spending more time together. At first, it was nothing more than conversation, the kind men have when they are trapped in the same place long enough to stop pretending they do not need one another. But over time, those conversations sharpened into something else. They became quiet strategy sessions, careful and guarded, never reckless, never loud enough to draw the wrong kind of attention.

Kremer was already fully committed to Jordan. He understood exactly how boys like Mitch were swallowed by the drug world, and he understood even better how men like Riley used them, shielding them when it was useful, weaponizing them when it was not. Jack, for his part, had been carrying his own plans for years. Revenge had lived inside him so long it had become less an emotion and more a structure, something built carefully in silence. Until Jordan arrived, he had assumed he would have to wait until he was free to do anything about it. Now he understood that some parts of the work could begin long before the gates ever opened.

Jack still had several years left under federal rules, but Jordan and Kremer were due to be released around the same time. That made Jordan the hinge on which everything would turn.

Outside the prison walls, life kept moving, indifferent and relentless. Tiffney had just finished her first semester of law school, and she was doing exceptionally well. She planned to visit during winter break and hoped to see Jordan in person over the Christmas holidays. Mitch, meanwhile, was nearing twenty-three and behaving with all the discipline of a spoiled teenager. He spent almost no time learning the business and even less with his family. His life revolved around parties, alcohol, and a growing dependence on both prescription pills and whatever else he could get his hands on. Riley had tried, more than once, to pull him back, but Mitch refused to listen. Even Dr. Moore had grown uneasy.

"Don't keep giving him what he asks for," Riley had warned.

"I've tried," Dr. Moore replied. "He doesn't listen. He's already dependent."

During winter break, Tiffney came home to visit her parents. Before she went to see Jordan, she stopped first at his family's place. Then she made her way to Greenville. When Jordan saw her, something in his face changed at once. Months of steady training had transformed him, and she noticed it before he even sat down.

"You look different," she said with a small, surprised smile.

He gave one of his own. "I've had time."

They talked first about her life, her classes, her professors, the demands of law school, the things she was learning and the world she was beginning to imagine for herself. Then, when she finished, Jordan told her about Jack.

"How long have you known him?" she asked.

Jordan leaned back slightly before answering. "I've been watching him for more than four years. He mostly keeps to himself. He works all the time. He notices everything, but he acts like he notices nothing. One day I told him about my case. When I said J.D. Callaghan's name, he stood up like he'd been hit."

His voice lowered.

"This has to stay quiet. No one else can know."

Tiffney nodded.

"He's been serving life for almost twenty-five years," she said softly. "Even if he survives all this, he still has years left."

After hearing Jack's story in full, she sat with it for a while, visibly shaken.

"I think we need a serious criminal attorney," she said at last. "Someone good enough to go after Riley and J.D. Callaghan."

Jordan shook his head.

"That's too dangerous. Callaghan still has too much reach. If we move too openly, somebody ends up dead."

Tiffney thought for a moment, then her expression changed. Jordan had seen that look before. It was the look she got when her mind began stitching a problem into something workable.

"Then we don't do it openly," she said. "We find an attorney who doesn't know who Jack really is. We file for early parole under the name Jonathan. We keep his real identity buried until he's out."

Jordan stared at her for a second, then nodded slowly.

"Good conduct. Federal review. Quiet and legal."

She nodded once.

"I'll find someone. Give me a week."

"Please," Jordan said. "The sooner, the better."

"I'll call you next Saturday."

When she left, Jordan sat for a long time with a feeling he had not trusted in years. It was hope, but not the soft, fragile kind. It had edges now.

Tiffney met with several attorneys over the next few days, taking free consultations, listening carefully, discarding anyone who sounded careless, eager, or too impressed with himself. By Wednesday, she was sitting in a downtown St. Louis office across from a man she finally believed she could trust.

"I'm a first-year law student at Harvard," she told him. "I recently visited my boyfriend at Greenville prison camp. While I was there, I met an inmate who has been serving a life sentence for more than twenty-five years. He's in poor health. He suffered severe burns in a fire years ago, more than eighty percent of his body. His prison record is spotless. Is there any realistic path to parole?"

The attorney leaned back in his chair and studied her for a moment before he answered.

"Yes," he said. "There's a chance."

Then, because he was a lawyer and not a dreamer, he added the rest.

"Normally, I'd charge ten thousand for something like this. But since you're a law student, I'll do it for five. Twenty-five hundred now. The other twenty-five hundred only if he gets out. If it fails, the second half is gone."

Tiffney nodded.

"I understand there's no guarantee."

He gave a short nod of his own. "I'll email you two documents. The fee agreement and the engagement letter. Jonathan has to sign first. Once he does, I can go see him."

"I'm visiting this Saturday," she said. "I'll bring them."

"Good," he replied. "I think I can get a judge to listen."

Before she left, she mentioned casually that her father was also an attorney in Farmington. The lawyer's respect for her became more visible after that. Not because she had tried to impress him, but because she had not.

That evening she called Jordan.

"I found someone," she said. "He sounds confident. Tell Jonathan to add the attorney's name to his visitation list. I'll bring the papers this weekend."

Jordan found Jack afterward and explained everything.

"You'll be released as Jonathan," he said. "We keep your real identity buried until you're out."

For the first time in a long while, Jack smiled without forcing it.

When Tiffney arrived that Saturday, she handed Jordan the documents. Jack read them carefully, then signed them and mailed them back.

"Nothing will move for a few weeks," Tiffney said. "The holidays will slow everything down. But the petition should be filed in January."

Jordan reached for her hand.

"You moved fast."

She laughed softly. "This is what I'm meant to do."

He looked at her with unmistakable pride.

"You're going to be a great attorney. You're going to expose people like Riley. J.D. Callaghan. Even Mitch."

"And I'm going to help people like Jonathan," she said. "There are thousands of innocent people sitting in prison because they never had access to a good lawyer."

Jordan nodded.

"That's how you change the world."

Chapter 46:
Hidden Wealth, Hidden War

Jack was deeply grateful to both of them, though he rarely said more than he had to. Half the legal fee had already been paid, and the signed agreements had been mailed more than a week earlier.

"Hopefully he has them by now," Jack said one morning.

Jordan nodded. "I'll ask Tiffney."

After a brief silence, Jack lowered his voice.

"As Jonathan, I still own five thousand acres of farmland."

Jordan looked at him, stunned.

Jack continued as if stating acreage and wealth meant nothing to him now.

"Jonathan's father died six months after the fire. Heart trouble. While I was in the hospital, burnt nearly to death, his condition got worse. He died before I recovered. Jonathan's mother kept visiting me in the hospital and later in prison, but she died within a year of him."

He stared down at the ground when he said the next part.

"The five thousand acres were leased to my cousin. He pays one hundred dollars an acre every year. That's five hundred thousand a year deposited into my account. My parents also left more than five million in savings. There's a farmhouse on the land too."

Jordan did the math without meaning to.

"After twenty-five years," Jack said, "there's around seventeen or eighteen million in those accounts."

Jordan let out a slow breath. "So when you get out, money won't be your problem."

Jack shook his head almost impatiently.

"I don't care about money. I care about my sister. And I care about exposing J.D. Callaghan and Riley. They stole, murdered, lied, and burned through other people's lives like it meant nothing. That needs to come back on them."

Jordan's jaw tightened.

"They ruined your life. Then they ruined mine. And probably more lives than either of us knows. I'm with you."

That weekend, Jordan spoke with Tiffney again.

"The attorney got Jonathan's signed papers," she said. "He plans to visit in a week or two. He wants to hear the whole story directly."

Jordan passed the message on to Jack.

"The attorney will contact the camp counselor. Once it's approved, they'll call you in."

Jack nodded slowly.

The pieces were moving.

And for the first time in decades, J.D. Callaghan's empire had begun to crack, not loudly, not dramatically, but quietly, legally, and from the inside.

A week later, the camp counselor called Jonathan to the office and told him he had a visitor. The attorney was waiting. Once Jonathan entered, the counselor closed the door behind them and gave them privacy.

The attorney introduced himself and listened for nearly an hour as Jonathan told the story in full. He took detailed notes, carefully marking dates, injuries, deaths, names, transfers of property, and every place the official record had been made to lie.

When Jonathan finally finished, the attorney leaned forward.

"I'm going to file a motion for early release in the Eastern District of Missouri. The judge may take two or three months to decide whether to give us a formal hearing. My guess is he will."

Jonathan nodded.

"If the hearing is approved," the attorney continued, "you'll likely appear by video through the camp counselor. I'm also requesting your full medical records from the Memphis hospital. The burns, the surgeries, the long-term damage, all of that matters."

Jonathan looked down at his scarred hands.

"My father died six months after the fire," he said. "My mother followed within a year. I don't have any family left."

The attorney's expression softened.

"I'm sorry."

Jonathan touched the edge of his damaged eye.

"I lost vision in my right eye because of the burns."

"I'll do everything I can," the attorney said. "These cases take time. Six months, maybe a year. But I'm not going to stop pushing."

Jonathan nodded once.

"And don't worry about the fee," he added. "That will be handled."

The attorney shook his head.

"Tiffney already handled half of it. The rest comes after the court decides."

When Jonathan walked back across the camp that day, he carried something he had not allowed himself in a very long time.

Hope.

Two months later, the court finally responded. The letter was brief but encouraging. A decision on whether to grant a formal hearing would be issued within sixty to ninety days.

Jonathan's attorney waited.

Just before the deadline ran out, the answer arrived.

The judge had approved a formal parole hearing, to be scheduled within the next ninety days. The government prosecutor had been notified and assigned to represent the state's position on Jonathan's early release.

Jonathan's attorney already knew the prosecutor. Within a week, they spoke by phone.

"I'm going to need everything," the prosecutor said. "Hospital records. Prison medical reports. Surgical records. All of it."

"You'll have it," the attorney replied.

Then he added, "My client has served more than twenty-five years. He lost both parents while in the hospital and in prison. More than seventy percent of his body was burned. He lost vision in one eye. His health is permanently compromised. He's no danger to anyone."

There was a long silence on the other end before the prosecutor responded.

"Once I've reviewed the records, come see me. Based on what you're telling me, this sounds reasonable."

Within days, Jonathan's attorney mailed complete copies of every prison and hospital document, Greenville records, Memphis hospital files, surgical reports, and photographs of the burns. One set went to the prosecutor. Another went directly to the district judge.

A month later, the prosecutor called back.

"I received everything," he said. "The injuries are severe. I don't see any reason to oppose his release. It'll come down to the judge."

Jonathan's attorney thanked him and ended the call.

Now there was only one thing left between Jonathan and the possibility of freedom.

Time.

And the judge.

Chapter 47:
Waiting for September

Tiffney and Jordan spoke on the phone almost every week. Unless she was buried under exams or some major assignment, he made sure to call every Saturday. Those calls became part of the structure of their lives, something steady they could both lean on through the long stretch of months and years that still stood between them.

Back home, Jordan's family was doing well. Lakesha was in college on a basketball scholarship and still dating Josh, the same boyfriend she had been with since Caruthersville High. Josh had enrolled in a combined college and police academy program and was training to become an investigator. He wanted to work serious cases one day, not spend his life writing traffic tickets and filling out minor reports.

Tiffney had just finished her first year of law school with strong grades. Her professors had already taken notice of her, not just because she worked hard, but because she carried a real sense of purpose into everything she did. Most of her classmates talked about corporate law, big firms, and the kind of money that came with them. Tiffney had no interest in any of that.

She loved criminal law.

That summer, she made another decision that surprised no one who knew her well. Instead of going home, she accepted an unpaid internship at one of the most respected criminal defense firms in the country. Jordan was proud of her. Her parents were proud of her. And underneath all that pride was something quieter and just as important. They recognized that she was becoming exactly the kind of lawyer she had always meant to be.

One Saturday, during one of their usual calls, she told Jordan the news she had been waiting to share.

"I spoke with Jonathan's attorney," she said. "The district judge set the hearing for September. He's optimistic. He really believes Jonathan is going to be released."

Jordan closed his eyes for a second and let the words settle.

"That's amazing," he said softly. "I'll tell him."

After all the waiting, all the secrecy, and all the years of careful patience, September was no longer some distant idea. It was real. It was close enough to count.

Jordan passed the news on to Jonathan as soon as he had the chance. The September date gave all three of them something solid to hold on to. By then, Jordan, Jonathan, and Kremer were spending more time together than ever. Kremer and Jonathan had already known each other for more than a decade, and Kremer was one of the very few people who knew Jonathan's true story from beginning to end. Other than Jordan and Tiffney, he was the only one who knew everything.

Kremer had one year left before he would move to a halfway house. Jordan had two years before he would be eligible for home confinement. Kremer had no relationship left with his ex-wife or his children, so he had already made arrangements to move into Jonathan's farmhouse once he got out. Jonathan had given the address to the case manager. He had offered Jordan the same place, but Jordan had already decided that when his time came, he would go back to his parents and his siblings in Sikeston.

Tiffney and Jordan's family still visited as often as they could. During summer break, Lakesha came to see him and brought her usual energy with her.

"You're still dating that white kid?" Jordan asked with a teasing smile.

"Yes," she said without missing a beat. "And we're serious. Same as you and Tiffney."

Jordan smiled. "That's good."

Then she told him that Josh was training to become a police investigator, and his expression changed slightly.

"I know what you're thinking," Lakesha said, her tone gentler now. "We've all been hurt by corrupt cops. I know that. But not everyone in that uniform is the same. Most of them really do want to do the right thing."

Jordan shook his head slowly. "I've seen the double standard my whole life. I've seen how police treat Black people and how they treat white people. But it's his life. I'm not going to judge him for wanting to do something decent with it."

Lakesha nodded, relieved to hear that.

"So," Jordan said after a moment, shifting the subject, "how's basketball?"

Her whole face brightened. "It's going great. Next year is going to decide a lot. I think that's when I either really break through or I don't."

"Then keep practicing," he said. "Get better every day."

"I will."

He watched her smile and felt something rare move through him there inside the prison.

Pride.

Chapter 48:
The Day the Door Opened

Both attorneys stood before the district judge in the Eastern District of Missouri. Jonathan's attorney spoke first, his voice steady, respectful, and without drama, as if the facts alone should have been enough to move the room.

"Your Honor, my client has spent twenty-five years in prison for a crime built on no eyewitnesses and no physical evidence. He was convicted of setting a fire that killed his best friend. Yet he himself suffered burns over more than seventy percent of his body and nearly died in that same fire."

He lifted the medical files and placed them before the court.

"He spent almost a year at Memphis University Hospital. He lost his right eye. He is permanently disabled. I ask the court to review these records and photographs carefully. This is not a man who set a fire and walked away from it. This is a man who barely survived it."

He paused, then lowered his tone.

"My client also lost both parents while incarcerated. He has no family left. If he remains here, he will die here. I respectfully ask for parole or probation so he may spend what remains of his life with dignity."

The judge gave a small nod and turned toward the other table.

"Counsel for the government?"

The prosecutor rose.

"Your Honor, after reviewing Mr. Jonathan's medical and prison records, the government does not object to early release. His condition supports parole."

The judge folded his hands and sat in silence for a moment, reading once more through the papers in front of him. When he finally spoke, the courtroom seemed to narrow around the sound of his voice.

"Based on the evidence before me, I order the immediate release of Mr. Jonathan from Greenville Prison Camp. He will be placed on parole and must report to his parole officer every ninety days."

Jonathan's attorney let out the breath he had been holding.

"Thank you, Your Honor. We will comply with all conditions."

The prosecutor gathered his files and added, "I will notify the Bureau of Prisons and the regional director immediately."

Within hours, the decision had been faxed to the warden. Jonathan's attorney left a message for Tiffney, then drove straight to Greenville. When the camp counselor paged Jonathan and told him a visitor was waiting, he walked to the office without knowing that the life he had endured for twenty-five years was about to break open.

The attorney looked at him, and for the first time there was no caution in his face, no lawyer's restraint.

"You're getting out," he said quietly.

Jonathan closed his eyes.

For a second he didn't move at all, as if his body could not catch up to what his ears had just heard. The camp counselor, who had seen enough men receive enough news to know when not to crowd a moment, spoke gently.

"You'll be out in a day or two. Paperwork takes time."

Jonathan found Jordan and Kremer as soon as he could. The change in his face was immediate and unmistakable. For the first time in years, Jordan saw real joy there, not guarded, not temporary, but something clean and almost disbelieving.

"I never thought I'd leave this place," Jonathan said. His voice had gone rough. "You and Tiffney gave me my life back."

"We're family now," Jordan told him.

Jonathan nodded once, then said, more quietly, "And we'll fight back. With money. With truth. With patience."

That afternoon, he called his cousin, the man who still leased the farmland.

"I'll be released tomorrow morning," he said. "I need a ride."

His cousin arrived the next day at 8:30. Before leaving, Jonathan hugged Jordan and Kremer both.

"We'll gather everything we can on Callaghan, Riley, and Mitch before you get out," he promised. "But I won't go near my sister yet. Kremer is right. We wait."

They all agreed.

On the drive out, Jonathan told his cousin only what was necessary, that the fire had damaged his memory and left much of his past broken and scattered. It was easier that way. Safer too. Because the cruelest part of freedom was this:

Outside those gates, he could never say his real name.

His cousin was waiting just beyond the prison entrance, older now, heavier in the face, steadier in the shoulders. But when he saw Jonathan step through those gates, something brightened in him all at once.

"Thank God," he said, pulling him into a careful embrace. "It's finally over."

During the drive home, they spoke quietly about his parents, about the years that had passed, and about how the land and the farmhouse had been handled while he was gone.

"After your mother passed, my wife and I moved into the farmhouse," his cousin explained. "We took care of everything. Kept it clean. Kept the place standing. We moved back to our own house last night so you'd have space."

Jonathan turned and looked out the window for a while before answering.

"Thank you," he said simply.

When they reached the property, he stood still for a moment before stepping toward the old garage. Inside were two heavy-duty pickup trucks and a luxury sedan. The sight of them hit him harder than he expected. One of the trucks had belonged to his father. One had been his own. The sedan had belonged to his mother.

He rested a hand on the nearest hood, then said, "I need clothes. And a haircut."

They drove to Memphis that same day. Jonathan bought new clothes, had his beard trimmed, and picked up groceries. By the time they returned to the farmhouse, it was close to five in the evening. His cousin's wife had dinner waiting.

"We're so glad you're alive," she said when she saw him. "And that you're home."

Jonathan thanked them both, then sat down at the table with the strange, unsteady feeling of a man relearning what ordinary life looked like.

After dinner, he spoke again.

"I have one request. Please don't tell anyone I'm back. I need peace for a while."

They both nodded.

Later, his cousin asked, "Are you thinking of farming again?"

"Not for a few years," Jonathan said. "So don't worry about the lease."

His cousin tried not to show how relieved he was, but Jonathan saw it anyway. The land had become the foundation of that household's livelihood. And for Jonathan, it was becoming something else entirely.

A refuge.

It took him more than two weeks to begin adjusting to freedom in any real way. He learned the rhythms of the house, the quiet of the land, and the pace of the nearby towns. He renewed his driver's license and began driving one of the trucks, but he was careful. He bought gas and groceries in larger cities rather than nearby towns. In small places, faces were remembered, questions were asked, and stories spread too fast.

He went to the bank in person. The manager nearly hurried out from behind the desk when he saw him.

"We've been waiting for you, sir," the man said, shaking his hand. "It's an honor."

Jonathan requested new debit and credit cards, along with new checkbooks.

"I'd like to submit a new signature," he said. "I'm concerned the old one may have been compromised."

The manager agreed immediately. Using Jonathan's new driver's license and Social Security number, he processed the request without hesitation. Temporary cards and checks were issued that same day. The permanent ones would arrive by mail in a couple of weeks.

After that, Jonathan contacted an interior design and construction firm about remodeling the farmhouse. Their estimator arranged to come the following week. That same afternoon, Jonathan drove out to the place where his old house had once stood. The fire had erased it so completely that there was nothing left now except open ground and memory.

He stood there for a long time.

The farmland itself looked almost unchanged after twenty-five years. That was the strange thing about land. It kept going. It kept growing. It remembered differently than people did.

He also drove past J.D. Callaghan's property more than once, slowing just enough to study the windows, the yard, the drive, looking for any sign of his sister.

He never saw her.

A week later, the contractors arrived with floor plans, material samples, and design ideas. Jonathan chose one and approved the renovation without much hesitation.

"It'll take a few months," they told him.

"That's fine," he said. "I won't be here much."

He paid one-third up front, then drove to an RV dealership in Memphis and bought a brand-new Class A motorhome.

Freedom, he realized, needed wheels.

Before leaving town, he made one more stop. Quietly, without telling anyone, he visited an eye specialist. Prison records listed him as legally blind in the right eye, which was true in part but not fully. The damage was severe, but not total. His left eye remained stronger. The specialist fitted him with tinted glasses that concealed the damage completely.

Now no one looking at him would know.

One week after construction began, Jonathan set out on a two-month journey across several states.

The war he had waited twenty-five years to fight had finally begun.

Chapter 49:
New Lives, Old Enemies

Time moved quickly after that. Tiffney completed her second year of law school with distinction. The same firm that had once given her a free externship now brought her back as a paid one. More than that, they quietly suggested that if she wanted it, a permanent position would be waiting for her after graduation. With more than a hundred offices spread across all fifty states, the firm even floated the idea that she could eventually work in Missouri if she chose to return there.

Back in Pemiscot County, Kremer was finally released from prison camp, and Jonathan picked him up himself. When Kremer first saw him outside prison, he stopped and stared.

"Oh my God," he said. "I wouldn't even recognize you if I passed you on the street."

Jonathan smiled faintly. "That's the point."

"How's Jordan?"

"He's doing well. Less than ten months left."

"That's good," Jonathan said. "By then, everything will be ready."

He drove Kremer toward Caruthersville and, on the way, laid out the next step in their long, quiet war.

"I've already set up a plumbing and HVAC company for you in Pemiscot County," he said. "I found two office spaces. We'll look at both today."

They ate lunch in Jonesboro, Arkansas, then crossed back over the state line. In the end, they both liked the same location, a small but visible building that sat not far from J.D. Callaghan's main office.

Jonathan nodded once. "What do you need to get started?"

"Three or four computers. Office furniture. A licensed plumber. Eventually a secretary."

"What about marketing?"

"I can handle that. I've got the IT and social media experience. We'll need billboards."

Jonathan smiled. "Done."

Within weeks, J.K. Plumbing LLC was registered and operating. Kremer hired a secretary and a retired master plumber who still held an active Missouri plumbing and HVAC contractor's license. The man agreed to let the company operate under his credentials while Kremer handled the real fieldwork. As the business grew, Kremer planned to hire assistants. For now, he did as much as he could himself, going door to door, offering free estimates, slowly building trust while quietly laying the foundation for something much larger than a business.

The war was no longer waiting to begin.

It had already begun.

For two weeks, Kremer called J.D. Callaghan's house. The first week, no one answered. The second week, a woman finally picked up.

"This is J.K. Plumbing and HVAC," Kremer said in a calm, professional voice. "We also handle computer and internet services. I'm calling to see if you need any help."

There was a pause.

"Well... yes," the woman said carefully. "My internet has been very slow."

"May I ask your name?"

"Mrs. Callaghan."

Kremer felt his pulse jump, but he kept his voice steady.

"When would be a good time for me to come by?"

"Any time between two and four."

"I can be there today at two-thirty."

That was the moment he and Jonathan had been waiting for.

The Callaghan estate was exactly what he expected and worse, white columns, iron gates, manicured gardens, the whole place carrying the polished ugliness of inherited power. Kremer parked outside, pressed the gatebell, and announced himself.

"J.K. Plumbing."

The gates opened.

A tall, elegant woman stood waiting at the front door.

"Mrs. Callaghan?" Kremer asked.

"Yes."

She explained the two problems, noisy air-conditioning at night and internet that kept slowing to a crawl. Kremer listened, nodded, and then asked to see the air-conditioning units first. She led him around the side of the garage, where several large HVAC systems were mounted.

After a quick inspection, Kremer straightened and looked at her more closely.

"There's something I need to tell you," he said quietly. "About your brother."

Her face changed instantly.

"Who are you?"

"I am a real technician," Kremer said. "But I'm also your brother's friend."

Then, more softly, "Your nickname was Pinky."

She froze.

"You need to stay strong," he said. "Jack is alive."

Her hands began to tremble. "That's impossible. I saw the body."

"It wasn't Jack," Kremer said. "It was Jonathan, his friend. He sacrificed himself so Jack could live. Jack pretended to be Jonathan so J.D. and Riley wouldn't finish the job."

For a moment she looked as though she had forgotten how to breathe.

"Can you keep this secret?" Kremer asked. "If J.D. or Riley find out, they will kill him."

"Yes," she whispered. "I swear."

He asked to see her ID. She brought him her driver's license, and after confirming her name, he nodded.

"It's true," he said. "Jack was treated as Jonathan in the hospital. After he recovered, they accused him of killing Jack."

Tears spilled down her face.

"My J is alive..."

"I need you calm," Kremer said. "Tomorrow. Northwest Mall in Memphis. Food court. Eleven in the morning. Tell no one. Not even Mitch."

She nodded, still shaken.

"Now let me fix the AC."

He worked for nearly two hours, cleaning the ducts, changing filters, and then moving inside to install a new router.

"You need a new computer," he told her. "This one's outdated."

"Buy it," she said, handing him five thousand dollars.

He looked at the money and then back at her. "I can't take this."

"It's J.D.'s money," she said softly. "And what you gave me today has no price."

So he took it.

As Kremer drove out through the gate, several black SUVs turned into the driveway.

J.D. Callaghan was coming home.

Kremer was already gone.

When J.D. stepped into the house, he looked at his wife for only a moment before narrowing his eyes.

"You seem unusually happy," he said. "Everything all right?"

Mrs. Callaghan forced a casual smile.

"Yes. You remember the strange noises from the air conditioner at night? I called a new plumbing and HVAC company. My computer was slow too, so they handled that."

Her voice remained steady.

"They fixed everything. The house is quiet again, and the internet is much faster. He also recommended a new computer."

J.D. waved a hand dismissively.

"You've got plenty of money. Buy whatever you want."

He loosened his tie.

"I'm starving. Have the staff set dinner. Riley and I have a meeting afterward."

Mrs. Callaghan nodded and said nothing more, holding her face still while the storm inside her gathered force.

Chapter 50: The Reunion

Kremer and Jonathan arrived at Northwest Mall just after ten in the morning. Jonathan had been waiting for this moment for more than twenty-five years, though even now, sitting there in the nearly empty food court, it hardly felt real. The place was quiet except for the soft hum of opening restaurants and the distant shuffle of early shoppers. Tables sat mostly empty. The whole mall seemed to be holding its breath.

Pinki was already there.

Kremer noticed her first. His eyes moved over the room automatically, checking entrances, corners, reflections in the glass, making sure no one seemed too interested in anyone else. Only when he was satisfied did he walk toward her.

"Follow me," he said softly.

Across the food court, Jonathan sat alone at a corner table. His hands were still, but his pulse was not. The moment he saw his sister walking toward him, something in his face changed, years of silence, fear, and distance giving way to something raw and immediate.

Kremer stopped beside her and pointed gently.

"That's your brother."

"Pinki," Jonathan said.

She froze.

Then she ran to him and threw her arms around him so tightly he could barely breathe. Her body shook with sobs.

"My baby J... you're alive..."

Jonathan held her and closed his eyes. "I missed you," he whispered. "Every day."

She pulled back just enough to look at him, her face wet with tears.

"I know it's you," she said. "No one else knows my nickname. No one else knows how easily I cry."

A faint smile touched his face. "Do you remember that crying doll Mom gave you?"

Pinki laughed through the tears. "I blamed that doll for years."

"I threw it to the dogs," Jonathan said. "They tore it apart. I told you, 'See? Even the dogs don't cry.'"

That made her laugh harder, the kind of laugh that comes from grief finally loosening its grip for a moment.

"I'm still Pinki," she said.

They sat together for hours after that, talking softly, sometimes holding hands, sometimes falling quiet just to look at each other and absorb what was in front of them. Kremer stayed a short distance away, keeping watch without drawing attention. Around noon, he came back with pizza and drinks for all three of them, setting the food down without interrupting the fragile rhythm that had formed between the siblings.

At one point, Jonathan leaned in and asked, "Is the farmland still in your name?"

"As far as I know," Pinki said. "I'll check. Quietly."

He studied her for a moment before asking the next question.

"How does he treat you?"

She looked away and shook her head. "J.D. and Riley are monsters. We've lived separate lives for years now. There's no love there. No trust. No intimacy. He's been with other women, girls young enough to be his daughters. I stopped caring a long time ago."

"And Mitch?"

Her face changed at once. "He's lost. Drugs. Drinking. Parties. Just like his father."

Jonathan lowered his eyes. "I'm sorry."

She took a breath and tried to steady herself. "I knew something was wrong when you died. I always knew. I kept dreaming that you were trying to tell me something."

Then Jonathan told her about Jordan.

Pinki cried again, but this time the tears carried anger too.

"Then we fight back," Jonathan said quietly. "We collect evidence. Jordan will be free soon. After that, we expose them."

She nodded without hesitation. "I'm with you. No matter what happens. Even if Mitch is my son."

They did not leave the mall until nearly five. When the time finally came, Pinki hugged both men. Kremer placed a new computer into her car before she left.

"A gift," he said. "From your brothers."

She laughed through the last of her tears.

"I'll see you tomorrow," Kremer added. "I'll install it at two-thirty."

The war had already begun. The difference now was that the Callaghans were no longer standing alone on one side of it.

The next afternoon, Kremer returned to the Callaghan estate with the new computer. Pinki watched him remove the old machine and set the new one in place with calm, practiced efficiency. Within minutes, her screen was brighter, faster, cleaner, and far quieter than before.

"Much better," she said.

Kremer nodded. "This one will last you for years."

Then he let a moment pass before speaking again.

"Pinki... do you have access to J.D.'s office building?"

She studied him carefully. "Yes. Why?"

"The computers in that building are old," he said. "I want to replace them. While I'm doing that, we make sure whatever happens in there can't stay hidden anymore, especially on the floor where Mitch holds those parties."

Her eyes narrowed slightly. "And J.D. and Riley? How do we find out what they're doing?"

Kremer lowered his voice. "I'll install hidden cameras and recording devices, especially on the party floor."

The room went quiet.

"After everything is in place," he continued, "you simply tell them you ordered the upgrades yourself. You liked your new computer and decided the business needed the same."

She thought about that for a long moment.

"They'll never suspect it came from me," she said at last.

Kremer's face stayed calm, but his eyes had gone cold. "There's a way to protect ourselves, not with force, only with truth. If we ever want to prove what J.D. and Riley have really been doing, we need access to what happens behind closed doors."

Pinki inhaled slowly. "I can get the keys."

"Good. When they're out of town, it'll be safest."

"They're leaving next week," she said. "J.D. and Riley will both be gone. But Mitch throws his parties on weekends. That floor turns into chaos."

"Then we avoid weekends," Kremer replied. "Tuesday and Wednesday. Quiet days."

Pinki nodded.

For the first time in her life, what she felt was not fear.

It was control.

Later that afternoon, she arrived at the office building with Kremer and introduced him to the company administrator as the technician she had hired herself.

"He's here to do a full inspection," she said calmly. "After hours, his team will handle the upgrades."

Then she turned toward the administrator.

"Don't lock any offices tonight. Give him full access."

The man hesitated only briefly before handing over the building keys.

"I'll come back later to check on things," Pinki added. "Make sure everything goes smoothly."

When she left, Kremer thanked her quietly and got to work.

The administrator walked him through the building floor by floor, office by office. He pointed out the aging computers, the humming air systems, the conference rooms, and the upper party floor where Mitch's weekends had become legends whispered about more than openly discussed. Kremer kept his face neutral, but his eyes missed nothing.

He unloaded sleek equipment and set up inside one of the offices, opening diagnostic programs and creating reports that looked complex enough to impress anyone watching. In a place like Pemiscot County, nobody was used to seeing that level of equipment or that kind of confidence. Even the staff, who had likely seen every kind of bluff and half-job before, seemed impressed.

By the time he finished the walkthrough, he had counted twenty computers scheduled for replacement.

And twenty doors that, for the first time in years, were finally opening.

Chapter 51: Moving Pieces

Kremer had made his decision long before the workday ended. Every outdated system in that building would have to go. Once the inspection was complete, he locked the office, left his work van parked outside for appearances, and climbed into the truck for the drive to Memphis.

The highway hummed beneath him as he called Jonathan.

"You did well today," Jonathan said. "That plumbing and HVAC business of yours looks convincing."

Kremer smiled. "It's more than convincing. It's solid work. Most people don't want dirt, sweat, and physical labor, but it pays. And more importantly, it opens doors."

Jonathan laughed softly. "Be careful. And don't forget to eat. You're not in prison anymore."

"I know, I know," Kremer said. "I'm trying to stay fit. No fast food. No soda."

Jonathan chuckled. "Right. The nutrition expert."

"Exactly."

By late afternoon, Kremer was on his way back, the truck loaded with what he needed. He had purchased twenty computers in Memphis, along with the hidden security cameras and recording devices that would turn the office building into something very different from what it appeared to be. He called Jonathan again.

"Come by around five-thirty," he said. "Between the van and the truck, it'll look like a full crew is working. You can see Pinki too."

"I'll be there," Jonathan replied. "We're in this together."

Kremer laughed. "I don't really need help."

"Good," Jonathan said. "Because I'm coming anyway."

As dusk settled over Caruthersville, the last pieces began sliding into place.

The administrator left just after five. Before heading out, he glanced once more at Kremer's truck and nodded with satisfaction.

"Looks like you've got a whole crew coming in. Good luck. And thank Mrs. Callaghan for finally replacing these old machines. I've been asking Riley for years."

Kremer smiled politely. "Your staff is going to love the new systems."

Once the building was empty, he unloaded the boxes of computers, cameras, and devices, then quietly swapped the truck for his work van so everything would still look routine if anyone happened to drive by.

When he returned, Pinki was already there.

"Sorry I'm late," Kremer said.

"I just got here," she replied.

"Jonathan's on his way. You two can talk while I get started."

She watched him work for a few minutes, clearly impressed by the calm precision of everything he did.

"You take this business seriously," she said.

"That's how I survive," Kremer answered. "Do it right every time."

Jonathan arrived moments later. He and Pinki exchanged a look heavy with meaning, but both kept their voices low. Kremer moved steadily through the building, handling the maintenance and upgrades he had promised. The hum of machinery, the shifting of boxes, and the soft glow of screens coming back to life made the whole operation feel ordinary, just another late night of work in an office that had never been honest in the first place.

Jonathan and Pinki stayed near each other, speaking softly, touching hands when no one was there to see. For the first time in decades, they were no longer powerless inside those walls.

They were there.

And that changed everything.

The new machines had already been unpacked and arranged in neat rows, waiting to replace the old systems one by one. Kremer moved through the second floor first, guiding the file transfers carefully so nothing would be lost and nothing would look disturbed. The business systems came back online faster and cleaner than before. On the surface, it all looked like nothing more than a long-overdue upgrade.

But the second floor was where J.D. Callaghan and Riley kept their private offices, and Kremer did more than install new computers there. Hidden cameras and recording devices were worked carefully into the space, placed in ways that would never be noticed unless someone knew exactly where to look.

He did the same on the third floor, the level used for parties, drugs, drinking, and everything else the family had kept hidden behind wealth and silence. He covered as many corners as he could. They had all agreed not to place any such devices on the ground floor. That level would remain untouched in that sense. The aim was not chaos for its own sake. It was exposure, and exposure required precision.

Hours passed.

By the time the systems were fully running again, the whole building felt subtly different, as though it had started breathing in a new way. Kremer finally turned to Pinki.

"You should go."

She nodded, squeezed Jonathan's hand once, and moved toward the door.

Then Kremer asked, "Do you think you could get us into Riley's house?"

She stopped and looked back. "I might. If not, I'll find a way."

"When do you think they'll be back?"

"Probably Sunday," she said. "They never miss their Saturday night parties."

Kremer smiled slightly. "That gives us time."

"And why do you need Riley's place?"

"I'll explain when it matters."

She studied him for a second, then nodded. "I trust you."

"Can you arrange it for tomorrow? Around noon?"

"I will," she said. "I'll meet you there."

When she was gone, Jonathan looked at Kremer and said nothing. He didn't need to. The pieces were still falling into place, carefully, quietly, and too late now for anyone to stop them.

Jonathan stayed occupied with the computer work while Kremer finished installing the hidden devices across the second and third floors. He tried to cover every useful corner he could. By the time night settled fully around the building and the silence deepened, the work was almost complete.

Jonathan moved through the offices with steady focus while Kremer tested each system, each feed, each point of access. One by one, the new machines came alive. The office resumed its rhythm, smoother and faster than before, unchanged on the surface and entirely different underneath.

Nothing had been erased. Nothing had been disturbed. The old machines had been placed neatly into storage exactly as the administrator requested. If anyone wanted to fall back on them later, they could. That was part of the point.

No alarms.

No suspicion.

No disruptions.

Kremer was deliberate about that. This was not the moment for destruction. It was the moment for positioning.

When they finally finished, he leaned against a desk and looked out over the darkened floor.

"This is only the beginning," he said quietly.

Jonathan nodded.

Twenty-five years of waiting had taught him one lesson better than any other.

Revenge was not loud.

It was patient.

And it had just begun.

The following day, Kremer and Jonathan tested all the hidden cameras and listening devices from Jonathan's new basement office. He had built the room out quietly, fitting it with new computers and large television screens so they could watch and hear everything happening inside J.D. Callaghan's office building.

The next day after that, Kremer set up the same kind of hidden devices at Riley's house.

When he arrived, he noticed Pinki already outside and quietly took a photograph of her as she went in, not for sentiment, but for documentation. Inside, the house was large and quiet. Kremer moved through it carefully, noting the layout without touching more than he had to.

Pinki turned toward him and said, "Be careful with Riley. He's clever."

Kremer gave a thin smile. "So is Jonathan."

She shook her head. "The two of you are dangerous in your own way. I've waited a long time to see the truth start coming out."

He looked at her for a moment, then asked the question he had been carrying.

"If this leads where we think it will, are you ready for what that means? Especially for Mitch?"

Pinki closed her eyes.

"I gave birth to him," she said. "But I lost him a long time ago. He chose a road I couldn't follow. What he did to Jordan, what he became, that broke something in me. I tried to stop him. He pushed me away."

When she opened her eyes again, her voice no longer shook.

"I don't want him destroyed. But I won't protect lies or crimes just because he is my son."

Kremer nodded once. That was all he needed.

"I've done what I can for now," he said. "If you learn anything, anything at all, call me."

She touched his arm lightly.

"Thank you. I haven't felt this steady in years."

Kremer stepped back outside into the sunlight knowing something fundamental had shifted. Not through force. Not through threats. Through patience. Through secrets. Through truth moving slowly enough to avoid notice until it was too late.

And now the balance of power was beginning to move with it.

Chapter 52: The Confession

Jordan had only seven months left before he would be transferred to a halfway house and then, eventually, home confinement. That should have felt like hope, but instead it made time heavier. Every day seemed to carry more weight than the one before it. The countdown never left him. It lived in the back of his mind, ticking through his work shifts, his meals, his sleep, even his time on the court.

One afternoon, while he was on the basketball court, he noticed a man standing off to the side watching him. He was thin, too thin, with the gaunt, hollowed look of someone whose body was losing a fight it could no longer hide. There was something about him that tugged at Jordan's memory in a way he could not immediately place.

He walked over slowly.

"Have we met before?" he asked. "You look like somebody I used to know."

The man's eyes filled almost instantly.

"My name is Corey," he said. "And yes... we have met."

Jordan felt his pulse kick hard in his chest.

Corey swallowed, and when he spoke again, the words came out trembling.

"I'm the one who planted the cocaine in your girlfriend's trunk seven years ago."

For a second, Jordan said nothing at all. The words hit him with such force that it felt less like hearing something and more like being struck by it.

Corey kept going, as if he knew that if he stopped, he might lose the nerve to continue.

"They transferred me to another prison after the trial. I got moved here last week. I needed to find you." His voice shook harder now. "I'm sorry. I lied. I testified against you. The Caruthersville police chief and Riley promised me a reduced sentence if I did it. I was looking at twenty to thirty years. They cut it to ten."

Jordan stared at him, stunned, trying to hold his face still while everything inside him shifted at once.

"Why tell me now?" he asked quietly. "And why should I believe you?"

Corey looked down for a second, then back up.

"I think I'm dying," he said. "I've lost thirty pounds. I'm bleeding inside. The doctors did a colonoscopy. They found polyps. Tumors. I'm waiting on the biopsy now."

His voice cracked.

"I don't care if they kill me for saying this. I'm not taking it to my grave."

Jordan stood there for a long moment, breathing through the rush of anger, disbelief, and something dangerously close to relief.

"Don't assume the worst yet," he said at last. "Wait for the biopsy. You might still be all right."

Corey let out a broken laugh that wasn't really laughter.

"The damage is already done," he whispered. "I ruined your life."

Jordan looked at him carefully.

"You told me," he said. "That matters. But don't tell anybody else yet. Not until I talk to my attorney."

Corey nodded at once. "I won't."

"You need to eat," Jordan said, noticing again how badly the man was fading. "You look like you're disappearing."

Corey swallowed hard.

"Please forgive me."

Jordan didn't answer. Not because he hadn't heard him, and not because he didn't understand what the words meant, but because forgiveness was too large a thing to force into that moment. He turned and walked away with his hands shaking.

That evening, he called Tiffney.

"There's someone here," he told her the moment she answered. "The man who framed me. He confessed."

There was a beat of silence, then her voice changed completely.

"Oh my God. Jordan, that changes everything." He could hear her already thinking ahead, already moving. "I'm calling Jonathan's attorney right now. We need a sworn statement immediately. Call me back in an hour."

Jordan closed his eyes after the line went dead.

For the first time in seven years, the truth had stopped hiding.

Tiffney called the attorney at once. His number was already saved in her phone. When he didn't answer, she sent a text explaining only the essentials. He replied within minutes, and when she called again, the urgency in his voice matched her own.

"I'll be there tomorrow morning," he said. "Before noon. This cannot wait."

"What about your retainer?" she asked.

"We'll deal with paperwork later," he said. "Right now this is about preserving the truth."

Tiffney sat there for a moment after the call, overwhelmed by a rush of gratitude. She trusted him completely, and for the first time in a very long while, that trust felt like it might actually lead somewhere.

The next morning at ten, Mr. Thompson arrived at Greenville prison camp. The counselor escorted him to a private room and paged both Jordan and Corey. It was the first time Thompson had met Jordan in person. He shook his hand firmly, then turned toward Corey.

"Tell me everything," he said.

Corey did.

He gave a full sworn statement, and though his hands trembled the entire time, his voice did not fail him. He explained the arrest, the deal, the police chief's involvement, Riley's role, the planted cocaine, the false testimony, all of it. Then he handed over a written confession, already signed and dated.

"In case something happens to me," he said quietly.

Thompson took it, read enough to understand the weight of what he was holding, and nodded.

"You did the right thing."

By noon he was back in his office in the Eastern District of Missouri, drafting an emergency motion. He didn't leave it to staff or the mail. He personally delivered it to the clerk and explained that a critical witness was seriously ill and might not survive long enough for an ordinary hearing schedule.

Because of the urgency, and because Thompson had the kind of reputation that made judges pay attention when he said something mattered, the court moved quickly.

A hearing was set for the following week.

Greenville was ordered to transport both Jordan and Corey to federal court.

Thompson called Tiffney as soon as he had confirmation.

"This is as fast as it gets," he told her.

She nearly cried from relief.

"I'm so impressed," she said. "You actually care."

He laughed softly. "Some of us still do."

"I'll try to be there Thursday," she said. "But don't tell Jordan. I want it to be a surprise."

"I like that," he said. "See you then."

For the first time in years, the truth was no longer buried under paperwork and fear. It was moving toward open court.

Chapter 53:
Truth in Open Court

The hearing was set for Thursday at one o'clock.

Jordan and Corey were brought in through a side entrance by prison guards in green uniforms. They were led to the defense table, where Mr. Thompson was already waiting. Jordan glanced toward the gallery out of instinct more than expectation, and the moment he did, he froze.

Tiffney was there.

She had flown in from St. Louis that morning and taken an Uber straight from the airport to the courthouse. Their eyes met across the room, and in that one look, everything passed between them, the years, the waiting, the pain, the refusal to give up.

The bailiff called the room to order.

"All rise. The Honorable Judge William presiding."

Everyone stood. The judge entered, nodded, sat, and said, "Please be seated."

Mr. Thompson rose first.

"Your Honor, thank you for hearing this matter on such short notice. My client was under eighteen when local law enforcement and a DEA agent fabricated charges against him under the influence of powerful interests in Pemiscot County. At the time, he was a high-school senior, a two-time state champion, and the recipient of a college basketball scholarship. Those records are before the court."

He lifted a folder.

"The government's case rested almost entirely on one witness, a man who claimed he worked for my client and planted drugs at my client's direction. That witness is here today, under oath, prepared to tell the truth."

The judge turned toward the prosecution.

"Any objection?"

"No, Your Honor."

"Motion granted. Call the witness."

Corey stepped forward, raised his right hand, and took the oath. Mr. Thompson approached him without drama, letting the seriousness of the moment carry itself.

"Tell the court what actually happened."

Corey drew a breath and began.

"The Caruthersville police arrested me for selling cocaine. It wasn't my first arrest. I had already done ten years in prison before and I was on probation. This time, I knew I was looking at twenty to thirty years."

He swallowed and kept going.

"The Pemiscot County police chief came to me and asked if I wanted help. He said if I cooperated, they would cut my sentence in half. We agreed on ten years. Their instructions were simple. I had to put the cocaine in Jordan's girlfriend's car. They showed me which car it was. It was parked in front of Jordan's house."

The courtroom was silent.

"I opened the trunk and planted the two packets they gave me. The same person who showed me the car was filming it. I lied to the DEA. I lied in court. I had never met Jordan until last week."

Mr. Thompson asked, "When was the first time you actually met him?"

"Last week. At Greenville."

"And why tell the truth now?"

Corey's voice grew rougher.

"I'm very sick. And I've been carrying this guilt for years. I ruined an innocent kid's life. I can't carry it anymore."

The prosecutor rose then.

"How does the court know you're telling the truth now?"

Corey looked exhausted, but he did not back away.

"Jordan's already served almost all of his sentence. Letting him go doesn't help me. It changes nothing for me. I just want to do one thing right before it's too late."

The judge raised a hand.

"That's enough. Thank you."

Then he turned to the prosecutor.

The prosecutor gave a small nod. "The government does not oppose immediate release and dismissal of the remaining charges."

The judge leaned back and reviewed the file in silence. When he finally spoke, every word seemed to land with its full weight.

"Under the plea agreement, this court cannot reopen the original investigation in the way the defense has requested. However, in light of this sworn testimony, the time already served, and the interests of justice, I order Mr. Jordan's immediate release and the dismissal of all remaining charges."

A hush fell over the courtroom before relief rushed in behind it.

Jordan's breath caught in his chest. He stood, not quite trusting what he had heard, then turned and embraced Mr. Thompson. After that he reached Tiffney, and the two of them held each other laughing and crying at the same time.

As Corey was escorted away, Jordan reached out and touched his arm.

"Thank you," he said softly.

Corey nodded, tears on his face.

A guard stepped up beside Jordan and placed a hand on his shoulder.

"You're free."

And for the first time in seven years, Jordan walked out of a courtroom not as a defendant, not as a prisoner, not as a man being led somewhere against his will, but as someone who had finally been given his life back.

Outside the Eastern District courthouse, reporters were already waiting.

Ethan and the STL Dispatch team stood at the front with cameras and microphones ready. Tiffney had warned Mr. Thompson they would be there. He stepped forward first.

"After seven years," he said, "justice has finally been done. A young man who was wrongfully convicted has been freed. The truth came from the very witness who once accused him under pressure from the Pemiscot County police chief, a DEA agent, a local businessman named Mr. Callaghan, and his son, Mitch."

Ethan lifted his microphone.

"This was a high-school basketball star whose future was taken away from him. Today he walks free. The questions now are simple. Who failed him? What does justice mean after seven lost years? And how does a man rebuild a life that was stolen from him?"

By evening, the story was everywhere.

The STL Dispatch ran it on the front page, Jordan standing beside Tiffney and Mr. Thompson, sunlight on his face for the first time in years. Television stations picked it up next. Then interviews, legal panels, online commentary, and social media. Ethan pushed the story across every platform he could reach, and what once would have taken weeks to spread through Missouri now moved overnight.

Radio stations repeated it every hour.

"Former state basketball champion freed after wrongful conviction."

Jordan's name was no longer tied to a crime.

Now it was tied to a question the state could not easily outrun:

How do you answer for seven years you can never give back?

Chapter 54:
When the World Finds Out

Kremer and Jonathan learned the news the very next morning, and for a long moment neither of them quite knew how to react. They were stunned, relieved, and shaken all at once.

Jordan was free.

Jonathan called Mr. Thompson immediately, then reached out to Mr. Moreland to piece together the full story. Mr. Thompson, understanding at once why Jonathan was calling, gave him Tiffney's number. When she answered, his voice was gentler than usual.

"This is Jack," he said. "Jordan's friend."

Tiffney smiled the moment she heard him. "I'm glad you called."

"I just wanted to congratulate you," Jonathan said. "What you did changed everything. We're grateful to you in ways I can't even explain."

"Thank you," she said softly. "Jordan's with his parents right now, but I'll give him your number. He'll call you later today."

Kremer called too, offering his own congratulations in that dry, steady way of his. Tiffney thanked him and told both men the same thing. She wanted to meet them properly soon, not through stories, not through Jordan's words, but face to face.

By then, the story had already exploded far beyond Missouri. Local television ran it all day. Newspapers across the state followed. Then the national outlets came in behind them, CNN, FOX, NBC, all chasing the same headline. Jordan was finally being called what he had always been: a state-champion basketball star whose life had been stolen by a fabricated drug case.

Now he was free.

But freedom did not silence the larger questions. If anything, it sharpened them.

How do you repair seven stolen years?

Who gives them back?

Where does justice even begin for someone who never should have gone to prison at all?

And beneath all of that, the question no one in power wanted asked too often:

Would the law ever touch the people who made it happen?

J.D. Callaghan and Riley were in the office when the phone rang. It was J.D.'s brother, the congressman, and he didn't bother with pleasantries.

"Have you seen the news?" he demanded. "This is not some little local embarrassment, J.D. It's everywhere. Local stations, national stations, papers, online, all of it. The Callaghan name is tied to this mess."

J.D. kept his voice cool, though his jaw had already tightened.

"I don't know enough yet. Reporters always make noise. We'll deal with it."

"This isn't noise," the congressman snapped. "Other members of Congress are calling me. The governor's office is asking questions. Mitch's name is being mentioned. This is an embarrassment."

Then the line went dead.

J.D. stared at the phone for a second before slamming it down hard.

"Riley!" he barked. "Get in here."

Riley came in carrying a stack of newspapers, the STL Dispatch folded on top. The headline stared up at them like an accusation that had finally found its audience. J.D. skimmed the article, and for one strange moment a tight, almost admiring smile crossed his face.

"Whoever wrote this did a good job," he said. "They wrote it well. They just don't know who they wrote against."

Riley gave him a careful look. "Do you know who the journalist is?"

"No."

"He's the grandson of the same Shirley who published the story about Mitch, Jordan, and Tiffney."

J.D.'s face hardened immediately. "I don't care who he is."

Riley said nothing, so J.D. kept going, his anger beginning to spill over in every direction at once.

"I still haven't forgotten Rick," he muttered. "That slap. I still have that ringing in my ear because of that son of a bitch. Tinnitus. Hearing loss. All because you talked me out of finishing what should have been finished."

He turned away, pacing now.

"We should've burned him and all of them. We should've wiped out that whole family. Instead, we burned a building and settled for seven years of restrictions. It wasn't enough."

His voice darkened further as his fury rolled over into confession without fully realizing it.

"We handled Jack perfectly. Burned him alive, blamed his friend Jonathan, made the whole thing stick. My wife still thinks she's clever, but she doesn't know I took her brother's land. She doesn't know I killed for that land. She doesn't know that if I could kill my own father over farmland, I can kill anyone."

Riley stayed still, saying nothing.

"I should have killed my brothers and sisters too," J.D. said. "I hate every one of them."

Then, as abruptly as it had risen, the rage shifted into wounded vanity. He paced the room and looked back at the paper again.

"Now my own brother is panicking. Senators. Congressmen. Even the governor is nervous because my name is in this thing." He stabbed a finger toward the article. "They forget who made them powerful in the first place."

Riley laid a steadying hand on the desk. "Sir, you need to slow down. Your blood pressure—"

"Everyone thinks they can question me now," J.D. snapped. "They forget this is still my ground."

Riley kept his voice level. "That's exactly why we have to be careful. This isn't just gossip anymore. It's turning into something else."

J.D. stared out the window at the town below, at the businesses, the roads, the land, everything he still thought of as his.

"Then we remind them who controls the ground they stand on."

Riley reached for the phone. "First, we make sure you're not about to have a stroke. Dr. Moore needs to see you."

J.D. didn't answer right away. When he finally did, it came out less as an order than as a bitter admission.

"We made mistakes with Jordan. We should never have gotten pulled into this stupid obsession over Tiffney. We built that whole fake case, and I went along with it. That was on me."

He exhaled sharply.

"And Mitch killing the coach... that's on me too. I should've stopped him years ago. He's a monster now."

For a moment, he seemed to cool, though not truly calm.

"I don't know what to do with that boy," he muttered. "Why were they even trying to rape those girls? There are other girls everywhere."

Then the old arrogance crept back in, ugly and casual.

"I haven't touched my wife in fifteen years, and I'm still fine. There's plenty available outside. I married her for the fifty thousand acres. That's all."

By then the secretary was at the door.

"Dr. Moore is here."

Riley waved her off. "Send him upstairs."

Dr. Moore came in a few minutes later, looking as uneasy as usual whenever he was summoned into the middle of one of J.D.'s moods. Riley asked him to check J.D.'s blood pressure. Dr. Moore did, then looked up with visible concern.

"It's one-seventy over one-ten," he said. "That's very high. You could have a heart attack or a stroke if you don't calm down."

He gave J.D. a small tablet to dissolve under his tongue.

"This should bring it down quickly. If it doesn't, you need monitoring in the ER."

J.D. glared at him. "I'm not going to some filthy emergency room. Those places are disgusting."

Then he leaned forward and spoke more quietly.

"We need to talk to you. Sit down and listen carefully."

Dr. Moore did.

"Stop giving OxyContin, Viagra, and Levitra to my brothers, the judge, the sheriff, and Mitch."

Dr. Moore blinked. "If I stop suddenly, they'll come after me. Especially your son."

"As of today, we're telling you it ends," J.D. said. "We're the reason you've kept your license this long. You think the BNDD and DEA stayed off your back by accident? We told you to keep them all supplied. Now we're telling you to stop."

Then his tone dropped into something colder.

"If you don't follow my order, I'll kill you."

Riley cut in immediately. "Sir. Relax."

He turned to Dr. Moore. "Check his blood pressure again. If it's improved, you can go."

Dr. Moore did as he was told. "It's one-fifty over ninety-five now. Better, but still high. Please try not to get this worked up again. I don't want to end up dead, in prison, or without my license."

Riley nodded. "Go."

Then he turned back to J.D.

"Go home. Don't talk about any of this with your wife. Act like everything is normal."

J.D. left the office early, and when he got home, Mrs. Callaghan looked surprised to see him.

"Are you all right?" she asked. "You're home early."

"I'm fine," he said. "Just tired. Thought I'd spend a little time here."

But she had already heard the news from his sisters, and she wasn't willing to pretend.

"They called me," she said. "Both of them. They said the whole family is embarrassed. Ashamed, because of Mitch."

J.D.'s face twisted. "What the hell are they talking about?"

"Jordan's case. The same thing everyone is talking about."

"Stop it," he snapped. "I'm sick of hearing about that stupid Jordan case. My brothers called me. Now my sisters are doing it too. Sometimes I don't believe they're even my real family." His voice rose again, wild and ugly. "I should've killed them when I killed my father."

Mrs. Callaghan went still.

"What did you just say?"

He turned too quickly, realizing what he had let slip.

"I said they should've died with him. That's all."

But the damage was done. He left the house almost immediately and went back to the office.

Riley looked genuinely surprised when he walked in again.

"What happened? Did you fight with your wife?"

"She's another headache," J.D. snapped. "My sisters called her and filled her head with the same garbage. They say this whole thing is an embarrassment. Shameful. That they're ashamed to be related to us."

His eyes had gone flat now, which was often worse than when he shouted.

"I should've killed my brothers and sisters when I killed my father."

Riley studied him carefully, then said, almost too evenly, "You need to cool down. If killing them ever becomes necessary, we'll decide that when it benefits us financially and politically."

That seemed to settle something in J.D.

A few moments later he let out a breath and muttered, "I'm feeling better now. It's been a long time since I had a young girl in this building. I need that now."

Riley gave him a look. "You had one last week."

J.D. poured champagne anyway.

Kremer and Jonathan watched all of it from their monitors and heard every word with perfect clarity. The technology had worked better than either of them could have hoped. They hadn't even had to wait long for what they needed. The timing had been almost perfect.

Not long after that, Jonathan spoke with Jordan and asked him to meet for dinner in Memphis.

"Kremer will pick you up at Sikeston Walmart around five," he said. "Bring one extra pair of clothes. You'll stay overnight. I want to show you something."

Jordan agreed and said he would wait in the food section.

But for all the progress they had made, both Jonathan and Kremer were more troubled by one thing than anything else J.D. had said.

Pinki.

Jonathan looked at Kremer and said quietly, "I can't lose my sister. Without her, I don't think I have a reason left."

Kremer's answer was immediate.

"You won't lose her. I won't let that happen. But if we're going to break this thing, we start with Riley. He's the brain. Then Mitch. Then J.D."

Jonathan nodded. "I agree. Can you connect me with Pinki? I need to hear her voice."

Kremer made the call.

"Hi, Pinki," Jonathan said when she answered. "It's me."

Her voice softened at once. "Hi. How are you?"

"I'm all right. But I'm worried about you."

"Stop worrying," she said. "I'm fine. I'm actually enjoying J.D.'s absence."

Then her voice changed.

"He lost his temper badly after I told him his sisters had called. He said the whole family thought this was embarrassing and shameful. He was furious."

Jonathan didn't wait.

"He also told Riley he wants to get rid of you one day. Because the farmland is still in your name. If something happens to you, it transfers to him."

There was silence on the line for a moment.

Then Pinki said, very quietly, "One day, you're going to show me all those recordings."

"I will," Jonathan said. "Kremer did incredible work."

He told her that Kremer had already left to pick up Jordan and that the three of them would be in Memphis for dinner.

"You need to act fast," she said. "I don't want to spend the rest of my life in this hell."

"You won't," Jonathan said. "Kremer will call you tomorrow. He has a few things he needs from you. Take care of yourself. I love you."

"I love you too," she whispered. "Take care."

Chapter 55:
Secret Planning

Kremer picked Jordan up outside the Sikeston Walmart just after noon. For a second, the two of them only stood there, almost as if neither quite trusted what he was seeing. Then they laughed and pulled each other into a hard embrace.

"You're really out," Kremer said, stepping back to look at him. "No chains. No guards. No one telling you where to stand."

Jordan smiled, still carrying that strange lightness that came with freedom. "It still feels unreal."

They drove straight to Jonathan's house. When Jonathan stepped outside and saw Jordan coming up the drive, he did not try to hide the emotion in his face. The three men met in the yard and hugged like people who had survived the same long storm and somehow found one another on the other side of it.

"It still amazes me," Jonathan said, shaking his head. "All your charges dropped. The judge finally did the right thing."

Jordan nodded. "I couldn't have done it without you and Kremer. And without Corey. Somehow his conscience finally woke up."

Jonathan let out a slow breath. "Your story is everywhere. That article Ethan wrote opened a lot of eyes."

"It should have," Jordan said. "Too many powerful people still use money and influence to twist the justice system into whatever they want it to be. It's like a quiet mafia, only everything looks respectable from the outside."

Jonathan held his gaze. "Maybe not forever."

Jordan gave a faint smile. "Maybe the next generation will be better."

For the first time in years, the three of them were not talking about how to survive. They were talking about what came next.

On the drive in, Kremer's work phone lit up with a missed call and a voice message. He pulled over at a gas station off the highway and listened to it while Jonathan and Jordan waited beside the truck. When he finished, he looked up.

"It's Riley," he said. "He says the air conditioner at his house is making strange noises. He wants me there tomorrow morning at nine."

Jordan raised an eyebrow. "That's convenient."

Kremer smirked. "Very. I left a little trash in the duct system when I put the devices in. Just enough to make him uncomfortable and just enough to give me a reason to go back."

Jordan laughed. "You should've worked undercover for the CIA."

They all laughed at that, and for a moment the sound of it felt almost unreal, men who had spent so many years cornered by other people's power now sitting in a truck, smiling over the first real opening they had ever had.

They had dinner together that night and returned to Jonathan's place a little late. Down in the basement office, Kremer and Jonathan showed Jordan the recordings and the camera feeds they had already collected. The screens lit the room in a cold glow, and as Jordan watched, he felt the full weight of what they had built.

"We got lucky early," Kremer said. "Your release, the media coverage, the timing. It all hit at once."

Jordan stood in front of the monitors and watched J.D. Callaghan pacing in his office, Riley trying to calm him down, both of them talking as if no one in the world could hear them. Confessions. Plans. Threats. Rage. It was all there.

J.D. Callaghan had said too much.

Much, much too much.

Kremer leaned back in his chair and told them what he intended to do next. As he explained it, both Jonathan and Jordan felt that same dangerous excitement rising in them again. The plan was bold, but it was not reckless. It depended on patience, on listening, on letting the right people say the wrong things in their own time.

The next morning, Kremer arrived at Riley's house exactly at nine. Riley opened the door, glanced at his watch, and gave a dry little smile.

"Right on time," he said. "Did you work in the military?"

Kremer gave him the answer he had already prepared. "Contractor, technically. But the work was different."

Riley stepped aside to let him in. "What kind of work?"

Kremer met his eyes without blinking. "Off the record?"

Riley gave a small nod.

"I was a contract killer."

Riley studied him carefully, more curious than alarmed. "Then how did you end up doing plumbing and air-conditioning work?"

Kremer shrugged. "Long story."

"If you don't mind, I'd like to hear it," Riley said. "Believe me, I can keep a secret. You can trust me."

Kremer let just enough silence pass to make it believable.

"My last contract was in Istanbul," he said. "The target was an Iraqi ambassador who knew too much. The order was to kill him and his family. I didn't kill the wife. I didn't kill the little girl. They were innocent. After that, the CIA found out and buried me under a drug case. Twenty years. I learned HVAC and plumbing inside prison."

Riley looked at him with even greater interest now.

"I appreciate the honesty," he said. "You do good work. Can I trust you?"

Kremer nodded. "You're the first person in this region who knows the truth."

Riley seemed to like that. "Do you drink?"

"At night," Kremer said. "Not during the day. Not on a job."

"How about coffee?"

"Coffee's fine."

Riley led him into his office and asked, "Black? Cream?"

"Black. No cream. Thank you."

When Riley came back with two large cups, Kremer took a sip and nodded. "That's good."

Riley sat down across from him and got to the point.

"I need your help with something highly confidential. If you do it, you won't need to crawl under houses or clean ducts ever again. You'll make millions."

Kremer set the cup down carefully. "Before you say anything else, let me make one thing clear. I never kill children. If there are children involved in whatever this is, then I'm out."

Riley actually looked relieved by the question. "No children."

Then he lowered his voice.

"I need two jobs done. The first involves four people, two married couples. The second is one middle-aged woman."

Kremer said nothing, waiting.

"I'll pay one million per target."

Kremer leaned back as if calculating risk. "That's five million total. Fifty percent up front. Fifty percent when it's done."

Riley took a couple of minutes to think, then nodded. "Done."

"What do you need from me?" he asked.

"Current photos. Addresses. Schedules if you have them. And one more thing." Kremer kept his tone flat. "How do you want it done? House fire? Vehicle accident? Something else?"

"No bullets," Riley said at once. "No gunshots. Either a crash or a fire."

Kremer nodded. "Is anybody else involved in this? Who else knows?"

"Only J.D.," Riley said. "Three people. You, me, and J.D."

Kremer held his gaze a second longer. "And why, exactly, do you and J.D. want these people dead? Sometimes there are other ways to handle problems."

Riley's mouth tightened. "You raise a fair point."

He leaned back and answered more openly now.

"The four people are Mr. Callaghan's two brothers and two sisters. I got legal notice from them yesterday. They want their share of the family property. According to the original will, they believe the estate should have been divided. If J.D. doesn't deal with it, they'll take it to court."

Kremer let him continue.

"One brother is a politician. The other has federal connections too. One sister is married to a judge. The other to the county sheriff. If they move together, they can do real financial damage."

"And the woman?"

Riley gave him a meaningful look. "J.D.'s wife. You've met her."

Kremer understood immediately. "She still legally holds the fifty thousand acres."

Riley nodded. "If she dies, it all goes to him."

Kremer sat in silence for a moment as if thinking through logistics.

"Let me work up something smarter," he said. Then he tilted his head. "I think someone's at the door."

He had heard the bell before Riley had.

"Show me the air-conditioning units," he said. "I'll handle that first."

Riley led him out through the garage and toward the units. Kremer thanked him, crouched down beside the equipment, and waited until Riley had gone back toward the house. The moment he was alone, he moved quickly, opening Riley's SUV and planting what he needed before closing it again as if nothing had happened. Then he went back to the units, changed filters, cleaned out the ducts, and removed the trash he himself had hidden there before.

A few minutes later, Riley came back outside with Mrs. Callaghan. She had arrived while they were talking and now followed him into the garage. Kremer kept his expression neutral and continued working. He replaced the filters, vacuumed the venting, and by the time he came back inside, the system sounded normal again.

"Fixed it," he said.

Then he nodded toward Mrs. Callaghan. "Good to see you again."

Riley waved him off. "You didn't disturb anything. Mrs. Callaghan just stopped by for coffee. Send the invoice and I'll mail the check."

Before Kremer could answer, Mrs. Callaghan stepped in and handed him cash.

"I forgot your name," she said lightly, "but here. A thousand. Thank you."

Kremer looked at the money. "That's too much."

"Keep it," she said.

Back at Jonathan's basement office, Jonathan and Jordan watched all of it unfold on the screens in front of them. Every word. Every glance. Every shift in posture. Every lie spoken as if it were ordinary conversation.

Jordan stared at the monitors.

"Oh my God," he muttered. "Kremer's unbelievable."

Then his face darkened.

"I knew Mitch was bad. But Riley and J.D... they're worse than anything I imagined."

Mrs. Callaghan soon left Riley's house, and Riley followed a few minutes later in his SUV. When he saw her still on the driveway, he stopped.

"Everything okay?"

"My car won't start," she said. "Can you drop me at the house?"

Riley agreed at once. She mentioned that she had left the key inside in case a mechanic needed it later, then got into the passenger seat. As they pulled away, she turned to him and said, as if only just remembering it, "Actually, I need to go to the office first. There's something I want to check."

Riley turned the SUV toward the building.

Once inside, she asked him, "Can you show me the third floor? And J.D.'s room?"

The office staff noticed them at once, surprised to see her arrive with Riley and even more surprised when the two of them went upstairs together. Riley opened the large room for her, the one with the attached bath and the sofas. It had once been J.D.'s private room. Now it belonged to him half the time and to Mitch the rest.

Pinki stepped inside and looked around carefully while Riley waited outside the doorway. When she came back out, she said she wanted to go home before J.D. arrived. Riley drove her back, then returned to the office.

About an hour later, J.D. Callaghan arrived. Riley had been waiting for him.

He shut the office door, told the secretary not to disturb them, and then gave him the news.

"The plumbing man," Riley said, "the one who fixed the office and the house, used to work as a contract killer for the government. I think we can use him."

J.D. looked up sharply. "Can we trust him?"

"Yes," Riley said. "I already started the conversation. I told him about your brothers, your sisters, and your wife."

J.D. didn't even pretend to think twice. "I want them all dead as soon as possible. I won't share what's mine."

Then he leaned back and said the thing they had been waiting to hear.

"I killed my father to get this empire. I made the fake will. If I could do that, and get rid of my brother-in-law, I can kill anyone."

He looked almost proud when he said it.

"This belongs to me and my son."

After a moment, J.D. added, "Can I meet this plumber? I want to know for myself whether he can do the job."

Riley called Kremer immediately.

"Can you come to the office now?" he asked. "Mr. Callaghan wants to discuss further business."

Kremer, still listening to everything through the recording feed, answered in exactly the tone they expected him to use.

"Yes, sir. I can be there in thirty minutes."

Jonathan, Jordan, and Kremer sat together in the basement office for only a few more minutes. Then Kremer stood.

"This is going where we need it to go," he said. "I have to leave."

He arrived at the office precisely thirty minutes later. Riley and J.D. were waiting for him.

J.D. wasted no time.

"Have you killed before?"

"Yes, sir," Kremer said. "High-value targets. Government work."

J.D. leaned forward. "As Riley told you, I want my brothers, my sisters, and my wife gone. Money isn't the problem. Trouble is."

Kremer nodded as if this were a practical problem like any other.

"Do you own a private vacation place? Cabin, resort house, somewhere quiet?"

Riley answered. "Yes. Gatlinburg area. Very private."

"Perfect," Kremer said. "Invite all of them there. A family gathering. Tell them you need to discuss something important. Don't mention the legal notice. Don't hint at conflict. Let them walk in comfortable."

J.D. and Riley both listened intently.

"I'll study the place first," Kremer continued. "I need the address. It may take two to four weeks to plan this properly. No rush. If you move too fast, all of us get in trouble."

They both agreed.

"We do not discuss this on the phone again," Kremer said. "I don't want any chance of anyone recording us. Understood?"

"Yes," both men said.

"Good. And let me see that legal notice."

Riley handed it to him.

"I'll review it and get back to you. Once I've seen the cabin and finalized the plan, you deposit two-point-five million into my account."

"No problem," Riley said.

"Do not contact me about this anymore," Kremer added. "I'll contact you."

When he left, J.D. turned to Riley and said, almost admiringly, "He's smart. I like him. We'll use him again after this."

Riley nodded. "We need him right now."

Then, after a pause, he added, "Later, we get rid of him too."

Back in the basement office, Jordan sat staring at the screens in disbelief.

Then he turned to Jonathan and Kremer and said something he had been holding back.

"There's one more person you need to meet. My sister Lakesha's boyfriend. Michael. He's with the DEA now. He's solid. He's not like the others. I trust him."

They met Michael soon after, and both Jonathan and Kremer liked him almost immediately. Jordan and Kremer walked him through the plan carefully, showing him enough to make him understand what they were building. Michael listened without interrupting and then gave them his word.

"If Kremer helps us go after the distributors and the corruption behind them," he said, "I'll make sure he's protected."

For the first time since the war had truly begun, they were no longer fighting alone.

Chapter 56: Into the Web

Kremer and Jonathan finally traced the pattern.

For weeks, they had been quietly watching what happened inside Mitch's world, especially on the third floor of the Callaghan building, where the parties ran late into the night and the same faces kept returning. The same friends. The same suppliers. The same ruined rhythm of alcohol, pills, powder, and noise. It all flowed together until it stopped looking like chaos and started looking like structure.

Jonathan took on the work of following Mitch's inner circle. He did not rush. He watched the way a hunter watches tracks, patiently, knowing that impatience ruins a trail faster than weather ever could.

Jordan recognized two of the men almost immediately. Both had once been part of the nightmare that nearly destroyed Tiffney and Lakesha. The sight of them brought the old anger back so fast it felt almost physical, but Kremer and Jonathan kept him out of it.

"This is not your fight right now," Kremer told him. "You've already paid too much. Let us handle this."

One name surfaced again and again.

Chris.

He was one of Mitch's closest friends and, more importantly, the one who quietly controlled most of the flow. Jonathan followed him carefully through back roads, bars, parking lots, and private meetings until the pattern became clear. Chris was not the top. He was the doorway.

Past him stood the real source.

When Jonathan finally had enough, he handed everything over to Kremer.

"Now it's in your hands."

Kremer nodded and thanked him. Then he reached out through old contacts of his own, men who still moved in those circles and still knew who to trust for the wrong kinds of work. Through them, he made contact with the distributor.

The man's name was Jimmy.

They agreed to meet at a well-known nightclub in Jackson, Tennessee. Jimmy was younger than Kremer expected, somewhere in his mid-thirties, but he already carried himself like someone who had made enough money in dangerous rooms to stop fearing most people. He also knew enough about Kremer's old life to take him seriously from the start.

Kremer did not waste time.

"There's a big opportunity in the Bootheel," he told him. "I know a guy who can move volume if he's interested. We could run meth, cocaine, whatever is needed, and cover Missouri, Arkansas, Tennessee, and Kentucky out of Caruthersville."

Jimmy listened without interrupting. Then he leaned back and gave a short nod.

"If the man is real, bring him in. Fifty-fifty partnership between you and me on supply. I'm good with expansion."

Kremer thanked him and played his part well. He told Jimmy he was older, less interested in the front-facing work now, but still willing to help from behind the scenes if the money and the structure were right.

By the end of the meeting, they had exchanged numbers. Jimmy went a step further and showed him the main warehouse and processing site where the drugs were prepared. He even explained where his ingredients came from.

"Texas first," he said. "Then across from Mexico."

That was enough.

From there, Kremer approached Chris. He told him there was a major business opportunity for Mitch and his circle, and if they were serious, he wanted to meet both Chris and Mitch in person at the same nightclub in Jackson where he had met Jimmy.

Chris said he would check with Mitch and get back to him.

Kremer kept a separate phone for everything tied to the drug operation. Every call, every text, every meeting detail was being passed quietly to Michael, the DEA agent Jordan trusted.

Michael appreciated the work and kept his own replies brief.

"Keep me updated. If you need anything, call."

Chris and Mitch agreed to meet.

Before the meeting, Kremer sent instructions. No phones. No exceptions. He told them he would be wearing a red see-through shirt and asked them to come in similar colors so they could identify each other quickly without drawing attention.

"We need to be careful in this business," he told them.

Chris liked the idea. Mitch liked anything that made the whole thing feel larger, more expensive, and more dangerous.

When they met at the club, Chris recognized Kremer first and introduced himself. Then he introduced Mitch. Kremer apologized politely and said he needed to do a quick security check.

"Why don't you search me first?" he said to Chris.

He spread his arms the way a man does at airport security. Chris searched him. Then Kremer did the same to Chris and Mitch, careful, professional, and calm enough to make the routine feel ordinary.

After that, he led them to a booth in the far corner of the club, where the noise was low and the traffic lighter.

"Let's order first," he said. "Then we talk."

They looked at the menu, ordered drinks and food, and waited until the server was gone.

Then Kremer began.

"This is a multimillion-dollar opportunity, and it stays safe only if everyone follows protocol. There's no pressure here. At the end of this meeting, either of you can walk away and nothing happens. No hard feelings. But once we commit, there's no changing your mind. The one thing that destroys people in this business is cheating each other."

Both men listened.

"The model is simple," Kremer continued. "Jimmy and I supply bulk product to your warehouse. You move it down to smaller distributors and direct buyers. Business-to-business and retail. Half the money at delivery. The other half when you sell."

Chris asked the first real question. "And what if we don't move all of it?"

Kremer nodded as if he respected that.

"Good question. Some months you sell more. Some less. What remains rolls into the next month. We don't start with five million in product. That was just an example. We start with one million. Your initial investment is five hundred thousand. If you fail to move it in ninety days, you get back seventy-five percent of the value on the unsold product. Your real risk is only twenty-five percent."

Chris and Mitch both nodded.

"The only condition," Kremer said, "is that what comes back has to be exact. The people who get into trouble are the ones who dip into the product with their friends, then try to return short inventory."

He asked them twice if anything was unclear. Neither man seemed confused. If anything, both seemed energized.

Kremer leaned in slightly.

"Your location in Caruthersville is perfect. Water access. Four-state reach. Missouri, Arkansas, Tennessee, Kentucky. That alone gives you a serious edge."

Mitch smiled. "How much can you supply?"

"That depends on you. We can move five million a month. Ten. Fifty. It all depends on what you can handle."

Then Kremer asked the question he already knew Mitch would answer the wrong way.

"Do you have any protection on the law side? Police? DEA? Judges?"

Mitch laughed a little, too proud of himself to hear the danger in his own voice.

"Yes. The police chief and most of southeast Missouri law enforcement are under our influence. Judges too. Sheriffs too. We can sell in any high school across those four states if we want."

Kremer made a show of being impressed.

"Then the hard part is already solved. The biggest problem in this business is always enforcement. If you have that covered, and you already know the local market, then you can move fast."

He let that settle before asking the final question.

"How much can you invest up front?"

Mitch barely hesitated.

"Money isn't a problem. My father is J.D. Callaghan. He's rich and powerful in southeast Missouri. I can start with five or ten million."

Kremer gave a small nod, as if this answered everything he needed to know.

"That helps. We'll need a signed agreement before anything moves. Initial order, ten million. Fifty percent due at signing. Once the advance hits, delivery within thirty days. Do you already have a building in mind?"

Mitch nodded.

"Yes. Good access. Easy to store and move out from."

"Then we can move quickly," Kremer said. "Can you arrange five million within a week? I'll bring the contract."

"Yes," Mitch said. "I'll talk to the police chief and the others in the meantime."

"That's fine. Let's meet at this club again next Thursday night. We sign the agreement and get the money started. Text me the address for the building first. Text only. Then I'll call you back."

He handed Mitch his private number.

"Have a good night. I'm looking forward to working with you."

By the time the meeting ended, Chris and Mitch were visibly excited. Mitch, especially, looked as though he had already started spending money he had not yet touched.

Chapter 57: Easy Money

Mitch was glowing by the time he left the club.

To him, it felt like the start of something enormous, the thing that would finally prove he was more than just J.D. Callaghan's reckless son. He told Chris they were standing on the edge of real money now, serious money, and Chris, as always, let him talk. He knew better than to interrupt when Mitch was full of himself.

That afternoon, Mitch texted his father.

I need money. Big opportunity. My own business.

The reply came back almost immediately.

Come to my office tomorrow at two.

Mitch arrived on time. Riley was already there, sitting beside J.D.'s desk like he always did, half adviser and half shadow.

Riley studied him first.

"What kind of business?"

"Distribution," Mitch said.

"Distribution of what?"

Mitch's face hardened. "Not what you think. Healthcare-related. Four states."

Riley did not look convinced.

"I want to talk to my father alone," Mitch snapped. "Not to his employee."

The insult landed exactly the way Mitch intended it to. Riley stood up without a word and left the office.

J.D. waited until the door shut.

"How much do you need?"

"Ten million."

J.D. leaned back in his chair. "That isn't pocket money. What kind of return?"

"Fast," Mitch said. "Low risk. I need it next week."

J.D. hesitated, then nodded slowly.

"I'll arrange it. But you don't vanish from my business."

"Of course not."

J.D. looked at him for another moment. "Have you spoken to your mother?"

Mitch scoffed. "Why would I? She doesn't understand anything."

A thin smile crossed J.D.'s face. "We agree on that."

Mitch stood up, satisfied. "Tuesday," he said. "Don't forget."

As he walked out, the secretary stopped him and handed him a small package marked urgent. Mitch dropped it into his sports car and drove off. A few minutes later, his phone rang from an unknown number. He ignored it.

Then a text appeared.

Open the package. It concerns your mother and Riley.

He pulled over.

Inside the envelope were photographs. Clear, deliberate, impossible to mistake for anything accidental. His mother arriving at Riley's house. His mother sitting in Riley's car. His mother walking into Riley's private office. In one of the last photos she wore a familiar pair of earrings. In the next, one was missing.

A note was attached.

Check Riley's bedroom.

Mitch's hands began to shake.

Within minutes, he was at Riley's house. With the help of one of his friends, he went inside. What he found there finished the job the photographs had begun. The missing earring lay hidden in a place where, to Mitch's eyes, it could only mean one thing.

Something inside him snapped.

By the time Riley came home, Mitch was waiting.

Riley stepped through the door and stopped immediately. "What are you doing here?"

Mitch had already dragged a chair into the middle of the room. He pointed at it with the gun in his hand.

"Sit."

Riley's voice stayed calm, but there was fear in it now. "Put the gun down and let's talk. I know you were angry yesterday in the office. I know your distribution business is about meth and cocaine."

Mitch stepped closer and lifted the gun toward his face.

"You shut up," he said. "Yes, it's meth and cocaine. So what? That's not why I'm here."

His whole body was trembling now.

"What the hell was my mother doing in your bedroom?"

Riley blinked. "She was never in my bedroom. She came by once last week. We had coffee. That's all."

Mitch's expression darkened further.

"Coffee?" he said. "Or a date? Or sex?"

He reached into his pocket and threw the earring onto the floor between them.

"What was her earring doing there?"

Riley looked down at it and then back up, and for the first time he looked genuinely alarmed.

"You're misunderstanding this."

"My father trusted you his whole life," Mitch shouted. "He gave you everything. And you repay him by sleeping with his wife?"

He pushed the gun harder against Riley's face.

Riley lifted his hands slowly. "Nothing happened. I never looked at your mother that way. Nothing happened."

"Then why was she at your house? Why was she in your car? Why did she go to the third floor office with you?"

Riley tried to keep his voice steady.

"Her car wouldn't start. I gave her a ride. She wanted to check something in J.D.'s room. That's all."

Mitch fired before Riley could say anything more.

The first shot hit high. The second finished it.

For a moment the room was silent except for Mitch's breathing. Then the shock gave way to motion. His friends arrived quickly. He had already texted them what he intended to do. They brought large plastic bags and moved with the speed of people who had done bad things before and knew the value of acting fast.

They wrapped Riley's body with the sheets. They cleaned the room. One of them took the gun and told Mitch to leave.

"We'll take care of the rest. Go home. Relax."

Mitch did exactly that.

When he reached the house, both his parents were at the dinner table. J.D. looked up first.

"Where were you?"

Mitch ignored him and looked straight at his mother.

"What's going on between you and Riley?"

Mrs. Callaghan stared at him. "What are you talking about?"

"Are you cheating on Dad?"

Her whole face changed. "Absolutely not. How dare you even ask that?"

Mitch stepped closer. "Then why was your earring in Riley's bedroom?"

Without saying a word, she touched both ears and showed him the matching pair she was still wearing.

Mitch froze.

She looked at him with disgust now. "I went to his house because his air conditioner was acting up and I had given him the plumber's number. The plumber was there. Then my car wouldn't start, so Riley drove me. I stopped at the office because I wanted to check my diary in your father's room upstairs. That's it."

J.D. looked from one to the other.

"Why are you asking this?"

Mitch's voice came out flat.

"I killed him."

His parents both stared at him.

"You're joking," J.D. said.

"No. I killed him. I thought he was sleeping with Mom."

For a second, nobody spoke. Then both parents reacted at once.

"He was gay."

It came from both of them together.

Mrs. Callaghan felt something strange and complicated move inside her. She did not like that Mitch had killed Riley. She did not like that her son had crossed another line he could never uncross. But beneath that, deeper than she wanted to admit, there was relief. Riley had been the mind behind so much of the evil that had poisoned their lives, Jack, Jordan, the schemes, the lies, the manipulation. His death did not erase any of that, but it did end him.

J.D. was already in problem-solving mode.

"Where is the body?" he asked. "Did anyone see you?"

"My friends are handling it. No one saw me."

J.D. stood up immediately.

"Go shower. Pack a bag. Leave tonight. Take your friends. I'll call the hotel in Nashville and get you rooms for a few days. If anybody asks, you were there. You were never anywhere near Riley's house."

Mitch nodded as if this were just another inconvenience.

Then, on his way out, he added, "Don't forget the money for my business deal."

J.D. barely looked at him. "You'll get it next week."

Down in Jonathan's basement, Kremer and Jonathan had watched the entire thing.

Every word. Every movement. Every shot.

They said nothing for a while after it ended. They did not need to. The screen had said enough.

Chapter 58: A New Beginning

Jordan threw himself into training his younger brother for basketball. Watching Scott step onto the court as a freshman at Sikeston High brought back memories Jordan had spent years trying not to touch too closely, the early mornings, the hunger, the feeling that life was still opening rather than closing. Back then, before everything had gone wrong, the game had felt like a door. Seeing Scott now, awkward in some movements and gifted in others, made Jordan feel that old pull again.

Not long after, Jordan met with the principal at Sikeston High to talk about the future of the basketball program. Everybody in the building knew his name. They knew what he had done in Caruthersville. They knew what had been taken from him too.

"If you hadn't been pulled away," the principal said quietly, "you would've led Caruthersville to three straight state titles."

Then he leaned back in his chair and told Jordan the truth about Sikeston's program. They didn't even have a formal basketball coach. Parents and volunteers were doing what they could just to keep things alive from season to season.

"If you're interested," he said, "we'd like to appoint you. I'm not going to pretend the money is great. Our budget is small. But the opportunity is here."

Jordan did not need time to think.

"I'm in," he said. "The money doesn't matter."

The principal smiled, though his expression turned practical again almost immediately. "I'll need board approval. And the chairman's approval too. He's the biggest farmer and donor in the district."

Something in Jordan tightened at that, but the principal seemed to catch it.

"He's not what the rumors make him out to be," he said. "At least not in this situation."

Jordan nodded. "I'd like to start as soon as possible. Building a real program takes time. You can't just throw something together and expect it to last."

"That," the principal said, "is exactly why we want you. Let's meet again next week."

Jordan left the office feeling energized in a way he had not felt for years. It was not just excitement. It was deeper than that. Something inside him had begun to line up again.

When he told Jonathan and Kremer, both men were thrilled.

"This is where you belong," Jonathan said.

Tiffney sounded just as happy when Jordan called her.

"You're going back to what you love," she told him. "I'm proud of you."

Then she mentioned, almost casually, that she had been fielding job offers from several law firms.

"I'm still deciding," she said. "I want to hear a few more of them out before I choose."

Jordan smiled to himself. "Do what's best for your future."

For the first time since his arrest, the future did not feel like something stolen from him, something he might spend the rest of his life trying to recover in pieces. It felt like something he could still build.

Around the same time, Ethan received a remarkable offer of his own. One of the most influential newspaper companies in St. Louis, a media group that dominated both print and digital journalism across Missouri, had taken serious notice of his work on Jordan's case. The chairman and CEO had been especially impressed by the clarity and courage of Ethan's reporting. Within two weeks of the story breaking wide open, Ethan was invited in for a formal interview. Not long after that, an offer followed.

He sat down with Shirley and his grandparents in Poplar Bluff to talk it through, but all three of them were already leaning in the same direction. The company had reach, reputation, benefits, and more room to grow than Ethan had dared expect so early.

Shirley, who had only recently come through the last stretch of her professional restrictions, was free at last to return to journalism herself.

"Take it," she told him. "This is exactly the kind of place serious reporters hope for."

A few days later, the CEO called Ethan personally and asked him to come back to the St. Louis headquarters that Thursday at four o'clock. During that conversation, Ethan mentioned his mother.

"She'll be free to work again in April," he said. "She's one of the best journalists I know."

The CEO laughed softly. "I understand. And yes, when her restrictions are over, she's welcome to come talk to us too."

Ethan answered quickly, wanting to be clear. "That's not a condition of me taking the job. I just want her to have the same chance."

The CEO respected that immediately.

"That kind of loyalty says a lot about you," he said.

Ethan signed the contract later that week with a June start date. For him, and for the family that had spent years paying the price for telling the truth, it felt like more than a job offer. It felt like the beginning of a chapter none of them had been sure they would reach.

Back in Sikeston, the principal met with the school board and the board chairman later that same week. Jordan's name alone changed the energy in the room before any details had even been discussed.

"Bring him in," one board member said almost immediately. "We all know what he did at Caruthersville."

The chairman, who had been silent until then, finally asked the question that mattered most in practical terms.

"How much is he asking?"

"He hasn't named a number," the principal said. "I told him our budget was limited."

The chairman smiled. "Then we make room. Our basketball program hasn't cracked the top forty in years. Jordan took a weak school and turned it into a champion. That kind of leadership is worth paying for."

He looked toward the principal again. "What's the going rate for a strong high-school coach?"

"Fifty to sixty thousand."

"Offer him sixty," the chairman said. "And build in bonuses if he takes us deep into the tournament. Final Four, state run, whatever makes sense."

The principal left the meeting almost giddy. He called Jordan as soon as he stepped out.

"Come in tomorrow," he said. "I've got very good news."

The next day, Jordan sat across from him while the contract was laid out in full. Four years. A starting salary of sixty thousand. Incentives tied to tournament success. Jordan stared at the numbers for a moment, genuinely stunned. He had expected something far smaller, something closer to twenty or thirty thousand, especially after the principal had warned him about the budget.

"Our chairman is also willing to invest in equipment and renovations," the principal added. "He wants the program taken seriously. We all do."

Jordan signed without hesitation.

"Welcome aboard," the principal said, extending his hand. "We'll announce it Monday morning."

Jordan called Tiffney first. Then Jonathan. Then Kremer. After that he called his parents and Mr. Moreland. The excitement in every conversation made the whole thing feel more real.

Tiffney laughed when she heard the salary.

"You may be making more than some first-year lawyers."

Jordan laughed too. "You'll be helping people in court. That matters more."

That evening, he called Scott.

"Let's get everybody in the gym this weekend," he said. "I want to meet the players and talk about where we're going."

Scott was already halfway there in his own mind.

"I'll spread the word tomorrow. They'll come."

Jordan ended the call already seeing it, the gym, the drills, the sweat, the bark of sneakers on hardwood, the sound of basketballs hitting the floor in unison. For the first time in years, he was not trying to salvage his life from what had been done to it.

He was building something.

The official announcement came the next morning during school assembly.

"Our new basketball coach begins on Monday," the principal told the students. "His name is Jordan."

Any student who cared about basketball knew exactly who that was. The reaction moved through the room almost at once.

Scott wasted no time after the assembly ended. He went straight to the players he knew mattered most.

"My brother wants everyone in the gym tomorrow at ten."

The response was immediate. The serious players were excited. The less serious ones were curious. Either way, they came.

When Jordan met them that Saturday, he saw exactly what he had hoped to see. Hunger. Rawness. Pride. Unfocused talent in some, discipline in a few, and potential in more than he expected. Besides Scott, there were eight or nine boys he thought could become something real if they were pushed hard enough and honestly enough.

By Monday, the job was official. Jordan announced open tryouts for the following week and invited every student who wanted to compete to show up and earn a place. By the end of that week, he had formed both varsity and junior varsity teams. Fifteen players made varsity, not merely the most talented, but the ones who were willing to commit.

Then he laid down the rules.

Three hours of training every weekday.

Six hours on weekends.

No excuses.

Jordan had taken a four-year contract for a reason. He wanted to be there for Scott through all of high school, not only as a coach, but as something more steady than that, a guide, a witness, a brother who had already seen how quickly the world could turn and who refused to let the next boy walk into it alone.

Tiffney supported every part of it. Over the next four years, both of them would be building something, Jordan on the court, Tiffney in the law, each moving toward a future they had once feared might be gone for good.

Now, at last, the next chapter no longer felt imagined.

It had begun.

Chapter 59: A Quiet Death

On Thanksgiving night, J.D. Callaghan's sister dialed 911 from her home in Poplar Bluff. Her husband, the county sheriff, was unresponsive.

They had finished dinner and settled in to watch college football. He had poured himself a drink while she cleaned up the kitchen. When she returned, he was slumped in his chair, his eyes closed, the television still flickering in front of him as if nothing at all had changed.

She called his name and tried to shake him awake.

There was no response.

Paramedics arrived within minutes. They checked his pulse, checked his breathing, and began emergency measures right there in the living room. Nothing worked. He was rushed to Poplar Bluff Regional Hospital, but by the time they reached the emergency room, the truth was already ahead of them.

The ER physician followed every life-saving protocol. Still, there was no heartbeat, no breath, no sign that his body was coming back. After exhausting every measure, the doctor pronounced him dead.

Because of the sheriff's position, law enforcement was notified immediately. Blood and urine samples were taken. His body was examined for any visible sign of injury or assault. Nothing obvious appeared. No bruising. No struggle. No wound that would explain such a sudden death.

Then the physician turned to the widow and asked for a medical history, along with any medications her husband had been taking.

"I brought everything," she said, handing over a bag filled with prescription bottles. "I don't really know what he was on. I just know he had heart trouble and blood pressure problems. His doctor is in Pemiscot County."

The physician began checking labels.

Then he paused.

"Dr. Moore," he said quietly.

The medication list was long. Too long. High-dose painkillers. OxyContin, eighty milligrams, three times a day. Sedatives. Valium, ten milligrams, three times a day. Xanax. Viagra. Levitra. Heart medication. Blood pressure medication. Some were clearly intended for routine use. Others were written as needed, though the definitions were alarmingly vague.

The doctor began counting pills.

Something was wrong.

Some bottles were much lighter than they should have been. Worse, the pain medication appeared to contain mixed strengths, OxyContin 80 milligrams and 160 milligrams in the same supply. The hospital pharmacist confirmed it after reviewing the bottles himself.

"He took more than prescribed," the physician said grimly. "And with alcohol in the system, that combination can be fatal."

The sheriff's wife nodded slowly.

"He always drank."

The physician turned to the investigator who had already arrived.

"At this point, medication toxicity mixed with alcohol appears most likely," he said. "But the autopsy will confirm it."

The investigator handed the widow his card.

"Until the lab work and autopsy come back, this stays confidential. Don't leave town without notifying us. And if you remember anything else, call me immediately."

She agreed.

Outside the hospital, Thanksgiving night moved on in silence. Families ate leftovers. Football games rolled on. Towns dimmed into sleep.

But deeper inside Missouri, something darker had begun to move.

The next morning, the police investigator contacted a federal agent he trusted, DEA Agent Michael.

Within hours, Michael was standing inside Dr. Moore's clinic.

The color drained from Dr. Moore's face the instant he saw the badge. His confidence disappeared so quickly it was almost embarrassing.

"Is... is everything all right, Officer?" he asked, forcing a smile that never quite reached his eyes.

Michael did not return it.

"That depends on how honest you decide to be."

Dr. Moore swallowed and said nothing.

Michael requested the sheriff's medical records. What he found was thin. Not just incomplete, but alarmingly thin. The notes were sparse. The documentation was inconsistent. High-dose prescriptions for OxyContin, Xanax, and Valium stretched over long periods with little meaningful medical justification.

"When was the last time the sheriff actually saw you?" Michael asked.

Dr. Moore fumbled at the computer.

"I... I'm not sure. Maybe last year."

Michael looked at him steadily.

"And how long had he been receiving high-dose narcotics and anxiety medication?"

Dr. Moore hesitated.

"I don't remember exactly."

"Do you have imaging studies?" Michael asked. "Any documented justification for long-term pain treatment?"

Dr. Moore had no answer.

Michael already knew enough to understand what he was looking at. Jonathan and Kremer had warned him about Dr. Moore weeks earlier. This was not a surprise. It was confirmation.

Without involving the state board yet, Michael called in his federal colleagues. By the end of the day, agents had seized patient files and digital records from all three of Dr. Moore's clinics. Ten charts stood out immediately, all tied to the same circle of power: the Callaghan family, their associates, the judge, and now the recently deceased sheriff.

The clinics were sealed.

Dr. Moore sat pale and trembling in a chair that suddenly looked much too small for him.

"How serious is this?" he asked quietly.

Michael didn't soften the answer.

"Extremely serious. You're looking at decades in federal prison. But I'm not arresting you today."

Dr. Moore looked up in disbelief.

"You get one chance," Michael continued. "Tell the truth. Cooperate fully. Become a government witness."

"And if I do?"

"Then you might survive this with a lot less time."

Michael gathered the files and moved toward the door.

"One of your patients is already dead. We're waiting on the autopsy. If it confirms what we expect, your window closes fast."

He paused only once more.

"You have a day. Maybe two."

Then he was gone, leaving Dr. Moore alone with the sound of his own breathing and the weight of everything he had buried finally rising up around him.

Later that same day, Agent Michael followed the trail to a small pharmacy in Caruthersville.

Nearly every prescription written by Dr. Moore had been filled there.

Michael met first with the owner and then with the head pharmacist, a man named Randy. The moment Michael identified himself, Randy's composure started to break.

"I'm going to be very clear," Michael said. "You are facing the loss of your license and serious prison time. You have one chance to help yourself. Tell the truth and cooperate."

Randy's hands began to shake.

"I'll cooperate," he said quickly. "I swear I will."

Michael studied him for a moment.

"Explain why the sheriff's last prescription included mixed dosages."

Randy hesitated, then gave in.

"We were short on one strength," he said. "I contacted Dr. Moore. He approved substituting a higher dose to make up the difference. It wasn't the first time."

Michael's expression hardened.

"And why were nearly all of Dr. Moore's patients filling their prescriptions here?"

Randy swallowed.

"We had an arrangement. He got a percentage of the profits. Most of my business came through his clinics."

"How much?"

"Almost all of it," Randy admitted. "More than ninety percent."

Michael nodded slowly.

"That makes this very serious."

Federal agents moved in quickly after that. Computers were seized. Records were boxed. The pharmacy was shut down and sealed.

Michael handed Randy his card.

"You have until tomorrow," he said. "Call me. Bring a lawyer if you want. But understand this, the evidence is overwhelming."

Randy broke down.

"I'll cooperate now," he said. "I won't change my mind."

Michael slid a set of documents across the table.

"Then sign these. This is your cooperation agreement. If you back out later, the deal disappears."

Randy signed immediately. He surrendered his pharmacist license on the spot.

"I'll meet you tomorrow," Michael said. "Cape Girardeau. Three o'clock."

Randy nodded weakly.

"Yes, sir."

As Michael walked out, the pharmacy behind him felt hollowed out, as if the walls themselves knew that another pillar of the old system had just given way.

Dr. Moore drove straight to J.D. Callaghan's office, his hands shaking on the steering wheel the entire way. He barely spoke to the staff. At the desk, he asked for Riley.

"Mr. Riley is on extended leave," the administrator said. "But Mr. Callaghan is in his office."

Dr. Moore went in without hesitation.

J.D. Callaghan looked up, already irritated before the doctor had said a word.

"They took everything," Dr. Moore blurted out. "The DEA seized my records, my computers. They sealed all three clinics. I'm finished if you don't help me."

Callaghan's face hardened instantly.

"I'm already dealing with enough," he said coldly. "The sheriff is dead. And from what I hear, it's because of the medications you gave him."

Dr. Moore's voice wavered.

"I did what you and Riley told me to do. I prescribed what you wanted prescribed. I ignored the documentation because you promised protection. Every one of those patients, your family, your son, your people."

Callaghan rose slowly from behind the desk.

"We paid you," he said. "In cash. Very well. Don't stand there and act like this was charity."

Dr. Moore looked close to breaking.

"I protected your son," he said. "I kept him and his friends out of the rape case. I falsified the emergency room report. I switched their samples with false ones. I altered records when it would've destroyed him."

That was enough.

"Get out," Callaghan shouted. "Get out of my office and don't ever come back. I'm not protecting you."

Dr. Moore stumbled out, nearly in tears.

On the drive home, he pulled over and sat staring at his phone for a long time. When he finally made the call, his voice sounded smaller than Michael had ever heard it.

"I'm ready to cooperate," he said. "I'll testify. Against all of them."

There was a short pause.

"Come to my office in Cape Girardeau tomorrow at one," Michael said. "Bring an attorney if you want."

Dr. Moore exhaled shakily.

For the first time, he understood something simple and final. There was no way back. There was only forward, and forward meant walking into the truth he had spent years helping to bury.

That evening, DEA Agent Michael called Ethan.

"I thought you should hear this directly," he said. "Dr. Moore's clinics are shut down. All three. We also closed the pharmacy in Caruthersville. Records seized. Licenses surrendered."

Ethan went quiet for a moment.

Then he said, "So it's real. The whole thing."

"It's bigger than we expected," Michael replied. "And it's moving fast."

Ethan's instincts sharpened immediately, but he kept his voice controlled.

"Is this on the record?"

"Not yet. But it will be. Soon."

Ethan leaned back in his chair and stared at the wall for a long time. He thought of Jordan. Of his mother. Of every story that had been buried under fear, influence, and money.

"This isn't just corruption," Ethan said at last. "This is a system built on silence. And it's cracking."

Michael agreed.

"When it breaks, it's going to break loudly."

Ethan's hand was already hovering over his notebook.

"When it goes public, people are going to want answers," he said. "I'll be ready."

After the call ended, he sat there alone for a long time.

He did not feel excitement.

He felt responsibility.

Because this was no longer just a story. It was history moving in real time.

Around four that afternoon, the autopsy report came in.

The findings were conclusive.

The sheriff had died from a toxic combination of drugs. High levels of OxyContin, Valium, and Xanax were found in his blood and urine, along with significant alcohol content. There was no real room left for doubt.

The family was notified. The body was released for burial.

Earlier that same day, Dr. Moore had met with Agent Michael at the federal office in Cape Girardeau. By one o'clock, he had signed a formal cooperation agreement with the government and entered a guilty plea to multiple violations. Michael made it clear that the confession would need to be preserved properly, under oath before a magistrate judge. Dr. Moore agreed immediately.

Pharmacist Randy met with Michael as well. He too signed a plea agreement and agreed to provide sworn testimony.

Once the autopsy confirmed the cause of death, the government moved quickly.

Both Dr. Moore and Randy were taken into custody.

Michael reminded them that this had already been discussed. Because they were cooperating fully, the government would not oppose bail. Three days later, both men were released under strict conditions. They surrendered their passports. They were ordered not to leave the area without federal approval. And they were warned that any violation would immediately void their agreements.

The system that had protected them for so many years was gone.

Now every step they took would be watched.

Dr. Moore pleaded guilty to multiple federal charges, including prescribing high-dose narcotics without medical necessity, healthcare fraud, conspiracy, and falsification of medical records. The court sentenced him to eight years in federal prison, bringing an end to years of illegal practices that had fed addiction, corruption, and death.

His medical license and DEA registration were permanently revoked. He was also permanently excluded from Medicare and Medicaid, effectively ending any future in medicine and any access to federal healthcare reimbursement for life.

Pharmacist Randy also accepted responsibility for his role in the scheme. He pleaded guilty to healthcare fraud, illegal kickbacks, and criminal association with Dr. Moore. The court sentenced him to three years in prison, permanently revoked his pharmacist license, and barred him from ever practicing again.

With their convictions, a major pillar of the corruption network finally collapsed, marking a decisive step toward accountability and long-overdue justice.

Chapter 60: The Deal

J.D. Callaghan told his business circle that Riley had left on an extended trip overseas to explore new opportunities. He said it casually, as if it were nothing unusual. No one questioned it. In his world, people rarely did.

Mitch, however, felt like everything had finally fallen into place.

He came back to town full of energy, talking nonstop about the new distribution business. To him, it wasn't just another deal, it was his chance to prove himself. Riley had always been the obstacle, the one who controlled access, decisions, and timing. Now Riley was gone, and Mitch believed the path was clear. He already had the building, the office, and the warehouse. All he needed now was to lock in the deal and start moving product.

He called Kremer and told him he was ready, fifty percent upfront, no hesitation. Kremer kept his tone steady and professional. He told Mitch to meet in downtown Nashville at a hotel where he had rented a conference room. A projector and a large screen had already been set up. Jimmy would be there as well.

Mitch confirmed he would come and said he'd bring Chris with him.

By the time they arrived, everything was ready.

Kremer had already placed the hidden recording devices throughout the room, positioned carefully, nothing obvious, nothing that would raise suspicion. On the surface, it looked like a standard business setup. Clean. Organized. Routine.

They all showed up on time.

Jimmy started with a short presentation. He moved through it with confidence, clicking through slides that outlined the structure of the operation, the product lines, the delivery process, and the payment terms. It was polished enough to feel legitimate, if you ignored what was actually being sold.

Jimmy had never handled an order of this scale before, and it showed. There was excitement in his voice, a kind of restless energy. He was also clearly impressed with Kremer for bringing this opportunity together.

"As per the agreement," Jimmy said, gesturing toward the screen, "ten million dollars' worth of cocaine and meth will be delivered within thirty days to your warehouse in Caruthersville, Missouri."

He paused, letting that sink in.

"From that point forward, all communication runs through Kremer. No exceptions."

He looked directly at Mitch and Chris.

"You've got thirty days to prepare. Start marketing, line up buyers, collect advance payments wherever you can. If you move the full stock, your net profit should be at least ten million."

Mitch's eyes lit up.

Jimmy continued, his tone steady.

"And make sure you handle your local police and DEA contacts. That part matters just as much as the product. We'll notify you at least ten days before delivery. Both of us will be at your warehouse when it arrives. And if everything goes well, we can celebrate that night."

He leaned back slightly.

"Any questions?"

Mitch didn't hesitate.

"I appreciate this," he said. "Both of you. I already spoke with the local police chief. He's handling everything on that side."

He smiled.

"He's my five percent partner."

Jimmy nodded with approval.

"That's smart. Very smart. That five percent will save you a lot of trouble. In this business, the more you share, the smoother things run."

Mitch took that in like validation.

"Yes," he said quickly. "And we'll throw a party when the delivery happens. A real one."

Kremer stepped in at just the right moment.

"Then invite your police chief," he said calmly. "Invite your top buyers too. Let everyone see who's standing with you. It builds confidence. It shows you can move anything."

Mitch nodded immediately.

"Yes, sir. We'll invite everyone."

The meeting continued, moving through smaller details. Storage. Timing. Money flow. Every word Mitch spoke only tightened the case against him, but he didn't see it. He was too caught up in the moment.

When it ended, Jimmy suggested they head down to the bar for drinks. Mitch and Chris were eager to go. Kremer declined, saying he needed to rest. He even told them to take it easy, to get some sleep, as if he were looking out for them.

Before they left, Jimmy pulled Kremer aside.

"I'll send two-point-five million to the main distributor in Texas," he said. "The other two-point-five, we split."

Kremer gave a small nod.

"Let the check clear first," he said. "Give it a few days. Then call the supplier and let him know the order is confirmed."

Jimmy was still riding the high.

"Thank you, Kremer," he said. "This deal is because of you. After this, we should go to Texas and meet the supplier in person."

"We will," Kremer replied. "Have a good night. I'll talk to you tomorrow."

A few minutes later, his phone buzzed.

A message from DEA Agent Michael.

We got everything. Audio and video. Good job.

Kremer read it once, then slipped the phone back into his pocket.

The next morning, Kremer would remove all those hidden recording devices from the hotel conference room.

Chapter 61:
The Walk Through the Woods

Mr. Callaghan's brother-in-law, a Dunklin County judge, kept his life neatly divided. In public, he was disciplined and respected. In private, he had two quiet obsessions: fishing and gold. Neither was something he talked about, but both shaped how he spent his time.

Nearly every Saturday morning, he fished.

He owned a small cabin near Lake Wappapello in Butler County, about fifteen minutes from Poplar Bluff and roughly an hour from his home in Kennett, Missouri. Most weekends followed the same routine. He would arrive late Friday night, sometimes alone, sometimes with a couple of close friends. His wife joined him occasionally, but more often he preferred the quiet.

Privacy mattered to him.

That Friday was no different.

He left Kennett after dusk and reached the lake just as night settled in. Not long after, two of his closest friends—each with cabins nearby—arrived. They gathered near the water, drinking heavily, laughing louder than they would anywhere else, slipping into habits they kept hidden from the rest of the world.

By around eleven, the night began to wind down. Fishing required an early start.

Because the cabins were close together, no one bothered with cars. A narrow footpath cut through the trees, a shortcut they had used for years. It was familiar. Easy.

The front of the cabins faced thick woods and tangled brush. The back opened directly to the lake—dark, still, and nothing like the clear waters people imagined. The forest around it was known for snakes, especially copperheads that blended into the ground without warning.

The air that night was heavy. Hot. Humid.

As they stepped outside, one of his friends smiled.

"Need a ride, Judge?"

He laughed it off.

"Don't start. I'll take the shortcut."

Another friend held up a flashlight.

"You sure? It's dark."

"I know the path," he said. "I'm fine."

They said their goodnights and went their separate ways.

The judge walked alone.

The path narrowed as he moved away from the light. Leaves crunched under his shoes. Insects hummed around him. The breeze from the lake barely reached the trees.

A few hundred feet from his cabin, something struck his right calf.

Sharp. Sudden.

He stopped, thinking it might be a thorn or a branch, but the pain spread differently. It burned, deep and immediate.

He forced himself to keep moving.

Each step became harder than the last.

By the time he reached his door, sweat was running down his face. His leg throbbed. A wave of dizziness hit him.

He fumbled for his key. His hands shook. It took longer than it should have, but the lock finally turned.

He stepped inside.

The dizziness worsened. His vision blurred. His balance slipped.

He collapsed onto the cabin floor.

The woods outside fell silent.

The next morning, both of his friends were already at their usual fishing spot by 5:30.

The lake was quiet. The air was thick with humidity.

They waited.

Thirty minutes passed.

"He's late," one of them said. "That's not like him."

"It happens," the other replied. "But not this long."

They kept fishing, though both of them glanced toward the trees more often now.

Another thirty minutes went by.

"Enough," one of them said, standing. "Watch my line. I'll go get him."

He shook his head as he started walking.

"Next time we don't let him drink that much. He's getting older."

The walk took about fifteen minutes.

When he reached the cabin, the door was unlocked.

That didn't feel right.

He pushed it open and froze.

The judge was lying on the floor.

"Hey," he called out carefully. "Wake up. It's almost seven."

No response.

He raised his voice.

"Come on. We're late."

Still nothing.

His heart began to race.

He knelt down and checked for a pulse.

Nothing.

He leaned closer, searching for breath.

Nothing.

The color of the man's skin had changed. Pale in places. Dark in others.

Panic hit.

He ran.

Back through the woods, shouting, waving his arms. By the time he reached his friend, he was gasping for air.

"What's wrong?" the other man asked.

He bent over, trying to catch his breath.

"Just—give me a second—"

He straightened, his face drained.

"I think he's dead."

"What?"

"No… he's just asleep."

"No," he said firmly. "I checked. No pulse. No breathing."

They didn't argue.

Both men ran back.

Inside the cabin, it was clear.

"Oh my God," the second man whispered. "He's gone."

They noticed the mark on his leg.

"Do you think… a snake?" one of them asked.

Neither answered.

They called 911.

It took more than an hour for the ambulance to arrive. The paramedics examined the body and exchanged a look.

"He's been gone for a while," one of them said.

They transported him to Poplar Bluff Regional Medical Center. The two men followed behind in silence.

At the hospital, the ER physician conducted an initial examination.

"This appears to be a snakebite," he said, pointing to the wound on the judge's right calf. "Most likely a copperhead."

The friends explained the previous night—the drinking, the walk through the woods.

The doctor documented everything and notified law enforcement.

Once it was confirmed that the deceased was an active judge, the situation escalated immediately.

An investigator arrived and reviewed the details. Then came the call.

The judge's wife was notified.

"As standard procedure," the investigator told her, "an autopsy will be required. We'll release the body once all tests are complete."

She nodded, though the shock was still settling in.

News traveled quickly.

By midday, people across the region were talking.

A Dunklin County judge had died overnight—apparently from a snakebite.

Mr. Callaghan's sister called him and their other siblings, her voice shaking as she shared the news. Soon after, she drove to the hospital, desperate for answers.

Mr. Callaghan was shaken.

He had already lost one brother-in-law to a drug overdose not long ago. Then Riley. And now this.

Another brother-in-law.

Another sudden death.

Sitting alone in his office, he spoke under his breath.

"Why does everything collapse at once?"

"Why now?"

He called his sister and told her he was on his way.

Then he called Mitch.

"I need you to take me to Poplar Bluff," he said. "The judge is dead."

Mitch didn't hesitate.

"I'm busy. I can't go."

Mr. Callaghan's voice hardened.

"That judge helped you when you were in trouble. He protected you."

Mitch scoffed.

"He's dead now. It doesn't matter. I've got more important things to deal with."

The line went dead.

Mr. Callaghan stared at his phone, stunned.

Then he called his wife.

"The judge is dead. Meet me at my office. We're going to Poplar Bluff now."

"I'll be there in thirty minutes," she said.

They drove in silence.

At the hospital, they found his sister and her children. The grief was still fresh from the sheriff's death, and now it had deepened.

A few hours later, his other sister arrived.

No one spoke much.

The weight of it all filled the room.

Finally, the judge's wife spoke.

"The funeral will be next Sunday," she said quietly. "One week from today."

The words settled over everyone.

Another burial. Another week of mourning.

Another reminder that something dark was unraveling around the Callaghan family.

Chapter 62: The Perfect Setting

Kremer visited Mr. Callaghan's vacation home in Gatlinburg, Tennessee, under the pretense of discussing a possible family gathering. Because of the recent deaths, the meeting had already been delayed and was now tentatively set for the following month.

While he was there, Kremer installed the audio and video equipment, carefully placing each device so it wouldn't be noticed. The feed was routed directly to DEA Agent Michael, with separate access for himself and Jack.

After the judge's funeral, Kremer spoke with Mr. Callaghan in private.

"I've been trying to reach Riley," he said casually. "No response."

Mr. Callaghan dismissed it.

"He's in Europe. Looking into business opportunities. He won't be back anytime soon."

Kremer nodded and shifted the conversation.

"I visited the Gatlinburg property," he said. "It's ideal for what we discussed. Can we move forward next month?"

Mr. Callaghan took a moment before answering.

"Yes. Next month is better. After everything that's happened... I don't trust anyone right now. I saw them at the funeral. Every one of them. Watching. Waiting."

Kremer kept his tone steady.

"You don't need to bring up land or shares. Let me handle that part."

Mr. Callaghan seemed relieved.

"I trust you," he said. "Handle it."

Kremer then added, as if it were an afterthought, "I'll be in St. Louis next week. Cardinals game at Busch Stadium."

Mr. Callaghan's expression changed immediately.

"You're going to that game?"

"Yes."

"I'll be there too," he said. "I don't miss Cardinals games."

Kremer smiled.

"I'm staying at the hotel next to the stadium."

Mr. Callaghan laughed.

"That's where I'm staying."

"Then let's meet before the game," Kremer said. "I'll reserve a conference room. We can talk there."

"Perfect," Mr. Callaghan replied.

They ended the call, both satisfied.

Jack looked at Kremer and shook his head.

"You're a genius," he said. "Computers, surveillance, HVAC… you mastered all of it."

Kremer shrugged lightly.

"It's necessity," he said. "I already knew computers and surveillance before prison. That world required it. But inside, those skills didn't matter. So I learned something else. HVAC. Plumbing. Just to survive."

He paused, then looked at Jack.

"You helped me when I needed it. I won't forget that."

Jack waved it off.

"We're past that," he said. "We're family."

The words stayed there, between them.

On Saturday, Kremer secured the conference room at the hotel. The game was scheduled for six. They met at four.

Kremer spoke calmly.

"I have two plans."

Mr. Callaghan listened.

"Plan A happens on the road. Plan B happens inside the house."

Kremer paused.

"Do you have an unregistered automatic weapon?"

"Yes."

"I'll place it under the dining table. If things go wrong, you'll need it."

Mr. Callaghan didn't hesitate.

"If it comes to that, I won't hold back."

He handed Kremer $2.5 million in cash.

"Come by my office in two days," he added. "I'll give you the weapon."

Kremer took it and left.

Two days later, he returned to collect the gun, wrapped it carefully, and transported it to the Gatlinburg property. He placed it under the dining table, positioned exactly where it would be within reach.

Then he sent the letters.

They were written as if they had come from Riley.

Each one carried the same message. A private family dinner. A proposal to divide the land equally. A request for silence.

The response was immediate.

Greed erased doubt. They accepted.

Kremer scheduled the dinner for the same night as the drug celebration.

He already knew what mattered most to Mr. Callaghan.

Mitch. And the land.

Those weaknesses would soon destroy him.

Chapter 63:
A New Court, A New Fight

Jordan threw himself completely into his new role as head basketball coach at Sikeston Public High School. For him, this was never going to be just another job. It felt far more personal than that. It was a second chance, a way to reclaim the part of his life that had been stolen from him and twisted into something unrecognizable.

His younger brother Scott understood that weight too. Neither of them said it often, but both knew the truth. Results mattered. Effort mattered. Excuses meant nothing.

Jordan moved quickly once he took over the program. He finalized the roster with the kind of clarity that came from knowing exactly what he wanted. In private, he understood that this season was only the beginning. With barely four months left before tournament play, his deeper goal was to build the foundation for the year after this one. Still, he did not lie to his players or fill their heads with fantasies.

"If we make the Final Sixteen," he told them, "or even the Final Eight, that would already mean we've done something real this year."

From the first day, he made the standard clear.

"I'm available ten to twelve hours a day," he said. "But basketball is not just shooting and passing. Anybody can stand around and throw up shots. That won't make you a team."

He walked slowly across the gym floor as he spoke, making sure every player was listening.

"This game asks for everything. Running. Weight training. Conditioning. Repetition. Discipline. You have to be strong physically, yes, but that's only half of it."

Then he stopped and looked at them one by one.

"Mental strength wins games. Stamina wins championships. We're going to build both."

The practices became intense almost immediately. Conditioning came first. Endurance drills. Strength work. Constant repetition until good habits stopped being forced and started becoming natural. The skill work followed, sharpened day after day, but Jordan never let them forget that talent alone meant very little.

More than anything else, he demanded belief.

"When the moment comes," he told them, "we fight. No fear. No intimidation. No quitting."

The gym fell silent around him.

A new season had begun. But for Jordan, it was never only about basketball.

It was redemption.

Tiffney accepted an offer from one of the most respected law firms in the country, a firm preparing to open a new office in St. Louis, Missouri. They did not see her as just another young hire. They saw her as part of the foundation, someone they trusted to help establish the office and give it credibility from the beginning.

She would be joining the firm as a criminal defense attorney in Missouri, and even at that early stage in her career, they were giving her real responsibility. Few young lawyers were trusted that way so soon.

Everyone around her felt the meaning of it.

Her parents were proud in a way that left them almost speechless. Jordan was genuinely thrilled for her. Jordan's parents welcomed the news too, and more than that, they welcomed her as family. Even the geography seemed to carry its own quiet comfort. She would be only an hour from her parents and less than two hours from Jordan and his family, close enough for Sunday dinners, quick visits, late-night calls, and a life that no longer felt scattered across impossible distances.

After years of struggle, separation, and uncertainty, their lives were finally beginning to move in the same direction.

Not because they had been lucky.

Because they had refused to stop.

Ethan also formally accepted the offer from the St. Louis Post, one of the most influential news organizations in Missouri. The position placed him at the center of both print and digital journalism in the state, exactly where someone with his instincts and nerve belonged.

Shirley received an offer from the same network as well. Once she completed the final terms of her plea agreement with the government, she would interview directly with the CEO. The path in front of them was becoming clear. Before long, mother and son would both be living and working in St. Louis.

For now, Rick and his wife chose to remain in Poplar Bluff. They spoke openly about moving later, perhaps joining Ethan and Shirley once the time felt right. There was no urgency in them now, only the slow and hard-earned understanding that some parts of life could still be rebuilt.

Shirley and her parents were deeply proud of Ethan, not just because he had succeeded professionally, but because of the way he had carried himself. His reporting, whether in print or online, carried the same stubborn devotion to truth that had defined their family for years. In him, they saw continuity. Not imitation, but inheritance.

They had done what mattered most to them. They had raised someone brave enough to speak honestly.

Rick reminded him often that the road he had chosen would never be an easy one.

"Speaking the truth costs something," he told Ethan more than once. "Sometimes it costs a lot. You lose people. You make enemies. And you get tested in ways you never expect."

But Rick always ended in the same place.

"The reward is peace of mind. A clear conscience. No shame to carry when your time comes. We all die one day. The question is what you're carrying when you go."

He warned him, too, about the temptations that waited along the way, quick recognition, easy money, political access, quiet favors traded in back rooms.

"That path looks easy," Rick said. "That's why so many people take it. But it's empty. It's built on compromise, silence, and fear."

Ethan listened.

And he stayed on the same road.

Because truth, even when costly, was the only legacy worth leaving behind.

Jack met his sister, Pinki, at a shopping mall in Memphis, choosing a quiet corner far from the kind of faces that remembered too much. He spoke carefully, measuring each word before he said it. He told her about Kremer's long-term plans and the pieces already moving into place. He avoided some details, especially where Mitch was concerned, but he did not hide the truth entirely.

"Mitch is already involved in a drug distribution operation," Jack said quietly.

Then he showed her a few short clips. Nothing dramatic, nothing edited to force emotion. Just Mitch speaking plainly, and in those moments, speaking of her with resentment, contempt, and a coldness that no mother should have to hear from her son.

Pinki watched without interrupting.

Jack expected tears. Or anger. Or at least some visible shock.

He got none of it.

When the clips ended, she let out a slow breath and sat back.

"I'm not surprised," she said.

She had suspected for a long time that Mitch was deeper into drugs than anyone admitted. She had felt the distance in him too, the bitterness, the contempt, the emotional withdrawal that had been growing for years.

"This only confirms what I already knew," she said.

Jack studied her face. There was sadness there, yes, but not confusion. Not disbelief. More than anything, there was resolve.

Pinki had already made peace with the truth long before the truth had fully arrived.

Now she was simply ready for whatever came next.

Chapter 64: The Invitation

J.D. Callaghan's brothers and sisters received the invitation within days. One by one, they called to confirm they would attend. The tone of each conversation was nearly identical, gratitude, politeness, cautious optimism, and the kind of warmth people use when money is somewhere in the background, even if no one says it directly.

They thanked J.D. for arranging the gathering and praised him for everything he had done for the family over the years. He responded to each of them with the same smooth, measured charm, never letting his impatience show.

Privately, he was pleased.

Everything was moving exactly the way he wanted it to.

At the same time, Kremer handled the next part of the setup. Using forged stationery, he created a set of letters that appeared to come from a respectable law firm. The language was careful, formal, and convincing. The letters were written as though they represented J.D. Callaghan's brothers and sisters collectively.

Kremer handed the envelopes to Pinki.

"These came in the mail today," she told J.D. that evening. "I opened them before I realized they were addressed to you."

She passed the papers to him calmly.

"They're from your brothers and sisters," she said. "First, they confirmed that they'll be at the Gatlinburg dinner. Second, they thanked you for arranging it."

She paused just long enough.

"And third, they said the farmland and the business should remain entirely yours and Mitch's. They won't ask for any share. They said they'd rather discuss everything in person when the family gets together."

J.D. skimmed the letters, and a slow smile spread across his face.

"That's generous of them," he said. "They all called me earlier too. Very appreciative."

Then he looked up at Pinki.

"When are you planning to go?"

"Whenever you go," she said evenly. "I'll go with you."

J.D. leaned back.

"I've got an important business meeting around then," he said. "I'm not sure exactly when I'll arrive."

He let that sit for a moment before adding, "Why don't you go ahead of me? I'll meet you there."

Pinki had expected this. Still, she needed him to say it.

"No problem," she said. "I can drive up early and help get things ready."

"That would be perfect," he replied. "Though I already arranged catering. There's a company about fifteen miles away. They'll deliver the food a few hours before dinner and keep everything warm in heating carts."

He sounded almost proud of the detail.

"They'll come back the next day, clean up, and pick everything up."

"That's thoughtful," Pinki said quietly.

Inside, J.D. felt a kind of anticipation he had not felt in years. It sharpened him. Energized him. He had been waiting for this moment.

"If they ask for a share again," he muttered, almost to himself, "I'll kill them."

Kremer, standing nearby, gave a small approving nod.

"They shouldn't ask," he said. "You're the one who built everything, the businesses, the land, all of it. You and Mitch deserve it."

J.D. smiled, cold and satisfied.

"Exactly," he said. "I like the way you think. I'm very impressed."

The trap was fully set.

And no one except those who built it knew how deadly it would be.

Chapter 65:
The Final Preparation

Kremer spoke calmly, each word placed with care.

"Everything is already in place at the house," he said. "It would be better if you arrived a day early. Give yourself time to settle in and get comfortable with the layout."

He paused, then added the part he wanted J.D. to hear clearly.

"Let your wife drive separately."

J.D. Callaghan nodded at once.

"I was already thinking the same thing."

Kremer leaned forward, lowering his voice just enough to make the moment feel heavier.

"We finish this once and for all. No hesitation. Either on the road or inside the house, but no one walks away."

Then he slid a folder across the table.

"These are the agreements."

J.D. opened it slowly, giving the pages more attention than he gave most things unless money or power was attached to them.

"I printed two copies for each person," Kremer said. "Your brothers, your sisters, and your wife. Everyone signs both copies. They keep one. You keep the other."

He pointed to the body of the document.

"Each agreement states that the signer is acting voluntarily, without pressure or coercion. It confirms that all farmland and business assets belong solely to you. It also states that they agree not to demand, challenge, or file any legal claim now or at any point in the future."

His finger moved to the last paragraph.

"And here, they agree that if necessary, they'll appear in court later and confirm the same thing under oath."

J.D.'s eyes sharpened as he read. Then a slow smile spread across his face.

"This is brilliant," he said. "Absolutely perfect."

Kremer's tone did not change.

"If anyone refuses to sign, you kill them."

He let the silence after that sentence do its work.

"That will tell you everything you need to know about who is with you and who isn't."

Kremer understood J.D. well by then. He knew what kind of words fed his ego, what kind of provocation stirred his violence, and how easily the man confused control with destiny.

The night before the family gathering, J.D. arrived alone at the Gatlinburg house.

The very first thing he did was go to the dining room and check beneath the table.

The automatic AK-47 was there.

He pulled it out, raised it toward the empty chairs, and mimed firing at the people he imagined sitting there the next night. After a moment, he put it back where it had been hidden. He also carried a loaded handgun strapped near his ankle, a second layer of confidence he told himself was caution.

Three hours before dinner, the catering team arrived. They brought in the food, set up the warming carts, and arranged everything exactly as planned. By late afternoon, the house looked ready for a gathering that, on the surface, would seem almost ordinary.

One by one, the guests began to arrive.

Everyone came except his wife.

With less than an hour left before dinner, J.D.'s phone buzzed. He looked down and read the message.

My tire went flat in the mountains. No signal. I walked three miles and finally got a ride to a gas station. Road service is on the way to the car. I'm trying to get an Uber now. Please don't wait for me if I'm late. Start dinner if needed. I'll come as soon as I can.

He read it without expression, then looked up at the others.

"Her tire blew out," he said casually. "She's waiting for an Uber."

No one questioned it.

Everything, at least on the surface, remained on schedule.

And the house—quiet, prepared, and armed—waited for what was coming next.

Earlier that day, J.D. had tried calling Mitch more than once, but the calls went unanswered. He tried again. Still nothing. After several attempts, a message finally appeared.

Busy with the opening ceremony and celebration for my new distribution business. I'll talk to you tomorrow.

J.D. stared at the screen, his jaw tightening.

"Fine," he muttered, typing back.

Good luck.

He slid the phone into his pocket, but the irritation stayed with him. Things had not gone the way he expected. Everyone was still alive. That alone enraged him. A sharp resentment had already begun to gather against Kremer, though he hadn't yet spoken it aloud. The plan was supposed to be simple. Clean. Final.

Instead, nothing had happened.

J.D. paced the room, his anger growing heavier with every turn.

Patience had never been his strength.

By then, Kremer had already spoken to Jimmy and made his position clear. Jimmy had agreed to handle everything personally, meeting Mitch, running the celebration, and overseeing the business side of the operation. Given Kremer's past and the fact that he had spent more than twenty years in prison, there was always a risk that someone at a large public event might recognize him.

Kremer had made that clear from the beginning.

"You take the front," he had told Jimmy. "I stay in the background. That's how this works."

Jimmy had waved away the concern.

"No problem. I've got it. What do you want me to tell Mitch if he asks why you're not there?"

"Just show him my message," Kremer said. "You'll get it in a few minutes."

A moment later, the text went out.

My sister was just in a car accident. I need to go to her immediately. I don't know how bad it is yet. I'll try to make it later if I can. Sorry about this.

Jimmy responded almost at once.

Sorry to hear that. Hope she's okay. Don't worry about the celebration. Mitch and I will handle it. Take care and keep me posted.

Kremer set his phone down and said nothing more. Everything was moving exactly where he wanted it to move, and he didn't need to be seen for any of it.

Kremer sat quietly beside DEA Agent Michael, his phone still in his hand as the last of the messages came through. Michael said nothing. He didn't need to. He already understood why Kremer had stayed away.

For an entire week, Michael had been preparing for the operation with an intensity that left no room for error. The raid on Mitch's distribution center was one of the most delicate missions of his career, and secrecy mattered more than force, at least at first.

He had deliberately excluded local police and Missouri-based DEA teams. Too many of them were compromised. Too many of them had already sold pieces of themselves for protection, access, or money.

Instead, Michael handpicked agents with clean records—men and women he trusted enough to put into close-range danger. Most had been brought in from out of state.

Earlier that evening, as he stood before them, he had spoken with brutal clarity.

"There will be two raids tonight," he said. "One in Caruthersville, Missouri. The other in Texas."

No one moved. No one interrupted.

"Do not hesitate if you meet resistance," he continued. "We have overwhelming evidence. These are traffickers, corrupt officers, and men who are used to believing they cannot be touched. Your lives come first."

He let the silence absorb that.

"If anyone reaches for a weapon, neutralize immediately. I am not risking an agent's life for drug dealers or compromised law enforcement."

Now, in the final minutes before the operation began, agents moved into position.

The party at the distribution center was set to begin in less than an hour.

Michael watched the live feed. The warehouse sat near the river, lights glowing, music equipment coming in, cases of liquor being unloaded. A large boat floated nearby, already stocked with guests, alcohol, and armed guards.

Inside the building, Mitch and his security team moved around with full confidence, hosting officers, distributors, and buyers. They were drinking, laughing, congratulating themselves.

They felt untouchable.

Most of the local law enforcement people they relied on were already inside with them.

No one suspected what was coming.

No one imagined that the night they had planned as a celebration of power and profit would become the night everything broke.

Michael adjusted his headset.

"Move in," he said.

And the operation began.

Back in Gatlinburg, J.D. Callaghan stood at the head of the dining table, his posture stiff, his smile strained.

"Thank you all for coming," he said. "I appreciate you being here."

One of his sisters gave him a tight, polite nod.

"We appreciate you finally stepping up," she said. "And taking responsibility for the family."

Another sister was less restrained.

"The younger generation is out of control," she said sharply. "Mitch has embarrassed this family. He's damaged all of us."

His brother added quietly, "The fallout has been serious."

The room went still.

J.D.'s face hardened in an instant.

"What the hell are you talking about?" he snapped. "I don't care about your political reputations. All I care about is my son. How dare you speak about Mitch that way?"

One of his brothers lifted a hand.

"J.D., calm down—"

But he was already gone too far to be pulled back.

He slammed the folder onto the table and pushed two copies toward each person. His wife's documents remained separate, still untouched.

"What is this?" one brother asked, scanning the pages. Then his expression changed. "This is nonsense. I'm not signing this."

Another voice rose from across the table.

"We want our equal share. You cheated us. You manipulated Dad's will."

That was enough.

J.D. rose so fast his chair scraped violently across the floor. He bent down, reached beneath the table, and pulled out the automatic rifle. His hands were trembling, not only with rage, but with neglect. He had forgotten his blood pressure medicine that morning. Riley wasn't there to steady him. No one was.

"You all want truth now?" he shouted. "Fine. Here it is. Yes—I killed Dad. I changed the real will. He wanted the land divided. I didn't. So I ended it."

The room exploded in gasps.

"If I can kill my father and my brother-in-law," he shouted, his voice cracking with fury, "why not all of you?"

His siblings began pleading with him all at once.

"We're your family."

"Put the gun down."

"Don't do this."

"Turn yourself in. Stop now."

But J.D. no longer heard any of them.

He fired.

Panic tore through the room. Chairs crashed backward. Screams split the air. He kept shooting, wild with rage and years of buried poison.

"Yes," he shouted between bursts of gunfire. "I killed them. I'm a monster. I'll kill anyone—anyone—who stands between me and what's mine."

He staggered back, breathing hard, eyes wide and feverish.

"Everything belongs to Mitch and me," he spat. "The land. The brand. All of it."

Then he looked around the room again, searching.

"Where is she?" he snarled. "I've been waiting. After her, it's all ours."

The house fell silent, shattered, and changed forever.

At the distribution center, the DEA teams had already taken their positions with military precision. Helicopters remained on standby, waiting for a final signal if needed.

At first, the operation moved almost silently.

Teams came in from multiple directions. Some slipped inside the warehouse. Others moved across the roof. Within minutes, explosive devices had been quietly placed beneath cars, trucks, and SUVs parked around the compound. If anyone tried to flee in a coordinated rush, the exits would turn into death traps.

Michael led from the front.

Then the first gunshot shattered the silence.

His voice came through the comms, cold and controlled.

"If your life is in danger, neutralize immediately. Do not hesitate."

Inside, the celebration collapsed in seconds.

Music stopped. Glass shattered. Guests screamed as armed agents poured into the building. Heavy weapons were positioned near the main entrance, cutting off the most obvious escape routes.

Mitch shouted over the chaos, ordering his guards—and the local police chief—to fire back.

"This isn't us!" Mitch yelled at Jimmy. "Somebody on your side snitched!"

Gunfire erupted from every direction.

The firefight dragged on for nearly two hours.

Bodies dropped—guards, corrupted officers, dealers. The police chief died early. Jimmy went down not long after. Mitch was hit multiple times, collapsing against a concrete wall, bleeding heavily.

With trembling hands, Mitch dialed his father.

J.D. Callaghan answered immediately.

"How's the celebration going?" he asked, almost casually.

Mitch's voice broke the moment he tried to speak.

"Dad... it's bad. They raided us. Everyone's dead. I've been shot. I'm bleeding badly. Please help me."

There was a pause on the line, brief but heavy.

"Hang on," J.D. said. "Nothing's going to happen to you. I'll take care of it. I love you, my son."

Mitch was crying now, his words slipping out through pain and panic.

"I should've listened to you... and Riley. I thought you and Mom hated me. I love you too."

Then the call disconnected.

Back at the Gatlinburg house, J.D. kept talking into the dead phone for another second, either not realizing the line was gone or not caring enough to notice. Outside, sirens were beginning to rise through the mountains.

"I won't let you die," he muttered. "I'm a brand. I can do anything. No one kills us."

Then he laughed, low and unsteady.

"I killed my brothers and sisters. Your mother is next."

By the time police entered the house, J.D. was too far gone to hear anything clearly.

"Sir, stand up. Hands in the air."

He barely turned toward them.

"Who the hell are you?" he shouted. "Who gave you permission to enter my property?"

His hand moved toward the AK-47.

"I'll kill you all."

The officers gave one final warning.

"Put the weapon down."

J.D. screamed back and fired first.

"No one shoots me! Do you know who I am? I am J.D. Callaghan!"

The response came instantly.

Gunfire tore through the room.

J.D. Callaghan fell where he stood.

The house was secured within minutes. Five bodies were recovered, including his own.

The shockwaves reached far beyond the mountains.

A state senator.

A congressman's brother.

A criminal empire.

Gone in a single night.

The Callaghan legacy did not end in power. It ended in blood, sirens, and silence.

The story broke across the country within hours. Major news networks led with the same headlines: five high-profile deaths, tied to coordinated DEA raids in Caruthersville, Missouri, and Austin, Texas. The scale of it stunned the nation.

Authorities confirmed that no DEA agents or police officers had been killed. Every fatality had occurred on the criminal side. In the raids, agents seized more than ten million dollars' worth of cocaine and methamphetamine, dismantling what officials described as one of the largest drug-distribution operations in the region.

At the Gatlinburg house, officers were still processing the scene when Mrs. Callaghan arrived.

As planned, she waited until local police were already there before coming near the property. The timing mattered, and she got it exactly right.

She identified herself calmly.

"I'm Mr. Callaghan's wife."

The officers stopped her before she could get close to the house. One of them explained what had happened as carefully as he could.

"Five people are dead," he said. "One man shot four others. A neighbor heard gunfire and called us. When officers entered the house, the suspect was armed with an automatic rifle and threatened law enforcement. After repeated warnings, he opened fire. Officers returned fire and killed him."

He hesitated, then added more quietly, "The suspect identified himself as J.D. Callaghan."

She staggered slightly, as if the words had taken the strength out of her legs. One of the officers caught her arm.

"That was my husband," she said softly.

Then she began to cry, and she did it well.

"The others," she said between sobs, "were my brothers and sisters. He invited all of us here for a family dinner."

When they asked why she had not arrived with the rest, she gave the explanation she had already prepared.

"My car got a flat tire in the mountains. I walked almost three miles before a local officer gave me a ride to a gas station. I texted my husband to tell him I'd be late and that I was waiting for an Uber. It took too long."

One of the officers slowly shook his head.

"You're lucky you weren't inside," he said. "If you had been there, you might not have survived."

She lowered her head and let the tears keep falling.

Later that night, as the full shape of the disaster became clear, Pinki also received confirmation that Mitch had been killed in the raid.

The Callaghan empire, once treated as untouchable, had collapsed in a single night.

And the world was watching.

Regardless of everything, he was still her son.

He had not been a good son. He had become something cruel, careless, and dangerous. But he was still hers. She had made her peace with that truth long before this night arrived. Deep down, she had always known where his life was heading. It had been moving toward tragedy for years.

And still, beneath the grief, there was relief.

J.D. Callaghan had been the real monster.

Pinki called Jack and Kremer and asked them to come for her. Jack arrived within forty-five minutes. When she got into the car, both men saw the same thing in her face. She looked worn out, yes. Grief-struck, yes. But there was also something else there, something close to peace.

"He was waiting to kill you," Jack said quietly. "Even in his last moments. He said it himself before he died."

Pinki closed her eyes for a second.

"I know," she said. "It's not easy to lose a child. But he wasn't really my son anymore. He had his father's soul in him. All of it."

Jack drove her back to her home in Caruthersville. By the time they got there, television crews and reporters had already gathered outside. Cameras flashed. Microphones lifted. Everyone wanted the first words from the woman who had survived the collapse of one of the region's most feared families.

She stopped just long enough to speak.

"My husband, my son, and several members of my family are dead," she said calmly. "The police are conducting a full investigation. We will know more in the coming days. I'm exhausted and need privacy."

DEA Agent Michael stepped forward at once and motioned for the press to back away.

"Give her a few days," he said. "There will be official updates."

Back at Jack's house, Jordan, Kremer, and Jack sat together waiting. When they finally got word that Pinki was home safely, something in the room eased. None of them had expected the chain of events to move so fast or fall so completely into place.

It almost didn't feel real.

Again and again, events had turned in ways none of them could have forced if they had tried.

A judge had died from a snakebite.

A sheriff had died from a lethal combination of alcohol and high-dose narcotics.

The corrupt police chief, a compromised DEA agent, Mitch's friends who had tried to rape Lakesha and Tiffney, and several other local officers had all died during the DEA raid.

DEA Agent Michael, Lakesha's boyfriend, had turned out to be exactly what few people in that world still believed existed: an honest federal agent. He had handled everything with precision, discipline, and real integrity.

Riley had died at Mitch's hands because of one stupid, poisonous misunderstanding involving Mrs. Callaghan.

And J.D. Callaghan, in the end, had destroyed himself, killing his own brothers and sisters in a rage he could no longer contain.

Manipulating his paranoia and greed had been dangerous work, but Kremer had understood him almost perfectly. Most of the planning would never appear in any formal report. And once again, chance—or fate—had done what strategy alone could not. J.D. had forgotten his blood pressure medication.

By the time Mitch made that last phone call, his mind was already slipping. After that, there was no pulling him back. When police reached the Gatlinburg house, he was no longer rational. There was no safe way to end it except the way it ended.

It was better this way.

If he had lived through that night, he would have died soon enough anyway, from a stroke, a heart attack, a hemorrhage, and he would have taken more people with him before he went.

As the truth of it all finally settled over them, Jack, Kremer, and Jordan looked at one another across the room.

They had survived.

They had won.

And for the first time in years, justice, imperfect, brutal, and stained with blood as it was, had finally been served.

Quietly, they raised their glasses, not to celebrate death, but to acknowledge an ending that could not have come any other way.

Chapter 66: A New Beginning

Legally, Mrs. Callaghan now controlled all the property, farmland, and businesses that had once been ruled by her husband and son.

Her first major decision was both symbolic and just. She transferred the family farmland back to Jack, restoring what had been stolen years earlier through violence, deceit, and fear. It was not merely a legal correction. It was an act of moral repair.

Jack did not waste time once the land was back in his hands. He began planning a new house on the exact ground where the original family home had been burned down. He met with an architect, reviewed designs, and eventually approved plans for a five-thousand-square-foot residence. He did not want a monument to grief. He wanted something that stood for renewal.

By then, Jack had chosen to live with Kremer. The two men had grown close in the kind of way only hardship can create, not quickly, not dramatically, but steadily, with trust built over time. Pinki noticed it almost at once and teased Jack more than once, joking that Kremer had become his "boyfriend." Jack always laughed and let the comment pass without correction.

Later, Jonathan transferred five thousand acres of farmland to Jordan.

Jordan resisted at first. The scale of it felt too large, too generous, almost impossible to accept without discomfort. But Pinki, Jack, and Kremer refused to let him turn it down.

"You've suffered more than most people suffer in an entire lifetime," they told him. "What was done to you at that age, and what you survived because of Mitch, J.D. Callaghan, and Riley, cannot be measured. You earned this."

In the end, Jordan accepted. When he told Tiffney and his family, all of them were deeply moved, not only by the gift itself, but by what it meant. The land no longer represented theft, control, and blood. It had become something else.

Jack told Jordan that once the new house was finished, Jordan and his family should move there and oversee the farmland directly. Jordan agreed. He understood what Jack was really offering him, not simply property, but trust, belonging, and something lasting.

Meanwhile, Mrs. Callaghan took full control of the remaining businesses. One of her first official decisions was to appoint Jonathan and Kremer as her assistants, placing them at the center of day-to-day management.

She called a meeting with all employees and hosted a lunch at the very same building Mitch had once used for drug distribution. Standing in front of the gathered staff, she spoke calmly, but with unmistakable authority.

"Everything will remain the same," she said, "except the leadership."

Then she made the structure clear. She was now the Chairwoman. Jonathan would serve as the new CEO. Kremer would become COO, taking over the position Riley had once controlled. Together, they would oversee the company's daily operations.

"My office will always be open," she added. "If you have concerns, ideas, or questions, you may come to me during business hours."

Then she made the final change unmistakable.

"There will be no parties in this building. Ever."

The entire third floor, once used for drinking, drugs, and everything else the family had hidden there, was cleaned out completely and converted into proper office space. Jonathan and Kremer took over the executive offices on the second floor, replacing the rooms J.D. Callaghan and Riley had once used.

Mrs. Callaghan also met privately with the children of J.D.'s siblings. She offered them sincere condolences and explained that the original will, the real one, would finally be honored.

Each branch of the family would receive ten thousand acres of farmland, exactly as her father had once intended.

For the first time in decades, the land was being returned not only to its rightful owners, but to the truth itself.

What had once been held together by fear, corruption, and blood was now being rebuilt on something far steadier, transparency, accountability, and trust.

The era of Callaghan terror had ended.

And something better had finally begun.

Chapter 67: Full Circle

Lakesha and Michael announced their engagement first. It was not a loud celebration, but a deeply felt one, shaped by everything they had already lived through together.

Soon after, Tiffney and Jordan shared their own news. They would become officially engaged at Tiffney's law school graduation. Both couples decided they would marry within a year, not out of haste, but because, after all they had lost and survived, they no longer wanted to postpone joy.

As spring settled in, Jordan's basketball team entered the playoffs. Their first matchup drew immediate attention.

They were playing Caruthersville High School.

The anticipation around the game was electric. By the time Jordan walked into the gym with his team, the place was packed. Teachers, former classmates, old neighbors, families who had known him since he was a child, all of them filled the stands. The moment he stepped onto the court, the crowd rose and gave him a long standing ovation.

Many of them were openly emotional.

Their surprise deepened when they saw Scott take the floor. Jordan's younger brother moved with a style that felt uncannily familiar, the same instincts, the same confidence, the same quiet control. Watching him play felt like watching memory and possibility standing on the same court at once.

Sikeston won the game convincingly.

That victory carried them into the Final Sixteen of the Missouri State Tournament, a remarkable achievement in Jordan's first year as head coach. They did not advance to the Final Eight, but no one around them felt disappointment. What they felt instead was pride.

After the game, Jordan spoke to the press.

"I took over this program less than four months ago," he said. "This is only the beginning. Next year, we're aiming for the Final Four."

The board chairman and the principal were more than satisfied. Jordan, however, immediately turned his players' attention back to what mattered next.

"Focus on your exams," he told them. "Then we regroup. Summer is where we build next season."

That summer changed almost everything.

Tiffney and Jordan became officially engaged at her law school graduation celebration. Both families attended, along with Michael's family. Shirley, having finally completed the last of her seven years of legal restrictions, received full clearance. She interviewed with the CEO of the *St. Louis Dispatch* and accepted a journalism position that began in May. Ethan followed with his own start date in July. Tiffney began her work as a criminal defense attorney that same month.

For the first time in years, life began to feel almost ordinary.

A year later, both couples were married, Jordan and Tiffney, Lakesha and Michael, surrounded by family, friends, and a future that no longer felt overshadowed by fear.

That same year, Sikeston reached the Final Four. They lost to a powerful St. Louis team in the championship round, but even that loss felt historic rather than painful. The program had changed. The culture had changed. Jordan had done what he promised he would do.

Jack's new house was completed, and he and Kremer moved in together. Jordan and his family relocated to Jonathan's home and continued the farmland lease arrangement with Jonathan's cousin so the operations would remain stable.

Scott went on to win the Missouri State Championship in both his junior and senior years.

Then came a moment that felt almost impossible in its symmetry.

He received a basketball scholarship from the same college Jordan had once been meant to attend. The entire family celebrated that news with the kind of emotion only people who knew exactly what had once been stolen could fully understand.

Not long after, Jordan began receiving coaching offers from several colleges. He eventually accepted a three-year contract at the University of Missouri, taking the next step in a career that had once seemed permanently lost to him.

His ultimate dream had never changed.

The NBA.

And this time, nothing stood in his way.

For the first time in a very long while, every chapter ahead seemed open, earned, and full of promise.

All were finally free.

Epilogue

After seven years of legal restrictions, Shirley finally returned to journalism. Her first article, co-written with her son Ethan and published in the *St. Louis Dispatch*, marked more than a professional return. It marked a reckoning.

The fall of one tyrant, she made clear, did not mean the end of evil. Men like J.D. Callaghan still existed, in this country and everywhere else, men who used wealth, influence, and political power to break lives and bury truth.

The story exposed how such people manipulate systems that are supposed to protect the public. It revealed how corruption can spread through law enforcement, healthcare, regulatory agencies, and even the justice system itself. But it also exposed something more difficult and more important: good people and bad people exist in every institution. Police. DEA. Medicine. Courts. None of them are pure. None of them are beyond corruption. None of them are beyond courage, either.

Too often, justice bends toward wealth and power. The poor and the middle class are left behind. Poverty remains a quiet inheritance, passed from one generation to the next. Discrimination, addiction, and the exploitation of women and children continue to scar the country. Freedom of speech and freedom of the press are real, but only until they become inconvenient to those in power.

The justice system remains deeply uneven. Similar crimes produce wildly different outcomes depending on race, status, money, and access. Politicians speak beautifully about the public during election seasons, but remain silent while families struggle with rising food prices, unaffordable rent, and medical costs that break them. Millions of Americans remain uninsured. Millions more rely on Medicaid while being denied access to quality doctors, specialists, and hospitals.

Veterans wait months, sometimes years, for care in overcrowded systems. Nursing homes often operate in shadows few people bother to examine. Homelessness grows in plain view, visible on city streets and under bridges, yet it remains easier for leaders to look away. While the nation spends enormous energy debating foreign crises, urgent suffering at home is allowed to deepen.

America imprisons millions of people, disproportionately African American, under a system that too often prizes punishment over rehabilitation. Prisons are overcrowded, underfunded, and dehumanizing. Law enforcement and prosecution increasingly seem driven by numbers, arrests, convictions, sentences, rather than by restoration or justice. The evidence is everywhere. This system is not healing society. It is damaging it further.

Trillions of dollars are spent on institutions that repeatedly fail the people they claim to protect. Meanwhile, a small elite continues to grow wealthier, more insulated, and more powerful.

This story, then, is not only about revenge, justice, or closure.

It is a call for reflection.

And for change.

If this country wants a better future, it must confront its truths honestly. It must reform systems that punish without restoring, divide instead of lifting, and protect power more reliably than they protect people. The future depends on whether society chooses fear and control, or compassion, accountability, and reform.

Only then can justice become more than a word.

Only then can freedom belong to everyone.

THE END